The Wanderlust Diaries

It's a long way home from here.

To KRISTA
THAT IS ONE JUICY BUTT
♡ MM

MARIA MARTINICO

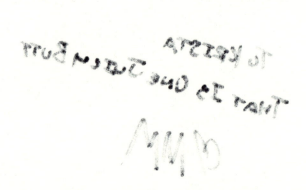

ISBN: 978-0-578-57744-9

TABLE OF CONTENTS

PART THREE: THE CITY

PART ONE:

THE JUNGLE

1 BANGKOK

It's only my second time on a plane…and I'm buckled in for 16 hours. I have a light backpack of clothes in the belly of this beast, 600 books on my Kindle and this journal. Not much else.

The only other flight was from Detroit, Michigan to Cheyenne, Wyoming. Some kind of summer program for "at risk" youth. A week eating quinoa wasn't going to keep us from the risks we faced every day, but poor kids don't say no to free vacations.

At first the big skies and bare cliffs Out West scared the crap out of me. Used to Michigan's low clouds and tree coverage, it felt like someone ripped the roof off and exposed us directly to the wrath of the universe. After I couple days I loved it though. The freedom to run a horse across a field without any street signs or traffic lights. Seeing stars instead of the 711's orange glow in the night sky. I felt small and significant at the same time. Coming home sucked.

I guess I'm chasing that feeling. With a round-the-world, ticket Aunt Mary's Claddagh ring on my finger and her "estate" in my bank account. I've got it figured out- if I average $120 a day (Asia days much cheaper than Europe days) I can be out for an entire year. Smell ya never, Flint.

I got the window so I could see the Pacific. I read once the Pacific Ocean has 75,000 volcanoes. I hope I see at least one. The joker in the middle seat is gorgeous and I'm trying not to look. He passed out right away and I'm going to have to wake him up soon to pee. Should I shove my crotch or my ass in his face? These are Coach Choices.

Damn, he's cute. Long, legs all scrunched up in the tiny seat. Eyelashes curled into a perfect semi-circle, like the smile on an emoji. Honey skin, and I caught a flash of greenish eyes while he settled in. Pile of nappy curls, bleached at the tips, either from sun and surf…or a kit. I snort, realizing my opinion of him will change entirely depending on which one it is.

I also am realizing I might think he's cute cause he kinda looks like me, like we could be cousins. Ok I really have to pee, but waking people up is so intimate. Good morning baby, how'd you sleep? Focus on the spray of blackheads on his big nose and the stream of drool.

Turns out his name is Gabriel. His t-shirt was crazy soft. And I went Crotch First. We talked for a long time after I got back, shared a couple beers. He's passed out again. Good start.

I've never felt jet lag before. Puke. It's all greasy and nauseous and headachy. Gabe followed me through customs. He's Gabe now, and his mother is Irish, and his dad is black (from England black), he loves papaya, the scar on his wrist is from a dog attack, he likes my ring and is visiting Thailand for a "vacay". It was a long flight. And his accent is adorable.

"That's a blank book you've got there," he said when they stamped my new passport.

I didn't hear that stamp, I felt it. CLunk. My first country. Grinning, I told him I lost my last passport.

He was in a big rush at baggage claim. I watched/didn't watch as he grabbed his light bag and took off with a long stride. Narrow hips, jeans barely hanging on, slightly duck footed. Fuck it.

"Want to share a cab?" I nearly shouted.

He stopped. "That's...not a good idea."

"Oh." Well fuck you too, Friend.

"I mean, sure, come on. Bangkok is intense your first time. Let's get you to the hostel district, that's where I'm headed."

Intense is the right word. Stepping outside the airport, mid-day humidity and heat instantly made my armpits prickle. The chaos of motorbikes, shouting people, bright signs, and intense smog bounced around my foggy brain, trying to register. I couldn't move, because I couldn't compute. There was foreign, and then there was this.

Gabe grabbed my hand, not noticing my sweaty shock. We piled into a cab and joined the river of honking traffic. I couldn't stop staring at the power lines. Hundreds of power lines, running all crazy back and forth across the street. What kind of system was that? What happened if one fell? All my mental preparation to be an impartial observer, a blank slate, absorbing new cultures without judgement, flew out that cab window. This place was loud, smelly and an electrical fire disaster waiting to happen! Was that a baby riding a motorcycle?! Sweet Christ.

We got out at Khao San Road, which Gabe explained was the place all the backpackers hang out in transition to somewhere better. By this point I think he realized I was a little out of it, mostly clued in by the fact that I sat down on the curb, retched a couple times, and almost passed out. Observant, this guy. He stationed me at an open-air bar in front of the world's most refreshing box fan and told me to eat something. I groggily watched as he crossed the street, went into a halfway decent hotel and exchanged high fives with a Chinese man in the lobby.

I ordered a green curry and a beer. I know. It should have been water. But…it was vacay. The curry shocked me back to reality a bit. Creamy, crunchy, sweet and savory at the same time, I didn't know food could be that many things at once. I ordered another plate before the first one was gone. And another beer. Gabe came back and offered to help me find a room. Good thing too, because when I stood up, I couldn't stand up.

He sighed and one-shouldered my pack for me, scooping the other arm across my sweat-soaked back. I wasn't so out of it that my ears didn't prick up nervously when the receptionist at the shoddy hostel next door asked if the room was for one or two.

"One," Gabe said firmly.

Fine, I think you're kinda sad too, Gabe. Get your warm and slightly calloused hands off me.

I sank gratefully onto the abused cot in the small room.

"Drink some water before you pass out," he said, tossing me a giant plastic bottle. "And if you're conscious later, my friends and I will be at Brick Bar at the end of the strip. Come by," he stopped at the door. "And if you go out alone…don't drink too much ok? There's a lot of

4

sketchy guys around here."

Thanks Gabe, I don't know anything about taking care of myself. Still it was kinda sweet.

Have you ever woken up in a panic, thinking you had forgotten something incredibly important, like, to breathe? I could somehow feel how far I was from home, mentally running down a rosary that ticked every mile, and it was unending. Also, so thirsty. So, so thirsty.

Gratefully chugging Gabe's water, I considered my options. My phone said it was 10:30 p.m. I could read (hide) in my room and wait for the train to Chang Mai tomorrow at noon. I read once about the Santika nightclub fire here. 66 people died and they were so crisped it took a week to identify all the bodies. I should really just chill out and rest.

The club was loud and blue. Gabe was sprawled across a low couch with a bunch of other hipster guys. Young Thai women in fuck-me heels floated around them hopefully. Ew.

He hopped up right away when he saw me, and settled me in his spot, shooing away a bro who looked like Scooby Doo with a man bun, then squeezing in next to me. He smelled like pot and sweat and curry. In a good way. He passed me a bucket with multiple straws.

"Knockoff Thai Red Bull, Coke, and vodka. A local favorite. It's rocket fuel for a party."

It tasted like bubble gum and bum piss. Wanting to play it slightly cooler than I had that afternoon, I sipped a beer from the iced bucket on the table instead. Gabe slid a long arm across my shoulders. Guess somebody warmed up from not wanting to share a cab. I felt a mix of annoyance at pretty much being peed on to mark his turf from the other guys, and a tug of excitement at the soft arm hairs on my bare skin. Doesn't take much to make a girl feel special, guys.

We kissed in line for the bathroom. In the close, dark hallway he gently lifted my chin and gave me a quick graze with his lips, then looked at me to see what I thought. Fuck it, is what I thought. I did what I had wanted to do for 16 hours on the plane and tugged one of his curls straight. Then I pulled his face down to mine and took it slow. We lost our place in line for the squatter toilets.

The night was still balls hot as we made our way back to his hotel. He stumbled a little dodging the crush of wasted 20-somethings on the street. At 1:00 a.m. the already busy road was a sea of tank tops, tattoos, sloshing Singha beers and hopeful whores.

Gabe grabbed my arm and pulled me into an alley. He pushed me against the crumbling wall roughly and kissed me softly. His breath started coming faster as he ran his hands up and down my waist, barely brushing the bottom of my breasts with his thumbs. I was having a little trouble breathing too, damn he was good. His mouth insistent on mine, I could feel him hard against my leg and it was definitely worth a grope.

"What the hell?" I yelled, whipping my hand out of his pants. Was there a bunch of a bubble wrap around his dick? Was it wrapped in Pillsbury dough?! What WAS that?

At the same time he gasped again, and hurled all over the alley. It smelled like bubble gum and bum piss.

I seriously considered running away, locking my hostel door and seeing if there was an earlier train out of this hellhole. Then I remembered how good his water tasted when I woke up. Dammit.

2 THE FIRST TIME

Gabe was heavier than he looked. Sweating through my tank top (again), I finally got him into bed. I forced him to drink some water and turned him on his side before he passed out for good. Aunt Mary's second husband died from vomit asphyxiation. No one was sad about it though.

The right thing to do was put a wastebasket by his head and leave.

I stealthily pulled down his worn cargo shorts and Lucky boxers. What the fuck was going on with his dick? It had all kinds of extra. I couldn't see the head, there was like…a skin blanket all around it. It looked like a supersized sausage roll. I stared for a long time. I guess when you only have sex with one guy since you were 13, you don't know everything about everything.

He woke up when the sun hit his joyful little eyelashes. My clock all messed up, I was reading his paperback copy of Alex Garland's *The Beach*.

The Beach, in Thailand? So freakin' basic Gabe. I read once that Garland was 23 like me when he started writing the book. If Gabe gives me a map and slits his wrists, I will shove it down his corpse throat and never look back.

Instead he moaned weakly and blinked. In the bright light it turned out only one of his eyes was celery green. The other was hazel.

He jumped and scrambled at sheets when he spotted me cross-legged at the end of his bed.

"Shit! Shit you scared me. What are you doing here?"

Making sure you don't choke on your own vomit, asshole. And visually molesting you.

"You got pretty sick, so I wanted to be sure you were ok." I said, getting up to leave. I saw the flashbulbs of memory pop one by one in front of his eyes…and could tell when the last one hit with a flinch.

"Oh. Oh man. I'm sorry. Wait, shit. Let me…like…clean up and get you breakfast or something."

"That's ok, I have a noon train I gotta get."

"No wait, I'll be two seconds."

He came out of the bathroom much more collected, with a white towel barely hanging on to his cut hips and knife-flat stomach, smelling like man soap. This guy. Not his first rodeo.

He sat down next to me on the bed and picked up the book.

"This book is crazy. You have to read it while you're here. If you like to read, I mean."

Kissing shut him up.

I expected things to go fast and got embarrassed when he took my hand away and said, "It's only 7 a.m. We have four hours till you have to leave. Let me look at you."

He stripped off my already grubby tank top (I had brought three for a year) and clicked open my bra with a snap. My breasts are good. Especially the right one. He inhaled slowly and laid me back on the bed. I felt them spread out and tickle the sides of my arms. The sun streak that lit his mismatched eyes was warm across them.

He knelt at the side of the bed and slowly ran the tip of his middle finger from top to bottom. The dark nipple reacted right away and I saw the tiny hairs around it stand straight up in the sunlight. Quick as a fish he licked both nipples with a single swipe, making me gasp, then stood up and turned on the overhead fan. The blades started a slow spin, kicking cool air onto the wetness.

He stretched out beside me and worked my thin cotton skirt off. I couldn't help leaning in to him, but he held me firmly away, stroking my waist and kissing my neck, gradually working down to fasten his wide mouth on the left nipple. Well that one's pretty good too I guess.

I had only been naked in front of one man. While I was packing practical backpacking underwear, I thought I'd be nervous the first time someone else saw me. Instead Gabe's gentle stroking, intense stare, short breath and giant hardon made me feel totally comfortable, in control and sexy as hell.

His tongue followed the curve of my waist, replacing his mouth with a gently pinching hand on my breast. I tried to hold still, as his tight grip on my shoulder and thigh told me to. Still I couldn't help arching and quivering as his light kisses moved over my thin underwear. His long pink tongue slipped between the fabric and my thigh and I yelped like a stepped-on puppy. His head shot up and he fixed me with two different colors of concerned eyes.

"Is that ok?"

It could be ok. I hadn't ever done it before though. Not that I wanted him to know that.

"It's good…I was surprised. Don't stop. Please."

He grinned cockily and went back to work. His curls tickled my inner thighs, making me stifle giggles with the back of my hand.

"You don't have to be quiet. I want to hear you," he said, slightly muffled. What did he mean, hear me?

Oh. That's what he meant. At first it was so sweet it almost hurt my teeth. I moaned and tried to wriggle away. He persistently hung on to my hips and held them tight. It rode the edge of being too much and not enough. He was determined, and when he would break to kiss my stomach or thighs, I could see he was excited as hell too. I was about to tell him to stop, worried I was taking too long or something, when his persistent licks slowed down excruciatingly, and he very gently inserted a finger into my slippery wetness. I could feel him beckoning toward my belly button and then Bangkok exploded.

I slowly came back to reality, the fan evaporating the sweat off the whole length of my body. Gabe, looking quite pleased with himself, ran light fingertips all over me, making me shiver in the heat.

"You are so soft," he said, running that middle finger down the inside of my arm, stopping to tickle my armpit briefly. I laughed and he finally let me feel his hard arms too.

"You're not so soft," I whispered. He laughed. Good. Aunt Mary always said you shouldn't have relations with someone you couldn't laugh with.

Turns out his lightly furred, honey colored skin went all the way down. His wide shoulders kept his skinny frame from being scrawny. His abs crinkled into tight waves when he laughed or stretched. I mostly liked the length of him; long, graceful bones and sinews close to the skin.

And damn if he didn't kiss like a choirboy possessed by the devil. I was drowning in his mouth and couldn't stop myself from sliding my hands all over his tight skin, lower and lower. He didn't stop me this time either. There it was again, the cock that had scared the pants on me last night. Now that it was erect though…nah erect is too a polite word for that veined, pulsing beast…now that he was boned out like a dog, it seemed totally normal. I wanted to ask but I wanted other things more.

I brushed it with my long curls and he took a sharp breath. I smirked at him and started south. He grabbed my arm.

"You don't owe me anything. I want you to know that. I spent half that flight picturing what I did to you and keeping the blanket on my lap. I'm happy I got to taste you...especially after I was such an ass last night."

Oh Gabe. You evolved man. You shining white knight. You have no idea what you would be missing.

I am very good at a few things in this life.

Taking care of dying people.

Driving fast.

Lying.

And blow jobs.

I knew I didn't owe him shit. But I really wanted to suck his cock. After a few deep swallows, stopping for a second at the top to make a neat circle around the tip with my tongue, I asked him if wanted me to stop.

"N- No!"

Thought so Gabe. I put my dark little heart and soul into that BJ, making him squirm and gasp, stopping short of him coming multiple times to brush his length with my breasts. Finally, jaw sore and very pleased with myself, I cupped his balls and nearly swallowed him, letting the back of my throat convulse around his tip.

"Glarg-u!" he shouted, tearing me off him so he could buck hard into his orgasm without breaking my nose.

I grabbed his hand to nibble on a fingertip and saw what time it was on his (crazy expensive) watch. 11:24 a.m.

Fuck.

I was dressed before he stopped shuddering. I still had to get my bag from my hostel, get a cab to the train station, buy my ticket and get on the noon train to Chiang Mai.

"Woah, did I do something? I'm sorry, I thought you wanted me to come…" he spluttered, still half hard and dazed.

I grabbed his stubbly chin and gave him a quick and deep kiss.

"You're fine. I've got to get to my elephants."

I ran out of his room, glancing back once to see him fall over trying to put shorts on to follow me.

Bye Gabe. You were the perfect kickoff. Minus the puke.

The street seemed more manageable than the day before as I half ran toward my bag.

I now had 30 minutes to make that train, and I knew I could do it if I hustled.

3 ELEPHANTS AND OLD BALLS

She had dark brown eyes and eyelashes to die for. I swear she winked at me as I came near with chunks of pineapple. The soft snout shot out and deftly took a piece out of my hand. It felt like a kiss and it was the best kiss of my life.

Fuck Disney, the Elephant Nature Park was the happiest place on earth. When I was little I saw an elephant for the first time at the Detroit Zoo. I remember thinking I has fallen asleep and was dreaming. No one animal could have a trunk, giant ears, tusks, and be that big at the same time. I refused to leave the Elephant Exploration Center and Aunt Mary said I cried the entire drive home till she smacked me.

I read once elephants are one of the only species who can recognize themselves in a mirror. They also mourn their dead, repeat musical melodies, live more than 70 years, remember each other after decades apart and have matriarchal society. Elephants are dope.

At the Elephant Nature Park, they are treated like Kardashians. I'd been following the preserve and it's roly poly pachyderms forever on Instagram, and I fell in love with each new baby born. When I first decided to leave I knew I was making a straight line to this place as my first destination. Seeing all of them IRL made my heart sing.

In the afternoon we went to the river with them and I got to witness what pure joy looks like. It is a baby elephant spraying herself and her friends. They were actually freakin' frolicking. Heart melt.

I realized how much I had kept to myself on the long train ride and night in Chiang Mai when I laughed out loud at Dok Mai tripping over her own giant padded feet. No wonder my voice sounded rough; it had been 48 hours since I'd last said anything.

I tried to imagine going two days at home not speaking. Everyone was always yelling every flimsy thought that floated across their brontosaurus brains. Work was 90% talking, asking patients questions and reporting out. Plus, the mindless chatter coworkers feel the need to pass back and forth. I learned early you had to catch the conversation ball and instantly bounce it back, whether you had something worthwhile to say or not, or be labeled "that stuck-up bitch". One time, still in that mode, I asked Aunt Mary about the weather.

"We're talking about the weather now? Sweet Jesus, come take me home to the Kingdom of Heaven immediately. I'm ready. Everyone here is boring me to tears."

I finished wiping her ass a little less gently and kept quiet after that.

I only had two days here. I wanted to stay for the rest of my life. I had emailed the director with my resume, highlighting I was a very accomplished Ass Wiper, and noting they had a whole lot of giant asses to be wiped. I guess they need more like "veterinarians" and "large mammal specialists" than registered nurses though.

I decided to break my vow of silence at the communal dinner for visitors.

Eyed my options.

Elderly Australian couple, softly bickering over a fish head. Nope.

Rowdy pack of young Brits, hiding their trust funds under boho clothes and dreadlocks. Nah guys, I can smell the rich on you under the BO.

Kinda sad looking older guy alone. Hi new friend.

"Can I sit here?" I asked, before setting down my tray of three different kinds of Curry Heaven piled around a rice mound.

He looked up and nodded, then went back to tucking away his portion. I sat and ate silently.

Three hours later we were BFFs.

"So I told Susan, 'Listen woman, I love ya. Still, I'll not rot in this backwater village walkin' yer poodles and fixing casseroles while ya work 14 hours a day in town.' And she left me. Tried to leave the damn dogs too. Heh, I shoved em into the boot before she drove away. Think she made it to Bristol before she realized they were back there!"

His name was Richard, he was a 64-year-old retired plumber, and he was so funny I didn't mind that he kept spilling his Singha down my leg each time we laughed. He had been married four times and I could see how he had charmed the ladies back in the day. Under the soft belly and wrinkles you could see outlines of a hot guy with bright blue eyes and a wicked smile.

"Here I am telling ya all my failures and faults and I've na asked ya nothin' about yerself. Hows it that you got here and whereya goin' next?"

"I've wanted to come here since I was little. I read about it one of those like, National Geographic for Kids magazines and promised myself I'd see the elephants in person someday. I don't know what's next...I have one of those around-the-world tickets, you know…where do you think I should go?"

It is shockingly easy to get people to talk about themselves instead of you.

"Well now that's a big question, ennit! Let me tell ya, I spent a week in Morocco in the 70's with the most beautiful woman in the world, Shirley Blackwell, and I'll ne'er forget the taste of the Alboran Sea on her skin…"

It was late by the time we stumbled back to the huts. I stopped, listening to the sounds of the elephants in the thick jungle air. The stamping and snuffling was loud and peaceful.

"Well ga night to you, Missy. It's been a lovely night, and you're a lovely girl."

Fuck it. I hugged the old bastard. He had a good light to him.

And damn if he didn't take the chance to grab my ass.

I wasn't totally shocked. Richard was joining ranks of thousands of men who appreciated my ass.

This thing I carry around is pretty fucking spectacular. It is big. Lots of women think they have a big ass. Mine is legit big. Like, disproportionate to the rest of my frame big. When I work out a lot it does not get any smaller, just rounder. It has been "vocally admired" by men on the street since I was 11 years old. And thanks to Real Ass Pioneers like J. Lo, I have always thought it's my best feature.

And now a 64-year old's strong plumber hands were on it. What would it be like to have sex with a guy 40 years older than me? On the one hand, he was not bad looking for his age, and would definitely know what he was doing. On the other…ew.

Old people are better at patience. A guy my age would have run if I didn't kiss him right away. Richard waited, card on the table, allowing me to make up my mind about my next move.

I kissed his cheek.

"A lovely night it twas, Sir. Sleep well."

He chuckled and gave me a brief hug, taking the rejection well. Hitting on a woman who could be your granddaughter takes some solid balls. I admired his cojones. I just didn't want them in my mouth.

4 INTO THE GREEN ROOM

I watched Khun Yai give herself a bath in the river the next day, wishing I could be an elephant. All power and inch-thick skin and sharp tusks. Maybe my next life. In this life I had to decide where I was going next.

For a half second I wished I had gotten Gabe's number or email. I wondered where his Heady Bro Gang was off to next. Probably Whore Island. Besides, the point of this trip wasn't to find a rando guy to tag along with. It was to do what I wanted to do.

I found the sanctuary director sipping tea on the deck of the kitchen hut. My bus back to Chiang Mai was leaving in 20 minutes. I read once the director won a Hero of the Year award from *Time* magazine. I probably should leave her alone and not bug her.

She was really nice and remembered reading my resume. They only needed vets for long-term volunteering though.

"You're the one with all the hospice experience, yes?

"Yes."

"Hmmm. Wait here."

She came back with a young Thai man in work khakis. His cut-glass jaw was set hard and his thick eyebrows bunched together.

"An elephant is being released from labor near Nomtok Mae Surin. This is Daw, one of our vets. He's going to get him and bring him to safety here. Do you want to go help him?"

"It will not be a tourist trip," Daw said in perfect English. "It is a two-day trek in the mountain jungle both ways. On the way out it may take longer walking with the elephant."

"Can't we ride it back?" I asked. The words came out a second before I remembered the strict No Riding rule that was a big deal in the Sanctuary.

Daw's face twisted like he'd taken a big swig of orange juice after brushing his teeth. He turned to go, and the bus driver waved at me to board.

The director grabbed Daw's hand and gently pulled him back.

"I think you will find her useful. I would like her to go with you." She turned back to me, "I will need you to sign some waivers. Daw is right, this is not a tourist activity. You said you want to really help. Are you sure?"

I nodded.

"Excellent," she smiled, "I will get the paperwork."

"Can you carry a 40-pound pack?" Daw asked. I knew that I was in, pack abilities or not. He clearly followed the director's orders. He was also clearly very cute, even while glowering at me.

Before dawn the next morning I climbed into the back of an open-air truck. Jenny, the youngest female, ambled by and eyed my banana. I held it out and she took it gently. I'm pretty sure she winked at me.

"Someone once told me you can hear through your feet. Is that true?"

She snuffled around looking for more food.

"Sorry that was my whole breakfast. But I'm going to bring you a new friend!"

"Assuming you don't get bitten by a pit viper. Or stung by a scorpion. Or kidnapped by drug traffickers near the Burma border," Daw chimed in, tossing gear into the back with me. "Hang on back there, I'd hate for you to bounce out along the way."

I think he likes me.

I was already sore after three hours of bouncing on a wooden plank. Then Daw added the pack.

"Hooof!" I exhaled as he pulled the chest and waist straps tight.

"I made yours lighter. I'm carrying most of the supplies. You only have the food. It'll get lighter as we go." He shouted to the driver in rapid Thai and waved.

All of a sudden it was me and him, and a wall of jungle. What the hell had I been thinking?

I am a concrete jungle animal. I know not to replace a battery right away if yours gets stolen, because the scummer will come back the next night to steal your new battery too. I don't know shit about vines and…undergrowth and whatnot.

I did read once all about the Golden Triangle and how the CIA gave guns to insurgents/opium traffickers in the Triangle in exchange for protection during anti-commie ops in China. Cool story bro, but not helpful right now.

Daw took off into the thick green brush at a legit clip. I wouldn't have spotted the trail entrance in a hundred years. Right away I noticed the sounds. Birds calling, insects humming, wind in the tall trees, random scuttling I didn't want to think about too hard. I thought of woods as peaceful. This was loud as hell.

I hustled to keep up with Daw. I wanted to stop and stare at the crazy plants growing on top of other plants, on top of vines, on top of trees. Then I wiped out and learned a quick lesson about keeping my eyes on the rocky, root-covered trail. Instead I trained my eyes on his butt, which looked pretty good in stained khaki.

Two hours in I was gasping, swatting bugs from my sweaty neck and questioning every decision that brought me to this tropical hell hole. I was incredibly grateful when Daw the Trail Eating Machine stopped at a small river and filled a filter bag with water.

"Take off your pack, this will take a bit," he said. It was the first thing he'd said to me since we hit the trail.

I felt like I was floating without the pressing weight on my shoulders. Finally being able to look around, I saw tiny purple orchids clinging on to the vines over the river, and a thousand tiny silver fish darting in the water. A bright yellow bird landed on a branch and looked at me sideways. A creeping sense of euphoria grew under my exhaustion. Or I was having a heat stroke.

Daw handed me the first liter of purified water. I chugged it and checked out the front side of the deer-fast guy I'd been following all morning. He was probably in his early 30's. My first impression last night was a hard face. His jawline and cheekbones were the kind that wannabe starlets tried to contour onto their faces with piles of makeup. Watching him relax by the water, I realized it must have been his expression of total disgust at having to take an American tourist with him. Without a scowl on his face he looked downright approachable.

"So you're a vet?"

"Yes. Large Animal Specialization."

"What's the craziest thing that's ever happened with an animal?"

He looked at me strangely.

"Like, tell me about something weird or funny that's happened while you were treating an animal."

"Funny? They are very sick when I see them. Or in pain. Not very funny."

It was going to be a long trek. After he got his liter of water and chugged it too, he waded into the river barefoot and stared up at the swaying canopy.

"One time there was a very rich landowner near the sanctuary. His favorite bull needed to be neutered to extend its life. However, the man was very proud of his bull's genitalia. He was very torn. I suggested we could cremate the genitalia, and he could keep the ashes. To this day if you visited his house you would see a very beautiful jar on his mantel, brimming with ashes of bull dick."

I barked out a laugh. Good one Daw, I didn't think you had it in you.

Once the water containers were filled we headed out again and didn't stop until late afternoon. I was dying. I also refused to ask for a break. I was gonna make this guy eat his words and be *glad* he had me along, not pouty.

We finally paused at a thick fall of vines over a large rock. Daw handed me a headlamp.

"There's still hours of light?"

"Not in there," he said.

WTF? In where?

He pulled back the vines and there was a black hole in the rock, barely taller than me.

"No one said anything about a cave!"

"You're a lucky girl. The cave trip is usually extra cost on the tour," he said mockingly. I liked Not Funny Daw better.

All my resolve to be a badass evaporated.

"I don't like small spaces."

"The other way around has a large river rapid that has killed many elephants. You want to try that way?"

5 THE VILLAGE

The best thing I can say about the cave was that it was a little cooler. The worst thing, neck and neck with my soul-crushing claustrophobia, was the spider that ran over my hand in the dark. It basically raped my fingers with the lightest, hairiest touch I've ever felt. I swung the light around just in time to see one of its legs. It was the size of a chicken thigh.

I didn't scream. But I think Daw heard the panic in my breathing, because instead of driving ahead without looking back, he took my hand and helped me navigate the uneven passages. The walls were close and wet and I swore I could feel the weight of the tons of rock surrounding us. The bats swooping through the beams of the light beams didn't bother me though. Our attic always had a bat problem and I was the best at catching them with a lacrosse stick and Dustbuster.

What did bother me? The Casket. That's what I called the super charming section where we had to take off our packs, shove them in front of us, and belly crawl through a tube the size of a damn coffin.

"I don't like small spaces."

"You said that."

"Yes. I did."

He was waiting with his pack already in The Casket. I could feel the patience draining out of him. I made a decision.

"When I was four someone put me in a wooden box, so small my neck was bent between my knees. They hammered it shut and left me in it for the night."

Daw's eyes grew big in the dark.

"That is terrible."

"I really don't like small spaces."

He nodded. Thought a moment. Took my pack and shoved it up with his. He went through pushing both packs, then came back so his face was peeking out at me.

"I will go through backwards. You come on, and only look at my eyes. Don't look away. Pretend you are crawling across an open plain, looking at my eyes."

"Why am I crawling across a plain? If it was wide open, I'd be walking."

His mouth hardened a little.

"Ok sure. Here we go."

It wasn't so bad. His eyes were lighter brown than I thought. They seemed to glow in the darkness and I concentrated on counting the sparse dark lashes on his lower lids, each one standing alone without touching a neighbor. I pushed with my boots and knees and before I knew it he dropped out on the other side and I followed. There was light coming from around the next curve.

"That was easy!" I crowed.

He grunted and strapped my pack back on with more muscle than necessary.

Soooooo happy to be back in the open air. The heat died down as the sun started to dip behind the ridge.

"Where are we gonna sleep?" I wondered out loud. It literally had not occurred to me before. An image of waking up on the ground, snuggling a Malaysian pit viper flashed through my mind.

"There are many hill towns in this area. We are close to the one where we will stay tonight."

It sprang out of the forest without any warning. We were deep in the green heart of the jungle, miles from any real road, and pop, there was a whole village. A cluster of huts on stilts surrounded a central fire pit, with longer huts spread out in a wider circle. Dogs and kids, both with a lot of ribs and not a lot of teeth, ran up to us on the path.

They all seemed to know Daw, and he scooped up a couple of both species in his arms, exchanging nuzzles. He was carried off with the pack and I didn't know where to go. A skinny young boy in a monk's orange robe stood by the gate to the village. He eyed me up and down and nodded like a king, allowing my presence.

Feeling like a lost puppy, I wandered around the compound,

inspected by chickens and suspicious eyes from hut entrances. One side of the village was completely cleared of the jungle brush and I could see out across the valley, to the next set of mountains. The landscape looked like a crumpled cloth napkin someone dropped after a good meal. It was hard to believe the same sun that was setting behind those purple mountains would rise over Flint's factories.

"It's time for dinner," Daw said.

I jumped. He was silent, that guy.

We went into a hut and my heart stopped. Honest to God, there was a mummy laying in the darkness. Her face was pale under a cross-hatch of deep wrinkles and the rest of her was bound in white muslin. Bats and spiders and mummies, fuck me, this was a House of Horror not a vacation.

"Daw...what...who...is that?"

"That is my grandmother. She has not been well lately. She is just getting older and needs more rest."

I sniffed, checked her pulse, and started pulling away the wrappings.

"Stop that, you have no business touching her!"

"I'm a nurse," I snapped, "And your grandmother is dying."

Daw left and brought in two village women, all of them talking in Thai at once. I ignored them and continued to check the woman. Stiff, cold appendages. Blood was collecting around the primary internal organs, trying to keep her alive. Viscous fluids in the mouth and nose. She stopped breathing and so did I. Ten seconds. Then she gasped without opening her eyes and started again.

"Ask them when's the last time she ate or drank anything," I said over my shoulder to the bickering sounds.

The dressing around her genitals was dark red. Not blood, distilled urine. Kidneys had stopped functioning.

"They say she has not taken food or drink for a day and a half," Daw translated through the noise, "Before that, she was doing much better. They are making a broth for her now."

"They can stop. She's not going to eat it, her digestive system shut down."

Daw said something to the women in rapid Thai. I knew it wasn't a direct translation of what I said.

"You should tell them the truth. Tell them to get the family together and do...whatever they do for a final goodbye here," I felt her pulse again, "She'll probably been gone by morning."

Daw grabbed me by the arm and dragged me out of the hut.

"Who do you think you are?" he hissed. His face was inches away and I could feel the angry heat coming off him. His blunt fingers dug into my upper arm, cords standing out on his forearm. "This is our family's business, not yours. I am a doctor! I was educated in Australia! I know dying when I see it. And the aunties think she will be better soon."

I was alone. No one knew where I was. This was his village, and I was the intruder. I should definitely not say, "Hey Doctor Dummy, your grandmother's not a fucking wallaby." The smart thing to do was back down and let them lie to themselves.

"Listen to me Daw," I said in my Nurse Tone, "I am very sorry to tell you that your grandmother's time is near. Her systems have shut down and all we can do at this point is be there for her during this transition. Did you know she can still hear us, even though she can't respond? Let's get all the people who love her to say goodbye, huh?"

My Nurse Tone is sweet as sugar. And the grip I used to take his hand off me was iron.

The fight went out of him. Tears sprang up and caught in the web of stubby eyelashes I had stared at earlier. He nodded and left me rubbing my sore arm.

Nearly everyone in the village piled into the hut. I stayed at the edge of the crowd as they sang to her, stroked her cheeks and took turns wailing over her body. Turns out death and goodbyes look the same whether you're in a sterile hospital room or a smoky hut.

Daw was missing for hours. I was getting spooked that he had abandoned me. Shit maybe I'd die in this village too, trapped by my inability to go back through the cave by myself.

He finally came back right before dawn. A younger version of him followed like a Daw Echo into the hut.

The man collapsed on the grandmother's feet, sobbing. I took the opportunity to slip through the crowd and check her pulse again. Shuddery. It was close.

"Go easy and I hope your next life is beautiful," I said in my head as I patted her shoulder. I'd probably said that little prayer to 500 people right before they died. I meant it every time.

The stars were fading and I could barely make out a line of mountain against the sky. Someone was singing now in the hut. Daw came out and sat next to me by the fire they had kept burning all night. He smelled like gas.

"That your little brother?"

"Yes. He is working across the valley. He would not have gotten to say goodbye if…Thank you."

"You're welcome. Tell me your favorite memory of her."

He took a swig of something cloudy in a jar and the gas smell intensified.

"Is that…booze?"

He chuckled. "It is our finest mountain moonshine. Special occasions only. Try it."

OMG it seriously tasted like gas and rotten meat. I choked. He laughed. We watched the fire for a while before he spoke.

"When I was a little boy I liked to chase her favorite rooster. It stressed the animal, to where its feathers were falling out. She kept swatting me for it, and I kept doing it. I don't know why. Maybe it felt good to be more powerful than him. To exert my dominance. She called me over one day. The rooster was letting her pet him in her lap. Animals love her…she's the one who taught me how to earn their trust.

She handed me a knife and told me to cut his throat. 'You want to cause him harm? You want to be the big man and bully him? Don't pick at him piece by piece. Have the courage to kill him all at once.' I remember how his eye twitched, following my hand with the knife. He didn't try to run. He was safe in her hands. There was so much blood it soaked us both. And she made me eat two plates of rooster at dinner."

"That is a badass parenting move."

"Yes. It was quite badass."

He hiccupped and started crying. He tried to hide it, pressing his face into his crossed arms. His shoulders were jumping though.

Shit. Ethically, you are supposed to "support the grieving individual with a minimal amount of physical contact."

I scooted closer and gently rubbed his shoulder. He took some deep breaths and wiped his face on his sleeve.

I usually spot things coming, so it shocked me when Daw's mouth landed on mine, urgent and hot. He tasted like that gross gas liquor and his lips were velvet soft. His face was wet from tears and maybe a little snot.

I shouldn't let this happen. I still had days in the jungle solo with this guy, and he was hurting. Most people don't know that horniness is a common reaction to death. Some people need to feel something other than grief; others want to connect with the source of life. Either way, witnessing death can give you a hell of a boner.

Case in point, Daw took my hand and rubbed it on the flagpole under his khakis. Despite myself I moaned a little into his mouth. He was a good kisser, even in his selfish agitation. And he grew even more under my hand.

He lifted me to straddle his lap, so I was pressed against it and wrapped his arms around me tightly, never stopping the breathless kissing. I couldn't help wiggling against him a little bit and he groaned, biting my lower lip. I ran my hand over his back and it was all ropy muscle. One hand released me to reach under my filthy shirt and circle my breast.

Right then I realized the singing had stopped.

6 CHAI SON

I don't know if it was the nipple pinch or the sudden quiet, but I froze. Bad! Bad Nurse! Having sex in the dirt with this grieving veterinarian was a terrible idea. I hopped off his lap, just in time for most of the village to come out of the hut. A couple more minutes and they might have seen their Golden Boy riding an American whore by the communal fire pit.

An auntie showed me to a floor mat under mosquito netting, and I passed out right away. I dreamed about dark holes and roosters spurting blood and came really hard. I woke up gasping and embarrassed, hoping I hadn't been making noise. If I had been, the only thing that heard it was the spider in the corner that was the width and weight of a Big Mac.

I got a lot of soft blessings and caresses as we left. After thinking these people might machete murder me for telling it like it was the night before, it was really sweet. Of course they made a big fuss over Daw, stuffing leaf-wrapped rice packages in every pocket and the men handing him wads of feather-shaped leaves.

We waved and set back on the trail, the day already half gone. Daw hadn't looked me in the eye yet. I tried not to care whether he was embarrassed or angry. After all, he had jumped me out of nowhere. It wasn't my fault I kinda liked it, then saved him from shame in front of all his aunties.

"What are the leaves?" I asked, mostly to break the silence.

"Kratom. Same family as coffee plants. Helps you stay alert. We've got a lot of ground to cover before we get to the animal, you want some?"

"Sure." His hands weren't totally steady and he was pale under his dark gold skin. Oh, Daw gots a hangover, huh? Well maybe you'll hike at a human pace today, Jerkwad.

Nope. He was still a machine. Fuck.

We rolled into a very different village at dusk. Even though his hill town had been poor it felt…homey. This place felt like a junkyard brothel. There was garbage everywhere and discarded humans too. Men watched us pass from doorways, murmuring to each other. Starving dogs picked at carcasses in the road. The hair on my neck prickled. I don't use this term lightly, but this place was hood.

There was no way in hell I was going to let Daw leave me alone here. I picked up my pace to walk next to him. He looked uneasy too.

"Are we staying here tonight?"

"Depends. How do you feel about getting your throat cut?"

"Not great."

"Then let's get the animal and go."

As the tears ran down my cheeks, I tried to remember the last time

I had cried. It wasn't at Aunt Mary's funeral (something all The Crows had commented on in their crackling, passive aggressive way). Oh yeah, it was when I first saw *Saving Private Ryan*. It was a sleepover in Missy Hernandez's basement. IDK why a bunch of 14-year old girls chose that one. Maybe we thought it was sophisticated of us to watch a WWII movie. I lost my shit after the first half hour of carnage, sobbing and struggling to breathe. I wasn't invited to Missy's again...and her table would chant "Save Private Pussy! Save Private Pussy!" when I walked into the lunchroom for weeks. Bitches.

Looking at the elephant I couldn't stop the wetness on my cheeks. Long red rips ran down the thick skin of his legs. There were circles of raw skin under the shackle on his back leg. It smelled infected and attracted flies. He was emaciated, humps of spine visible under the blistered skin of his back. One of his eyes was nearly swollen shut. This was one miserable bastard.

Daw was talking in rapid Thai to a Gollum. I guess it was actually a man who was so weather-beaten and twisted he could have been a piece of petrified wood. He had a large machete at his waist and red stubs instead of teeth.

I carefully walked up to the elephant and laid a hand on its side. He flinched. There were long, dark hairs speckling the thick hide and it was so warm.

The conversation got louder. Even though I didn't understand a word, I know a shakedown when I see one. The Gollum had his hand on his machete and Daw was shaking his head. He wanted money for the elephant. I knew the deal had been releasing this work animal to us now that he wasn't good for logging. Otherwise they'd kill him if they were being kind or let him starve to death if they weren't. There wasn't supposed to be a payment, and I doubted Daw had been dumb enough to carry a bunch of cash on the trek.

There was a pair of bolt cutters leaning against the fence. Seemed like one of us needed an insurance policy in this situation. I wandered over behind the elephant and grabbed the handle. The Gollum was stepping to Daw, nasty red mouth inches from his face, yelling. I didn't want to attack him with bolt cutters. I am a peaceful woman unless directly provoked. And they're too small to cut a good chunk off at once. What if…

Clever escapes are a lot easier in the movies. The bolt cutter barely nicked the surface of the elephant's chain on the first cut. I had to set it sideways and sit on it to generate enough pressure to cut the steel. I mean, I fell over multiple times in the process, but that chain got cut.

And good timing too. The Gollum and Daw were now shoving each other and a group of shady characters were wandering over in the dusk. They weren't going to side with elephant.

Now fucking what? What's Pachyderm for "You're free! Run away!"?

"Hey!" I yelled, "Hey buddy!" I jingled the broken chain as hard as I could. He turned to the sound of the chain, probably expecting pain.

I read once that the elephant cortex has as many neurons as a human brain. In the 70's an elephant named Bandula would unlock her shackles, then go around freeing other elephants in the zoo. She always made the first one she freed act as lookout for the zookeepers.

This one was no dummy either. He saw the broken chain in my

hand and took off. Daw and Gollum rolled on the ground, the enormous feet almost trampling them. They both looked stunned.

"Let's go!" I yelled at Daw. Guess he was a bit smarter than the inbred hillbilly, because he got off the ground and ran before the Gollum understood what was happening. It's a Great Escape, asshole!

The elephant was hauling straight out of town. We ignored the screams and barks and tried to stay close, choking on the dust he kicked up. He let out an earsplitting trumpet as the road entered the jungle. The sound almost knocked me over. I hadn't ever heard anything so happy.

It was so loud it covered the sound of the motorcycle. I barely saw it out of the corner of my eye before a dark black pain whipped from the back of my skull over my eyes.

7 ANTS IN THE PANTS

Everything I saw, I saw sideways. I tried to lift my head. It weighed 2,000 pounds so I gave up and laid in the dirt.

Gollum was back, with new wheels. Same machete though.

Daw turned and yelled something to me. No idea what. Maybe, "Get out of the damn road," because the elephant had turned and spotted Gollum too, and he looked pissed.

Gollum tried to nail Daw with the same golf club he laid me out with. I knew I was out of it because my thoughts wouldn't stop circling around where a Thai hillbilly could have gotten a golf club. Instead of like, getting to safety.

Daw barely ducked the swing. I yelled inside my echoing head, "Punch him Daw! Punch him right in the 'nads!"

Instead he ran. Super Veterinarian, yes. Super Hero, not so much. At least he ran toward me instead of into the jungle.

The elephant stood stock still watching us. Then he moved.

Have you ever popped a tick? That's pretty much what Gollum's head looked like when the elephant stomped it. He took three strides, knocked his abuser off the motorcycle and straight curb stomped him.

Daw was running toward me and didn't see it. To the guy's credit, he scooped me under the arms and was trying desperately to pick me up.

"It's okay."

"It is not okay! Whether is the money or he is angry at being fooled, he means to kill us. Can you move?" He pulled me up to standing.

"Daw, it's okay."

I turned him around and he saw the shattered head. It took a minute to sink in.

"We need to go," I said.

"We need to go fast," he replied. "Are you hurt?"

I gently felt the back of my head. A giant knot, and a minor cut. Head wounds bleed like crazy, if it wasn't gushing, the cut was superficial. I was more worried about concussion. So was Daw. He took his hands off my arms and I swayed a little.

"Do you know where you are?"

"No." He looked worried.

"I mean, I'm in a shitty village 40 miles from nowhere, in some Godforsaken Thai jungle, with a cute veterinarian. I couldn't point to it on a map though."

He grinned.

"You have a hard head. Come on."

"Wait."

I walked up to the dead man in the road. With all the death I'd seen, I'd never seen a head laid out like that before. I thought about Spaghetti-O's. Then I puked in the bloody dirt. Maybe I did have a concussion.

I grabbed an ashy foot and dragged the body into the undergrowth. Ha, now I not only know what undergrowth is, I've hidden a corpse in it! Travel really does expand your horizons.

Daw came to help. No, no, I've got this murder covered Daw, you go stand over there and file your nails some more. We got him pretty well hidden and kicked some dirt over the blood stain in the road. It still looked like a blood stain. Oh well. I picked up the golf club. You never know.

Daw checkout out the beat-up Honda motorcycle. Instead of an ignition there was a spaghetti tangle of wires.

"Must be stolen. Damn, he could have saved us a walk."

"There's no way that thing will go over the trail!"

"We were going to take logging roads back anyway. Chai Son would not fit down those trails."

"Chaison?"

"Chai Son. It means mischievous boy. Do you think it suits him?"

The elephant had been munching leaves peacefully since committing murder and saving our lives. He gave me a sideways glance and snurfed.

"It does! Will he follow us, even if we're on the bike?"

"Yes. Unfortunately, he is used to following human's orders. And he is smart enough to know we don't mean him harm."

I pulled gently at the ignition wires. Found the right two and twisted. The motor turned over.

Daw mumbled to Chai Son in soft Thai, stroking his trunk firmly. He worked his way to the back leg, patting as he went. He pulled a large can out of his pack, and very gently worked the analgesic salve into the shackle-bitten flesh.

Finally, he cut a number of leafy branches from the tree Chai Son had been munching on and stuck them through the straps of my backpack. He motioned for me to get behind him on the Honda.

"You're a carrot," he said, pleased with himself, then he made a loud, chirpy noise, and Chai Son magically followed us down the road.

We rode the bike through the night. We both wanted to be long gone from the Village of the Damned by the time someone missed Gollum. I tried to stay awake in case I did have a concussion, but the drone of the motor and the comforting rhythm of Chai Son's footsteps behind us in the dark made my head dip. I woke up every time we hit a bump (painfully shaking the lump at the back of my head), then drifted off again against Daw's back.

At dawn another sound entered my foggy brain. A big rushing. I realized we had stopped moving. And that a large, delicate penis was tickling my ear.

"Gah!" I snapped up, ready to bust some teeth.

Chai Son's trunk was gently pulling the branches out of my backpack. I watched the end of the trunk work with real precision to pull a single branch out. Damn, how could such a big sucker do such a small task? Daw was busy looking at a map. I hopped off the bike and followed The Hulk as he went for richer branches on a tree.

I wasn't scared of him, even though I'd seen very exactly what he could do to a human in a second. Chai Son and I, we had a thing. I could tell from the first time I put my hand on his side. He wouldn't hurt me on purpose. I stroked his front leg while he tugged powerfully on a branch.

At first it felt like someone poured a bucket of dark red sequins over me. They covered my eyes and hair and skittered everywhere down my body, into my clothes. Then the sequins started to bite.

I am not ashamed to say I screamed. It was some scream-worthy shit. The ants were everywhere. *Everywhere*. Each individual bite pulsed, then pulsed out to reach its friends, until every inch of my skin was on fire.

I tried to brush them off in swipes. No luck. Each tiny asshole had six sticky feet to cling on. Daw was there in a second, stripping off my clothes and pulling off the ants he could reach while I danced in a circle of pain. My hair was the worst. I could feel them crawling everywhere, especially over the tight knot. One bit the open cut.

"MOTHERFUUUUUUUUUUUUUCKER!"

Daw picked me up and threw me over his shoulder. This was not how I had pictured being aggressively taken by him in my underwear. Not that I spent a lot of time picturing that on long jungle hikes.

He ran to the rushing river around the bend and dropped me in the shallows. The cold water immediately helped the burning and made it easier to brush off the ants. We both worked fast and cleared most of my body in a minute. The hair though. They kept dropping out and biting my shoulders. I laid back in the water and let him fish the bugs out of my tangles. The gentle tugs gave me a flash of Aunt Mary picking lice out of my hair every spring.

The panic started to fade.

I was just a girl, in a scenic river, being held by a cute boy…with her tits out and covered in red welts. Sighhhhh. At least they looked fantastic in the cold water.

Daw took his shirt off and handed it to me without looking…for long, anyway. Very gentlemanly.

"Stay in the water. It will help. I will find your clothes."

Chai Son came down to the water, all innocent curiosity.

"You bastard. I trusted you."

What's it called when you put human reactions onto animals? Anthropormizing or something. I knew he wasn't a human. Doesn't mean he didn't look ashamed as he took a long drink from the river.

Daw chirped a few commands and Chai Son knelt on the river bank.

"Climb on his neck."

"What?! You looked at me like I was scum when I thought we would ride the elephant back."

"We do not believe in humans riding elephants for profit. However, do you see another way across this river?"

I looked across the crashing whitewater. It was littered with boulders and even in the shallows I could feel how strong the current pulled.

Daw ditched the bike in the brush, strapped my pack on top of his and easily climbed onto Chai Son's upper back.

Ok then.

My hands scrambled for a saddle horn when the giant stood up. There was nothing to grip on to, only expanses of smooth grey skin. I started to fall sideways, with eight feet of air down to the rocks below.

Daw grabbed me and pulled.

"Hold with your knees," he instructed.

He pulled me tight to him and pressed my knees down into the flesh.

We moved slowly, rocking as Chai Son picked the safest route across.

I felt a strange rush of adrenaline and extreme calm. My heart was racing and my senses sharpened as I completely surrendered control to this animal. He was in charge of the crossing. My job was to hang on.

The only sound I could hear over the river was the loud bird calls. Daw's soaked shirt clung to me, shoulders already drying in the hot sun. I tried to focus on my balance, keeping centered over the mountain moving beneath my legs. But I was…distracted.

I could feel Daw close behind me. Hands on my waist to keep me centered. Bare chest pressed against my back. His breath on my neck was steady and calm while his heartbeat sped up. I paid close attention to his thighs behind mine. They adjusted a half-second ahead of the next roll or pitch. I tried to move with him and it made a huge difference in stability.

I was starting to actually enjoy the ride when Chai Son stumbled.

I pitched forward like I'd been bucked off a bronco. I felt Daw grab for me again. Too late, I was a lost cause.

Thankfully we were most of the way across. If it happened in the middle, I would have joined Aunt Mary on the other side. Instead I got dumped into the shallows again. Soaked and rock scraped, I chose to lay there a minute and look at the sky. Scary dark clouds were rolling in. Fuck this. My next stop was going to be an all-inclusive in Indonesia. With monkey butlers.

Chai Son chose that moment to take another drink. And spray me with it. I will send to you to the Great Elephant Graveyard in the sky, Chai Son. Try me again, dickhole.

Daw pulled me up by both hands. Then his mouth was on mine. The stealth was strong with this guy.

I pushed him away.

"No thank you. I am soaked, sore and starving. Not horny." That

48

was a lie. Even after a cold-water dunk I was still super horny from the ride together.

"I told you this wasn't a tourist trip," he laughed, helping me to the sandy bank. "Let's eat."

There were sweet rice packets, beef jerky sticks and apples in my pack. We ate like wolves. He laid out on the sand and was asleep in a second.

I was free to stare. He looked younger with his intelligent eyes shut. His full lower lip sagged to the side. Patchy stubble had sprung up since leaving Chiang Mai. I held my thumb up to the width of his eyebrows. Yup, they were a full inch tall. The chicas in Flint would have their work cut out for them with those caterpillars. His bare chest looked like a topographical map of a harsh climate. Sharp ridges and valleys, with two landmark dark brown nipple mountains. And the start of a low forest right above the line of his pants. Poor dude looked exhausted. I should let him sleep.

Thunder rumbled from somewhere downstream. Chai Son, busy playing in the mud down the bank, lifted his head and perked giant fan ears.

I straddled Daw on the sand and put my face close to his. My dark hair made a curtain around our faces.

"Wake up," I whispered.

His eyes fluttered.

"A storm is coming," I whispered.

He turned his head, trying to hang on to unconsciousness. I got a chill up my back as the wind picked up and blew his soaked khaki shirt against my skin. Fuck it.

I took his chin and kissed him, sucking a little on that full lower lip. Like he had done to me by the village fire. I let the weight of my breasts rest on his hard chest and rubbed myself against his thin pants.

He opened his eyes.

8 NUDIE RIVER

The first raindrops hit the sand and my back with authority. The light turned bruised yellow. The trees shook their fists at the dark sky. The birds finally shut up.

Turns out a sweet rice pack and some jerky can really revive a lady. I didn't feel the hundred ant bites covering my skin, or the swollen contusion on my skull.

I only felt Daw.

He was sure as shit awake now. If he had been a gentleman about my breasts when picking fire ants off them, he was making up for holding back. He sucked the dark nipples hard through his own wet shirt while trying clumsily to undo the buttons. I helped and we were both quickly down to our functional black underwear.

He cradled a breast in his hand, like he was weighing it. Then he found my mouth. I felt the hard planes of muscle across his back, this time covered in sand. The arm propping him up was shaking a little. Maybe with exhaustion. Maybe not.

A teeth-rattling clap of thunder hit. We both jumped and down the river bank Chai Son made nervous noises.

I pressed against him, feeling the same response he had by the fire. This time I didn't feel guilty. My hips ground into him, pushing him into the sand and inviting him to meet me with equal force. He didn't disappoint. He dug his teeth into my neck and my back arched involuntarily. Fuck me, was that some secret Thai massage pressure point?

Daw rolled me over into the sand and I did feel my head injury bounce on the hard pack. I winced, and he looked instantly regretful, wadding his shirt under my head. Somehow in that maneuver my underwear was off too. Its official, the guy was a ninja.

He pinned me down with a sinewy leg over mine. I got to squeeze the muscles that guided my own on the river crossing, slick with the rain. He insistently kissed me, pressed himself into my soft hip and slid a slightly cold finger inside me. Oh hell yes.

We were going to fuck on this here riverbank and not even the resurrected corpse of Gollum could stop us.

But an elephant could. The water sprayed us head to toe. We yelled and looked up in time to see a crack of lightning split the sky in half. Chai Son snuffed and stamped.

Daw buried his face in my breasts and yelled in frustration.

"If I had to die, dying inside you would be ideal," he said, still sliding his finger in and out, "Let's not die today though."

He helped me off the ground and dug my pre-Ant Invasion clothes out of my pack.

"We need to find shelter."

I mentally said goodbye to the river. It was lovely being naked by you a bunch, Nudie River. Sorry you didn't get to see me fully bang.

We dashed into the coverage of the jungle canopy where the rain wasn't as intense. I wondered if being surrounded by a lot of tall trees was our best plan in a lightning storm.

Thankfully not too far down the road there was a ridge of rock with a friendly overhang. Daw and I scooted back into the depression and were mostly protected. Chai Son stood in front of us, providing a warm grey curtain against the storm. It was cozy under the rock and I hoped for a minute we could pick back up where we left off.

Daw was busy rummaging in his pack instead, taking out medical supplies.

"I wanted to wait until after the river to treat him," he said while meticulously laying out vials and the biggest syringe I'd ever seen. "Let the water wash out some of the leg wounds."

He handed me the salve. "You can use a little of that on your ant bites if they are bothering you. It is a numbing agent with topical antibiotics."

"Are you sure you're not giving me elephant tranquilizers to knock me out and take advantage of me?"

He looked at me strangely. "That would be terribly disrespectful."

I am good at making out. I am not good at flirting. I rubbed the stinking goo onto my bites and kept my mouth shut.

Watching him work was amazing. I thought my doctors had a tough job wrangling obese patients with dementia. This was next level.

Chai Son stamped, wiggled, trumpeted and even whacked Daw with his trunk while he cleaned the wounds and administered shots. His power to kill wasn't far in the rearview of my memory. Despite Chai Son's whining he seemed to know Daw was helping and not trying to hurt him. Daw kept up a soft patter of Thai while he worked, constantly providing firm pats along with the procedures.

The storm blew itself out by the time he was done.

"It is all I can do here," he said, reviewing his work. "We will give him a full treatment plan once we reach the Sanctuary."

"How close are we?"

"Two days walk."

"Oh." I had mixed feelings about that. On the one hand I wanted a beer and a bed so bad it hurt. On the other I had no idea what would happen when we returned. There was no scenario I could imagine that didn't involve saying goodbye to Daw and Chai Son. And that sucked.

"Now let's sleep though, yes?" He was pale and shaky. I almost felt bad for waking him up and making him finger me earlier. Almost.

"Yes." And as I said it I felt the exhaustion hit me too.

We made a nest under the rock with the backpacks for pillows and fell asleep. Right before I went under, I felt him take my hand.

I woke up groggy, itchy and thirsty. The goo had worn off and the initial sting of the bites was gone. It was replaced by intense, full-body itchiness. Fun.

Daw was on a satellite phone.

A. Fucking. Phone.

"You have a phone?!" I yelled.

He hushed me and continued talking rapidly. I had gone fully Dark by the time he hung up.

"You had a working phone this whole time?" I seethed.

"Yes."

"Why. Didn't. We. *Use* it?"

"Use it for what?"

"Calling for help maybe?"

Daw was very obviously not reading my mood. He laughed.

"What should I have done? 'Hello my peace-loving colleagues at an elephant sanctuary. I am being pursued by a very mean man with a golf club. Please get to the Elephant Chopper and come rescue me immediately.' We got there by walking because that is the only way to get there."

He made sense. However, I sure did not appreciate his tone.

"Why are you calling them now then?"

"We are close to a main road. The one truck that can transport an adult elephant can go on that road. They should meet us in an hour or so."

"You said it was a two-day walk!"

"It is. I did not know if the truck was available. I called to see. You are not in good shape. I thought you'd be happy for a ride."

I felt like three different rivers meeting in one narrow canyon.

"I have to pee," I announced haughtily, and marched into the jungle.

Instead of having two days to figure out my next move I had an hour.

I gave Daw a real kiss when I came back. It tasted good and lasted a long time.

For the last hour of our adventure I asked him to tell me about Australia. The landscape and animals sounded magical through his eyes. He was a careful observer, mindful of details. For a doctor, anyway.

Chai Son got a hero's welcome at the Sanctuary. The entire staff was there to greet him with boat-sized basket of fruit. I ran my hand down his side a couple times, trying to memorize the feeling of his skin. Daw was busy planning his treatment with the other vets.

The bus for the day tourists pulled in. I grabbed my bag from the reception area.

"Thank you for bringing us our new friend."

The Sanctuary director smiled brightly at me, taking in my bites, scrapes and general filth.

"I hope the trip was not too difficult."

"It was fun," I said, without sarcasm. "Do you know Daw's grandmother died?"

"Yes, I had a feeling Auntie Anong's time was near. And that you might be a help to his family. She was very famous around here for her skills treating animals…and her tolerance for moonshine."

"It was an easy passing with her family all around. The best kind."

"Wonderful to hear. You are leaving us then?" she nodded at my bag, "Are you sure you wouldn't like to stay the night? Perhaps…shower?"

I did smell terrible, she had that right.

"No, it's time for me to go. Thank you though. Thank you for everything. Someone will post pictures of Chai Son, right? On your social accounts? I want to be able to see him and know he's all healed up."

"Of course. And you can always email me if you would like an update on his health. Or the health of anyone else here at the Sanctuary." Winking was beneath her, but she laughed mischievously as she handed me her card.

"You're…a very good person," I blurted stupidly. It wasn't what I wanted to tell her. I guess it was the truth though.

"So are you. Be well."

You don't know me very well lady.

The sounds of the elephants faded as the bus merged onto the highway to Chiang Mai. I decided nothing better than Chai Son was going to happen in Thailand. It was time to move on.

PART TWO:

THE BEACH

9 THE CANADIAN EXPERIMENT

It was a very beautiful vulva and I had no idea what to do with it. I mean, I had *some* idea. I was pretty sure she wanted my mouth on her. Considering I only had it done to me once, I felt like a 10-year old boy faced with his naked babysitter.

Indonesia had been a fucking bust. All-inclusive resorts are not inclusive of fun. Also, no monkey butlers. After four days of reading on the beach surrounded by old cunts and couples, I was done. So it was Soekarno–Hatta International to Cairns.

I met Felicia on a boat trip to the Great Barrier Reef. I read once that the Great Barrier Reef can be seen from space. Seeing it up close is pretty amazing too. After my next life as an elephant I hope I come back as a sea anemone. I was hypnotized watching the hundreds of tentacles waving in the current. To be a fluid thing like that, maybe providing shelter to a little Nemo fish, living as one tiny part of the huge, interconnected reef...I bet it's peaceful.

Felicia's travelling solo too. We had beers on the ride back to shore and she told me all about Fiji. It might be my next stop. She's a freakin' Canadian Goddess. All white teeth and red cheeks and messy blonde braids. We went to dinner that night and have pretty much been hanging out for a week. Beaches and coolers of Victoria Bitter and nightclubs in Port Douglas.

I didn't realize she was a lesbian until she looked me right in the eye caressed my ass at the club. It was not your mother's ass caress. When I didn't pull away, she kissed me. It was just like kissing a guy I guess, except she smelled sweeter.

We stumbled back to the hostel last night too drunk to do anything except share some chips and pass out. Now it was morning, the sun was bright in our room and we had until check out at 10:00 to do whatever we wanted. I wanted to do a lot of things. I just wasn't sure exactly how.

I ran my fingertips over her thigh. The sun highlighted the blonde peach fuzz on her tan skin. Good. I don't trust women who consistently shave above their knees. I kept going, tracing lightly over her neat little folds. I giggled thinking about all the giant clams we'd seen on the reef.

I also realized I'd never really looked at myself. I'd have sooner died than have Aunt Mary bust in the bathroom and catch me straddling a hand mirror. As soon as I was done getting this British Columbian lesbo off, I was going to have a good long look.

No sense beating around the bush. "I want to make you feel good...I don't know how though."

"You've never done it before?"

I shook my head. She took my hand, licked my fingers and guided them with hers.

"No problem. I'll teach you. Start lightly stroking me, top to bottom," she moved my hand with hers.

"Now a little harder. Oh. Yep. Like that."

I stared, amazed. Her pink skin was darkening and her clit was swelling right before my eyes. This shit was magic. Her hips started moving with my hand

"I'm getting wet. Don't stop petting the top with one hand and put a finger in me, slow."

I put in two. Very slowly. She gasped.

"Quick learner. That's it."

She moved against my hand as I leaned forward to suck her breasts. They were small, perfect mounds. I traced the line where her dark tan and white skin met with my tongue. I didn't know nipples could be that light. They tasted like her lemon essential oil.

She pulled me up to kiss me, pressing my hand to keep it busy and making use of her own over my soft cotton nightie. I had picked this piece out carefully for the trip. Modest enough to wear to communal bathrooms, sexy enough to make me feel good. It was black with a low back and a little pink lace. Checking myself out in the Victoria's Secret dressing room at the Lakeview Square Outlets, I could not have imagined this would be its first outing.

"I want you to taste me," Felicia gasped into my mouth.

She was already slippery as seaweed. I was doing a pretty good job, might as well go for gold.

I slid down the bed and took a minute to look at my handiwork. She was so full, the neat little package unwrapped into flushed folds. Her clit was twice the size as when I started and a little white goo slid out of her. Whether it was the kissing, or her hands on me, or seeing how crazy turned on she was, I started to throb myself.

I straddled one of her legs and ground down on it for a few strokes. Not yet. If I was going to love on a lady, I wanted to be a generous lady lover. I tucked my hair behind my ears and lowered my face to her. I had a whole plan for a gentle approach like Gabe did with me. Instead she grabbed the back of my head and shoved herself onto my nose.

I pushed her back a bit, not appreciating the assault. This is happening on my terms, honey. I circled her full clit a couple times with my tongue and sucked it hard. She came instantly. I could feel the tendons in her inner thighs quiver uncontrollably and her legs kicked like she was being electrocuted. She was whispering "Oh God, Oh God, Oh God" over and over with her eyes closed. I stuck to my position, enjoying the success. I tried to keep sucking but she pulled me off like a leech.

She rolled to her front, hands between her legs and face buried in the pillow. Guess I'd have to wait for my turn. I wiped my mouth with the back of my hand. That was fun, and I was good and turned on. I wondered why Diego had never done it to me.

10 THIN BLUE LINE

I am fully done with Felicia. Turns out if you spend every minute with someone, they can get super annoying, even if you're only doing super fun stuff. She makes slurpy noises when she eats and says "literally" too much and might be racist against Jews.

Plus, she was acting all girlfriendy. I didn't mind the hand holding in public, even though it felt showy. I sure did mind her acting pouty if I spent too long talking to the bartender or went for a walk without telling her. And she kept posting pictures of me on Facebook when I asked her not to. And she was asking more questions about what it was like to be a marine biologist at Sea World than I was prepared to answer.

I'm also sick of going to the beach and not swimming. Between the box jellyfish and undertow, lifeguards keep kicking me out of the ocean every time I tried to take a dip. Like they were bouncers keeping me out of a Club Pacifica.

A trip to the Daintree Rainforest was fucking wonderful (blue butterflies the size of dessert plates!). But every time the canopy closed over me, I got a little anxious. I realized I was hoping to see an elephant and his friend around every turn in the trail. So, no more of that.

It's been real Cairns. Time to roll out.

One morning at a coffee shop I said I had to go to the bathroom. We both had our packs, and she was too deep in her phone to notice I took mine with me. Bye, Felicia.

I caught the Oz Bus down the coast. It was built for backpackers with stops everywhere you'd want to go if you were young, horny and ready for adventure. I went "quad biking" at a sheep station in the Outback (they're called 4-wheelers, you convict weirdos), toured the ruins of an 1800's mansion being slowly eaten by the rainforest and hit a bunch of sparkling beaches and scrubby hostels down the Gold Coast.

I made the mistake of hooking up with one of the tour guides at a popular stop. He was mean under his thin crust of charm and got really mad at me when I wouldn't have sex without a condom. Sorry Chlamydia Chris, I'm not trying to catch every strain of STD known to man. No more tour guides.

By the time we hit Byron Bay I was ready to find a halfway decent room and chill for a while. It was also where I would learn how to surf. *Blue Crush* is my all-time favorite movie. Badass surfer chicks who have to work as maids to support themselves. Kate Bosworth looking gorgeously athletic instead of skeletal. NFL player cameos. What's not to love?

My dad's favorite movie is *Point Break*. I'm pretty sure he thinks he's Patrick Swayze minus the mullet and plus 30 pounds of Midwest chub. He can dance pretty good for a big man. Point is I'm ready to stop watching surfing movies and get a board wet.

I was doing great on my budget. Between my free "adventure trek" in Thailand and letting Felicia pay for most things in Cairns I was way ahead of the game. I felt bad for a hot second about how many bar tabs I let Felicia pay...then remembered her dad "literally owns half of Whistler" and didn't feel bad anymore.

I treated myself to a private room at one of the nicer hostels on the main strip in Byron Bay. Nicer meaning a private bathroom and a 10% chance of bedbugs instead of a 90% chance. I was tired of falling asleep wondering if the creepy 50-year old German in the next bunk was struggling with his sleep apnea machine or masturbating.

I plunked down a credit card at the best rated surf school in Byron. I asked for weeks' worth of private lessons with their most experienced instructor. The bro who signed me up warned that a week in the breakers would be tough on a total newbie. I said I'd deal.

I woke up the first morning before dawn with worms in my stomach. I remembered the feeling from my short career as a track star in middle school. I was really fast and had good wind. Turns out you need a bunch of dedication and technique to consistently win though. It was game over when I got hips and discovered weed.

Walking out to Belongil Beach I felt that same mix of excitement and anxiety I always had at the starter line. Except instead of crouching on a crumbling track wrapped in rusty chain link I was standing at the edge of infinity.

The Pacific has been my ocean since the first time I saw her out the plane window. We're soulmates. There's something about her size and mystery that makes me stupidly happy. We have no idea what lives in her deepest parts, and I bet she likes it that way. I read once that less than .05% of the ocean floor has been mapped in detail with sonar. That's about the size of Tasmania.

Lots of people are freaked out by not knowing what lies under that thin blue line. I am seriously shocked at how many people I've met travelling who spent thousands of dollars to get to the "best beach in the world" and never actually go in the ocean. I like not knowing. It's a whole different world, right here on the same planet.

I was in love with the Pacific, and I wanted to learn how to dance with her. I spotted a guy with two boards and the surf school logo on his rash guard. Let's do this thing.

11 CONFESSION

His name was Shane and he was going to be a problem. I was serious about learning to surf and he was serious about looking like a Chris Hemsworth/Kelly Slater mashup. He kept flirting with me during his "dry land sesh," complimenting my pop ups and adjusting me physically into the right crouch. Finally, he grabbed my hips and pulled them down firmly, demonstrating how low I needed to stay. That was it.

"I'm not going to pay you to fuck me. I want to learn to surf."

He laughed so big I could see the fillings in his molars.

"You're true blue, huh? Don't you worry love, I'm happily married. And not a whore. You ready to catch your first wave?"

I paddled out on my giant foam board. Shane insisted it was easier to learn good technique on this beast instead of the sleek little shark board of my dreams. He got me in position and when a low roller came through, he gave me a push. I paddled like crazy as the momentum built behind me.

"Pop up!"

Wipe out. It was a lot easier to get from your belly to your feet on solid land. Repeat for the next two hours.

I almost crawled onto the sand. Laying on my back, Shane's golden head eclipsed the sun.

"You alright True Blue? It's a lot of work to learn, you're doing a good job for your first time. Let's take a lunch break and try again."

"It's only 10:00. I'll take five." I rolled onto my stomach, closed my eyes and tried to slow my breathing. I mentally reviewed each fall, and Shane's shouted instructions. Paddle harder. Pop more smoothly. Set my feet like I mean it. Bend my knees, not my back.

The first time back in the water I stood up. The wave was laughably small and I probably rode 15 feet before it petered out. I was the fucking champion of the world!

Shane gave me hoots and high fives and we were off. I had the rhythm now, even if I slipped or timed it wrong, I knew what it was supposed to feel like. And it felt like heaven. Speed and salt and the motion in the ocean. I was hooked. By the end of the day I was consistently getting up and had some ability to drive where I wanted to go.

Shane called that a great success for Day One. It's your job to tell me I'm doing a good job Shane. Guess I'll take it. We had a beer at the beach bar when I officially couldn't paddle anymore.

"You snowboard?" he asked, checking out my legs in what I now knew was professional interest. "You look like you have the instinct to cut."

"No. Never had money for a lift ticket. I skated a lot growing up though. Plenty of free concrete."

He nodded, "That's it then. I bet tomorrow you'll be able to carve more, and we may even try a real board Wednesday." He checked his phone. I checked his legs. Dark tan and calves so stacked there were raised veins crossing his shins. I was actually glad he was married.

"Perfect conditions here for beginners tomorrow too. Don't drink too much tonight, and if you have a tub take a cold soak. It'll help you be less sore. Eat a banana tomorrow morning for potassium. You're going to have a lot of lactic acid build up in your shoulders and calves. Drink plenty of water and go to bed early. I want you in shape to work. Eight a.m., ya?"

"Ya." I don't like being told what to do. I did like being coached.

I was stretching in the water at 7:30. My shoulders felt like lead. I bounded up to Shane when he arrived at 7:45 anyway, helping him pull the boards off the roof rack. There was a hot pink real board up there too. He saw me eyeing it.

"I thought maybe you'd be ready for it by this afternoon. First you gotta show me perfect form on the foam board though."

I got straight up on the first try and, if I say so myself, killed it all morning. Everything hurt and I didn't care. I was the best surfer in the universe. The waves died down around noon and we took a break on the sand. He had a packed lunch for us, some sort of amazing brown chicken over rice in little tin boxes.

"You're progressing really well, I gotta say when I first saw you I didn't know how serious you were about learning all week."

I cocked my head and looked directly into his bright blue eyes.

"What about me doesn't look serious?"

"Oh, you're serious as a heart attack, I see it now. My apologies for misjudging you. I get a lot of silly girls through here who think they want to surf and back out the second it gets hard."

"I bet."

He licked brown sauce off his fingers happily and laid back on the warm sand.

"So where are you from?"

Oh no Shane. We're not playing Get To Know You Bingo.

"You don't really care, and I don't really want to tell you, so why don't we talk about surfing? When did you learn?"

He chuckled and stretched his bulky shoulders.

"I like you, True Blue. You're real. I grew up here. My parents surfed. I swam before I walked, and I could catch a wave on my own by the time I was four. It's in my blood."

I realized I hadn't actually seen him on a board. He would stand in the chest deep water to help position me and give me a push.

"Where do you surf around here?"

"Locals secret," he winked. "I'll never tell you where I ride with my mates. I take my family to Cosy Corner, in the national park. We can go there if you're sick of Belongil already."

"I'm not sick of it," I said, looking out over the miles of breakers sparkling in the sun.

You know how I said I wasn't scared of surprises under the thin blue line? When I fell off my board and something as wide and solid as a guardrail slid past my leg I screamed real loud.

Shane laughed from 20 yards back.

"Quit whinging, it's a dolphin. There's a whole pod coming in!"

The sleek grey bodies sped all around me. I held my breath on my board watching them jump and chase each other. One came close enough to touch, cruising on its side and giving me the eye. I started crying and gave it the finger. But, like, playfully. I've cried more on this trip so far than I have my entire life. Maybe it's because no one I know is watching.

Getting up on a real board was starting back at Square One. I had no idea how much stability the wide foam was giving me. I spent most of the third and fourth days eating shit and muttering sarcastic comments to Shane under the sound of the waves.

"What's that you said, True Blue? I'm the best surf instructor this side of Burrumbuttock? That's right love, I am. Now paddle your wide ass back here, there's a nice set coming in."

Finally, finally, at the end of the fourth day I got up and stayed up. I was able to find the sweet spot on the board and felt how much more responsive it was to shifts in my body weight. I made a few solid turns and as I felt the wave start to peter out under me, I threw my whole weight into a full cutback.

Shane hollered and swam for shore. He took my two-million-pound board and grabbed me in a bear hug as I dragged my sorry ass out of the wash. His chest felt like a suit of armor. Mrs. Shane was a lucky lady.

"You are my masterpiece! A cutback on a real board four days in. And a Sheila to boot. What will it take for you to write up your experience on TripAdvisor for me?"

Ignoring the casual sexism, I demanded beer and food.

"I promised my son I wouldn't miss his rugby match at 4. Come to my house after and we'll cook you a feast. Ya?"

My brain said hard no. Somehow my mouth made a noise like "Sounds great". Goddammit.

As I sat in Shane's cozy and airy living room I realized I hadn't been inside someone's home in almost three months. It felt weirdly personal. Like every tossed paperback or child's drawing was a glimpse into the family's soul.

His wife Mary called from the kitchen, "Iced green tea or beer?"

"Um, can I have both?"

"Certainly honey, we believe in eating and drinking all the good things in this house!"

She was a petite Filipina with black hair to her waist. Years of working with old people gives you a crystal ball for how people will age. I could tell Mary would be one of those elegantly beautiful old women with silver hair and lively eyes, no matter how many wrinkles creased her smooth skin.

Their three children all looked like nature had Photoshopped them. I also hadn't been in close proximity to children in a while. I forgot how they could be obnoxious and engaging at the same time. I colored with the littlest one while Mary banged out a four-course meal. Or the little one colored, and I studied how long her eyelashes were and how cute her tongue was when she stuck it out the side of her mouth like a kitten.

Shane lit up at home. The kids seemed to gain strength from touching him. Whether it was a kiss after a fall or a tag while one of the boys sprinted through the kitchen, they never went more than 10 minutes without tapping into his reassuring physical presence. I thought it must be exhausting but Shane looked even happier here than in the ocean.

After an epic Filipino meal and five beers, I was happy to lean back in a saggy chair by the outdoor fire pit while they put the kids to bed. Shane and Mary came back out with fresh mint mojitos and did not look ready to call it a night. They settled into a hammocky seat with Mary curled into Shane's side and lit a joint.

"For real True Blue, what's your story? I can't quite figure you out."

I fidgeted with the bright silver Claddagh ring on my right hand. The words were out of my mouth before my filter could kick in. And they were baldly true.

"I killed my aunt. Her name was Mary too. She was dying painfully and she asked me to kill her. So I did. I'm a hospice nurse so was easy to make it look natural. Her friends found out though and think I did it for her money. Which is stupid. She was my only real family left. I wouldn't kill my only family for money. So, I left my shitty town and I don't think I'm going back."

12 MAYBE NOT SUCH A GREAT IDEA

I wasn't sure what reaction I expected from Shane and Mary. They seemed to skim over the homicide confession pretty quickly.

"You don't have any other family honey?" Mary asked.

"My dad is a trucker and he was gone a lot. Now he has another family in Kentucky and he's gone a lot more."

"What about your mom?"

Mary, if I wasn't so wrapped in your web of warm hospitality I'd shut down this Spanish Inquisition right here.

"My mom was a really fucked up alcoholic meth head and she left us when I was little. I'm pretty sure she's dead now."

"Well that sounds like a difficult journey. And here you are today, a beautiful, strong young woman travelling the world on your own. That counts for something."

Mary was stoned and a little drunk. Her words still made my chest hot.

"So you killed your aunt?"

There ya are Shane, all caught up now.

"I gave her a release from the terrible pain of pancreatic cancer and a peaceful exit to the next life."

It suddenly occurred to my foggy brain that they could report me to the police. I was in Australia, not Mars. I could be extradited and charged with homicide. Fucking beer. Why did I open my stupid mouth? Fight or flight instincts poured through me. I wanted to run. I had to poop.

"That sounds like the right thing to do honey," Mary said. "My father was a devoted Catholic and a rural doctor. He believed in relieving people's suffering in many ways when they were close to the end."

I looked at Shane. He was absentmindedly playing with a tassel on a throw pillow. I tried to tell if it was a "Burn this witch!" kind of fidget.

"My dad died of lung cancer. It wasn't pretty. He was such a big, strong guy and at the end he was an empty shell. I don't think I could have done what you did. Not because I think it's wrong. I just don't think I have the guts."

My pulse stopped banging in my ears. If they were going to narc me out, it wasn't going to be tonight while they smoked weed on the patio. I changed the subject to them and sat back, enjoying Shane's tall tales of his dad's surfing heroics.

As he walked me out Shane suggested a day off.

"You've got to be shattered from four days of wiping out."

Thanks guy. There was, like, 30 minutes of actual surfing in there too.

"Why don't you take tomorrow off, and we'll go to Cosy Corner Saturday? If you don't mind that Mary and the kids are there too."

If I let you hang with your family while I pay you, will you promise not to tell the cops I murdered my aunt?

"Deal. See you there."

The next morning, I didn't know what to do with myself. I bummed around the hostel eating vegemite with a spoon and reading. I walked around Byron trying to be interested in shopping. I kept hearing the waves crash in the background. Shane was right, I was super sore everywhere and it was probably a good idea to rest.

Clarke's Beach was quieter than the main ones and the waves were bigger. There were a few surfers bobbing out in the middle distance. I gauged their size against the waves and decided they were three-foot swells. I could totally handle that.

The rental board felt heavy on the paddle out. A breaker rose in front of me and I dove under. There she was. The ocean pulled and shushed and tiny shells skittered across the textured sand floor. I felt the low-grade anxiety melt out of my stomach. Before I had too much time to Zen out I broke the surface and faced another wave. This set was tight.

I made it out to the break, keeping my distance from the other surfers. Shane taught me enough about etiquette to know a newbie should never get in a veteran surfer's way. I paddled for my first wave and popped up no problem. The board was more stable than my pretty pink wonder. The waves were strong and more like four feet than three. My shoulders burned as I tried to get back in position for the next set. One of the surfers down the line waved at me. Friendly guy. I waved back.

I turned and paddled like hell to catch the next wave. I popped up and made it a few yards before losing my balance and wiping out hard. Directly into a bed of coral.

My shoulder and hip smashed into the spiky rods. My yelp made giant bubbles and I lost most of my air. I struggled with my good arm up to the surface. Another wave. Back down. Up again. I needed a deep breath now. I gasped for one and tried to pull my board toward me with the leash. I could almost grab it when another four-foot wave crashed down on me. This time I swallowed water on the way down. I tried to wait out the roll of water above me before trying for the surface. I couldn't tell if my lungs or puncture wounds burned worse. Streamers of blood floated past my face while I waited for the crush to pass.

I made it up for a breath and ducked back down before the next wave. I was getting exhausted quick. I needed a strategy. Ok next wave I would try to go sideways out of the swell. I needed to get my hands back on my board. Where was it?

Something surfboard shaped crashed into my skull. There it was. Pain and black.

13 THE PINK DEMON

You know how in the movies the heroine wakes up and the rescuer who pulled her from the heaving ocean is a totally dreamy?

My lifeguard had boiling acne and was missing a tooth. He was also fully furious.

"Hello? Good morning. You have a nice dip there, Birdie? Lovely bit of surf this morning? I hope so because I nearly broke my neck saving your arse."

Oh God I didn't feel good. Waves of pain crashed through me from my temple to my right side, pinging my stomach as they went. I rolled over and puked salt water and vegemite onto the sand. It was even grosser coming up.

My homely savior sighed and grudgingly patted my back.

"Get it all out. The ambulance should be here shortly."

"I don't need…" I croaked.

"Have ya taken a look at yourself, Birdie?"

I glanced down at my right shoulder. It looked like ground beef under the shredded rash guard and there was a piece of white something that I hoped was coral. Or it could be bone. I gagged. Nope. Nopeity nope nope. No more looking.

I woke up to the sound of a very delicate and long fart, ending in a high note. The guy in the next hospital bed over was snoozing peacefully despite the bandage covering half his face. I sat up and the yellow room spun. Oh, right, coming off morphine. Lay back down before you puke some more.

"That's some gnarly coral rash ya got there, True Blue."

Gah! Was I hallucinating? I blinked stupidly at Shane on my other side. He almost glowed in a hot pink tank top and his oversized frame looked absurd in the tiny chair.

"What are you doing here?"

"Turns out when they pull someone out of the drink half dead, wearing my school's rash guard, they call me."

I closed my eyes. Maybe if I couldn't see him, he couldn't see me. The morphine was making me super logical.

"What the HELL were you thinking? Going into the water in a spot you don't know, ALONE, without telling anyone? Barely off training wheels! You're an idiot. Truly. A true idiot."

I nodded. The pain was creeping through the drug curtain.

"I wanted to catch a couple waves." I hated how meek I sounded.

Shane sighed. "Well you aren't the first hard headed idiot to get banged up chasing the high, and I'll bet you won't be the last. Get some rest. They'll call me when you're ready to be discharged and you'll stay with us."

"They don't need to call you. I'll be fine. And your tank top looks stupid."

"Shut up True Blue."

Yeah ok.

Mary may not have been a virgin, but she was a saint. I nested on the couch in their den for three days, getting up only to pee. She brought me every meal, helped me change the dressings and made sure I took my thousand antibiotics every day. She would have made a killer nurse.

The room was the perfect place to heal. Mary kept dozens of fat succulents and leafy vines in colorful pots. In the late afternoon gold light came through the west windows and hanging crystals shot rainbows around the white stucco walls. At night they left the windows open and I could hear the ocean and get enough of a breeze to want the soft family heirloom quilt.

Reading was hard with the painkiller fog so I happily watched old Sesame Street episodes with the kids when I was awake. Maybe I could learn a thing or two about sharing. According to Count Chocula, sharing is caring.

When I could walk around without my head spinning I started thinking about my next stop. Part of me wanted to ask if I could be a Sister Wife to this happy little unit. Nah, I had bugged them enough between a homicide confession, liability concerns from the surf school and Mary washing my ass stitches with peroxide.

I owed them a goodbye whether I liked it or not. Everyone spilled into the driveway when my cab showed up.

"Go get it!" Mary hissed to the boys

They ran into the garage and came out with a women's board. It started dark pink on one end and bled into a flame design at the other. She was gorgeous. They boys walked it over and presented it to me.

"To take? I can't do that!"

"I know it's a pain to carry around. If you want it, though...it's no big deal," Shane said, "Mary got a new one from a shop sponsor last season and these silly boys won't ride this one because it's pink. It's just taking up room."

I ran my hand over the design. "I love it. I'll call it the Pink Demon."

"Good. Be safe on it. Take more lessons. Group ones are cheaper than private. I know I'm a pricey whore," Shane laughed, "And promise me you'll never, ever, go into a break you don't know alone, okay?"

"Okay Dad." I hugged all of them, thanked Mary especially and pulled the oldest boy aside. I passed him the paperback of *Ready Player One* I'd found at one of the hostels and couldn't resist re-reading.

"This is an awesome book about a virtual reality video game. There's some dirty parts so don't let your kid brother read it till he's old enough."

He nodded; eyes wide.

We somehow got the board in the cab and took off. I waved out the window. Goodbyes aren't so bad I guess. I just wished I knew where I was going next with 21 stitches and a new, six-foot best friend.

14 ISLAND RHYTHM

The seaweed smells like rot and sex in the early morning air. As long as I rake it off the beach every morning before dawn the resort workers pretend not to notice my tent behind their housing. I visited the resort on a day trip, decided this place was heaven, realized I couldn't afford to stay, went to the main island, came back with a tent and made myself useful. So far it's working just fine.

I mean, I poop in the woods and have so many bug bites I can't count them...still, it's pretty much paradise. Every morning I get up before dawn, rake the beach and hit the left-hand swell a little north of the resort. It's perfect for me: consistent three-foot sets, accessible from the beach and no stag coral in sight.

No matter what time I get to the beach Tukai is already there. He sits on a *masi* mat under the same palm every day. He's always carving a piece of wood with a battered knife. His legs are so gnarled I don't know if he can walk. Somehow, he's gone by the time I come back from surfing every day though.

After a couple days I started giving him a little something on my way to grab the Pink Demon. A pretty shell I found or a fresh coconut that fell on my tent and scared the crap out of me in the night. He never acknowledged me, or even glanced at me. The gift was always gone with him when I came back.

I liked to imagine he was a Sea God and the tide washed him in and swept him away each day. More likely he was a senile burden that his granddaughter deposited on the sand before heading in to clean toilets. But I liked to think if I gave him offerings for his treasure chest I'd be protected from sharks and riptides.

After surfing I'd take a nap in the communal hammocks during peak heat. When I woke up I'd snorkel the reef or explore the trails into the island's interior. At night I'd join the rotating cast of backpackers in the open-air bar for beers and story swapping.

Once in a while I'd let a particularly cute surfer come with me to the north swell. For some reason I called them all Jerry in my head. Most of the Jerry's were there for the big break to the south where you needed a boat. We'd get to talking at night and I'd let Jerry buy my beers and if he asked really nicely, I'd take him out to my spot when the big swell was quiet or the boat needed maintenance. The following things would happen like clockwork:

1. Jerry would try to show off in the "junior" waves.
2. The fourth wave of almost every set would break way earlier than the others and dump him.
3. I would laugh my ass off.
4. Jerry would be pouty with me.
5. Jerry would try to make out with me on the sand afterwards.

Sometimes I'd let him, sometimes I wouldn't (the decision mostly depended on his abs and his cutback). It never left the sand though. Partly because I wasn't in a position to take anyone back to "my place," seeing as my place was a nylon cocoon built for one. Partly because I didn't want the locals running the resort to see me coming out of guest rooms, think I was a prostitute and kick me off the property. And partly because of Malakai.

He was from the village on the other side of the island. I got the idea he'd left the community for a while and now was back for good. He drove the boat for surf and supply runs and seemed to be a general maintenance and handy person for the resort.

Everyone loved him, you could tell by how they flocked to wherever he sat at quitting time. He would tell the best stories, and even when he sat back quiet, his presence felt good to be around.

If Tukai was a Sea God, Malakai was a God of War. I thought he looked like a linebacker so it made sense when someone told me he was a rugby star growing up. His teeth were perfect (maybe fake??) but his eyebrows and hands were zig zagged with scars. He had huge shoulders and tree trunk thighs. Both grapefruit biceps were ringed with traditional tattoos and more crept out of his board shorts up his back.

Sometimes he talked to me!

One time I was raking and he was out early to do some boat maintenance. The stars had faded and it wasn't balls hot so it was probably 5:30 a.m.

"That's hard work," he said as he walked by.

I grunted.

I made sure to be out working by 5:15 for the next week. He didn't make another early appearance.

Another time he saw me leave Tukai a piece of wood.

"That wood is too hard for carving," Malakai said, walking by with a bag of concrete on his shoulder.

"Oh," I said.

Things were getting pretty hot.

One night we had a good group of storytellers in the bar, all trying to one-up each other. He told a whopper about surviving a great white shark attack that I half believed. Mostly it was fun to imagine him locked in a battle for life or death with a creature as strong as he was.

He pointed to me and said, "You haven't ever told us a story. No good at it?"

Screw you, Prince of Polynesia. I got tales.

"One time I knew an elephant name Chai Son…" I started, and by the time I got to falling in the river everyone was dying. I skipped the part where the elephant killed someone. Snitches get stitches.

I happily watched Malakai laugh with everyone else out of the corner of my eye. Sideways was the only way I could look at him. Front-on was too intense and embarrassing.

One week the entire resort was booked for a wedding. No one in the group surfed so Malakai had more time on his hands than usual. I got to my beach one morning and he was out in the waves. I felt equal parts excitement at seeing him and annoyance I would have to share the breaks.

I paddled out and nodded to him. Let's see what you got Local Hotshot.

Dude put on a clinic. He looked light in the water despite his bulk. I wasn't sure if I wanted to fuck him or be him. Correction: I definitely wanted to fuck him. But watching him paddle out, as much a part of the ocean as a seal, I felt a longing to be that at home anywhere.

My turn. Don't show off. Ride like he's not here.

Okay, I showed off. I'd come a long way since eating shit in Byron. I knew these waves; my arms and abs were stronger than they'd ever been and Pink Demon and I were ready to play.

I tried not to wheeze as I joined him on the beach after. Imagine, all that badass surfing and she's barely out of breath! What an impressive young lady.

"How long have you been surfing?" he asked.

"About four months." I looked at his wide feet. Eye contact would be risky.

"You look pretty comfortable for a beginner."

Don't throw your back out heaping praise on me buddy.

"Maybe you'd want to try the big break to the south?"

He wasn't looking at me either. If we hadn't been the only two people around, I would have asked, "Who, me?"

"You mean like, go out on the boat?"

"Yeah, if no one at the resort wants to go. I'd only charge you for the petrol."

Chivalry isn't dead, ladies.

"Yeah maybe."

I grabbed Pink Demon and headed back down the beach. I'd been on worse dates.

That night was the wedding. I climbed up the ridge a bit so I could watch from above. Between my ratty clothes and questionable personal hygiene, I probably looked like a creeper these days. I figured I'd save the bride from thinking a tropical ax murderer was spying on them from the foliage.

It was a beautiful ceremony combining Western and Chinese traditions. At one point bride and groom put two different colored flower petals in a basket, mixed them together and threw them into the wind. The red and yellow petals blew over the crowd, representing the joining of two families.

These joined families knew how to party. I managed to fall asleep eventually, then woke up again when the staff gave up on them at two or three in the morning and came into their huts.

Up again at 5:00 to rake, I didn't feel as warmly toward these newlywed jerkwads. Keeping the whole damn island up half the night. And damn if there weren't two guys still at it! I could see them out in the water and hear singing above the wind. Black forms dancing against the grey dawn sky. Go to bed dummies.

The singing changed. I looked up from the seaweed sprinkled with beer bottles. There was only one form against the sky.

That other drunk fuck fell into the drop off!

You could walk 100 yards into the water in front of the resort and still only be up to your chest. Then there was the reef and a sharp drop into deeper ocean. The reef acted as a natural safety check, since *most people* knew not to walk on the coral. This asshat, however, must have climbed right over the delicate ecosystem and into the deep.

His friend was shouting loudly and splashing back to shore. In the brightening light I could see waving arms out in the surf. There wasn't another soul around except Tukai, and he wasn't going anywhere fast.

I grabbed Pink Demon from her stash spot in the palms and paddled like hell. His friend screamed at me in Mandarin as we passed.

"Go get help," I yelled back.

I kept my eyes on the arms. By the time I hit the break at the reef they had disappeared. I made sure my leash was on and dove into the water where I thought I'd last seen him. Lucky guess, I spotted the struggling body less than 10 feet away. I popped up for more air and positioned the board right above him.

I dove down and grabbed a hand. He looked up at me and I saw the complete terror in his eyes. It made my stomach go cold. I pulled on him and kicked. He wasn't a big man, maybe outweighed me by 30 pounds. Dragging him up in the water he felt plenty heavy though. Pink Demon was right above us and it gave his Animal Panic Brain a bright idea.

He started pulling me down, climbing me to reach the board faster.

I. Am. Helping. You. Fuckface! I screamed bubbles when he kneed me in the gut. A wave came across the surface and washed the board away from us. I was running out of air fast.

I had a flash of memory from a hospital First Response training course. There weren't a lot of active shooter situations in the hospice center. Still, I thought it was smart to keep up on things. "You never go into the water with a drowning person without a personal flotation device." Thanks for that brain, only 30 seconds too late to save my life.

I did remember something else though.

15 KAVA AND JADE

The man's nose crunched under my left fist and let out a rush of blood into the water.

He stopped struggling. I yanked the leash and managed to get us both to the surface before the black closed in. After a couple heaving breaths, I started trying to drag him onto Pink Demon.

A huge hand appeared and pulled him straight up. I wiped the water out of my eyes and saw the resort canoe next to us.

"You ok?" Malakai asked. A young resort worker named Sam started CPR on the guy. When he started coughing and vomiting, I breathed easier.

"Yeah I'm ok," I answered. I actually didn't feel anything except adrenaline zipping through my body.

"Get in the boat and we'll tow your board," Malakai instructed, holding out a meaty paw.

"I can paddle in," I said absentmindedly.

He grabbed me by the neck of my shirt and plopped me in the canoe.

"Hey!"

He undid my leash and examined the skin there. It was raw and white from compression. I didn't realize I'd been pulling against it so hard during the struggle. His face was dark when he looked up.

"What else hurts?"

I looked down at my funny-feeling left hand. The pinky was curled awkwardly toward my palm.

He picked up my hand and examined it.

"We'll get this guest back to shore and I'll take you to Viti Levu for a doctor."

By this time a loud crowd had gathered at the shore. The guest in question hid behind his hair, looking down as blood dripped onto his formal pants. He was either still recovering or too ashamed to look at any of us.

I nodded at Sam and he paddled us in quickly with Pink Demon bobbing behind. The seawater and blood and beer vomit splashed over my feet. The only other time I'd talked to Sam, I'd had to ask the 15-year old kid to bring me back Tampax and razors from a supply run. I was furious at this drunk asshole who tried to kill me and the set of Malakai's shoulders felt like a storm about to break. Beaten up or not, I still would have preferred paddling back.

There was a lot of yelling at the shore line. Malakai shocked the shit out of me by doing some of it in Mandarin. People hugged the victim and got him inside. The bride cried dramatically while the friend from the water beat his chest over his failure. Nei Talei, one of the eldest resort workers, gracefully slid between the crowd and Malakai. One guest getting punched was going to be plenty of trouble for them.

Another woman named Litia took me by the arm and guided me to sit in the shade with Tukai. She looked me over and shook her head.

"Should I not have gone out there?" I whispered to her. I was starting to get worried they were going to kick me out for causing trouble.

"Oh no, if that man had drowned we would all be having a very bad day. Stay here and rest, I'll get you some juice."

I realized I was shaking in the growing morning heat. Adrenaline leaving the bloodstream. And probably a little shock.

I jumped as someone took my left hand. Tukai had reached out and was very carefully feeling the joint and trying to look at it with his cataract-clouded eyes. First time he acknowledged my existence and he was making a fuss over me. Aww.

Malakai brought me the papaya juice. He still looked angry. Tukai spoke to him in Fijian and he sat beside us.

"He says it's dislocated, not broken."

I slugged some of the juice for a sugar boost and examined it myself. I tried to bend it and pain shot up to my eyeballs.

"Well something's not right, that's for sure," I gasped.

"We'll go to Dr. Levi on Viti. Finish your juice and we'll go," Malakai stated with authority.

I gritted my teeth and felt the joint more carefully.

"No. Tukai's right, it's dislocated. If it was a boxer's fracture, I would be able to feel the bone up over the knuckle. I need to pull on it this way and it will go back. Sooner the better. Do you guys have anything stronger than Tylenol around here? It's not going to feel good."

"I say we go to Dr. Levi," Malakai said stubbornly. "You're not a doctor."

"I am a nurse," I said, getting pissed. "Which is like 50% of a physician's assistant, I don't need to go to a hospital for a simple dislocation. I'm not letting this thing swell for hours then paying hundreds of dollars for a PA to pull my damn finger! Do you have anything stronger than Tylenol?"

Malakai and Tukai both blinked at me. I guess almost being drowned by a panicking wedding guest and having a painful dislocation makes me a little crabby. I drank some more juice and looked back at them pointedly.

Tukai nodded at Malakai and he left, returning quickly with a wooden bowl and three coconut shells. Tukai mixed grey powder with bottled water in the wooden bowl and poured it neatly into the three coconut shells. I'd seen people drinking kava all the time here. I hadn't tried it yet cause I was scared it would be too psychoactive for me. I didn't want to have a bad trip here and have Nei Tali find me naked, wrapped in seaweed and screaming, "I am the Qween of the Sea!" one morning.

"It's not, like, peyote, right?" I asked Malakai.

"No, no it is a very light buzz, you will feel a little numb and... floppy, I guess. You must cross your legs, face the *tanoa* and clap before you drink it all in one."

I followed instructions and gulped the muddy water, which tasted exactly like it looked. I swallowed back the papaya juice, salt water and kava retch my stomach tossed up.

Tukai spoke again and Malakai translated.

"Good. You'll drink more after, and then you will have a nice rest."

My lips did feel numb already. Let's do this.

"Hold my arm and don't let it move," I instructed Malakai.

He clamped my left forearm between his tattooed bicep and his warm ribs. It wasn't going anywhere.

The kava was slowing things down and heightening them at the same time. I swear I could feel his heartbeat through my arm. It pulsed in time with the dull throbs in my hand. One. Two. Three.

I pulled the finger as hard as I could out and up. I felt a horribly crunchy pop and let go. I gasped a few quick breaths and managed not to yell out. Somehow my foggy mind decided it was the master of the pain and pushed it through my skin into Malakai's strong side. I swear he flinched.

I felt the joint again and it was aligned. I nodded to Malakai and he let go. The rush of constricted blood made the whole hand throb heavily. I downed another cup of the kava Tukai offered.

"I would like to lay down now," I said very formally while keeling over into the sand.

Malakai picked me up and laid me in one of the hammocks. Litia reappeared, face bobbing with the palms.

"Here's a Percocet."

Without waiting for permission, she shoved the pill in my mouth and fed me a sip of water.

The last thing I remember is her rubbing something nice on my chafed ankle.

I woke up at sunset feeling like a desert had taken a dump in my mouth. There went that day in paradise. Someone had very neatly splinted and buddy taped my finger. There was also a clean wrap around my ankle. I was viciously hungry and had to pee or die. I got up cautiously. Why are hammocks so damn swingy?

The dining area was unusually empty. I remembered the wedding party had left that afternoon. Good. I didn't want to have an awkward conversation with my *Survivor* castmate.

Nei Talei came out of the kitchen with a steaming plate of rice and pork.

"Hey! Surfer lady!" she called happily. "You hungry?"

It was the first time she'd really talked to me, even though we'd shared lots of polite nods and *bulas* in greeting. I said I was and she yelled back into the kitchen. A plate like hers appeared and I dug in.

All the workers sat together and it felt much more relaxed than dinner time when the resort was full. Sam begged me to tell the whole story from start to finish. Litia claimed a hero's credit for patching me up and in her version, she sewed my partially severed hand back on.

I understood why they were opening up. I had been another

tourist, likely to leave on any boat on any given day. You don't show yourself to someone who could leave at any time. If you're smart, anyway. They had given me their Tourist Relations Mask for weeks. But now it was different.

Malakai handed me a small package.

"What's this?"

"A woman from the party handed it to me before she got off the boat. She asked me to give it to you."

I unwrapped the delicate blue and white printed paper. There was a simple and stunning circle of jade in the wrapping with a note.

"To the girl who pulled my husband out of the ocean: thank you. My mother gave me this bracelet and I planned to give it to the daughter in my belly. Instead I will tell her about the woman who saved her father. Jade represents courage, compassion, modesty, wisdom and justice. Wear it in good health."

I pulled the sea green circle over my good hand. The color jumped out against my dark tan. Even though it was from the other side of the world from the Irish Claddagh ring, they somehow complimented each other. I promised myself I'd wear it anytime it would be safe on my arm.

16 THE LEGEND OF MAUI

For the first time on the island, I was bored. I hadn't realized how much surfing was the focus of my time here. I tried to paddle with my splinted hand and immediately knew it was a bad idea if I wanted it to heal right. I'd massaged enough arthritis-mangled hands to know the value of letting things heal.

I could still rake pretty well. Once I was done, I didn't know what to do with myself though. The fish on the reef looked at me like, "You again?". The other resort workers were still more friendly with me, but they had their hands full all day and into the night. I tried to help in the kitchen but kept getting shooed out by Nei Talei. I read the entire *Game of Thrones* series and embarrassed myself by talking with an Olde English accent for a few days. A stretch of ideal conditions had Malakai out with surfers all day, every day.

After raking one morning I sat by Tukai. He nodded at me now when I left him gifts.

"So, anything else to do on this beach?" I asked. He poured me a cup of kava from his *tanoa*.

Alright then. "Cheers!"

I was seriously considering leaving when the calm hit. I hadn't realized how constantly the wind was blowing until it stopped. The bay was glass and it was stupidly hot anywhere inland. The bugs rose up like a guerilla army and tried to overthrow me. I was thinking about how to disassemble my tent when Malakai walked up.

"What are you doing today?"

Getting off this hellhole spit of land and finding a nightclub where I can cause some trouble. After I pluck my eyebrows for a good long while.

"Nothing. You don't have anyone going out?"

"Nah, it's glass to the south too. Should only last another day or two though."

A crab the size of a volleyball wandered out of the palms and picked its way into my open tent. It was missing a claw and it still looked lethal.

"What the hell is that thing?!"

"It's a *ugavule*. Coconut crab. They're tasty if you can get past the pinchers."

"I bet." So, I wasn't going to be peeing at night around here ever again.

"You want to see something?" he asked.

More than I want to take a nap with Pinchy in there, I guess.

The wind on the boat felt amazing. It was the first time in days I'd felt anywhere near cool. We shot past the spots I knew dotting the southern coast. The big ridge behind the resort. The smaller inlets and beaches I'd explored on foot. It didn't take long to get to where I didn't recognize any landmarks. The southern end of the island was a tangle of undergrowth and sharp volcanic rock.

We slowed and headed toward shore. Malakai cut the engine and drifted, leaning out to grab an almost invisible plastic jug. The disguised buoy blended perfectly with the water as he tied up.

"You only know it's there if you know it's there," he smiled at me. "Don't want a bunch of tourists crowding this spot."

He took off the wide-brimmed woven hat he always wore on the water and started rinsing snorkel gear.

"Where are we going?"

"You'll see. You like caves?"

Motherfucker.

I watched his broad back as he prepped gear. It looked like a freakin' bag of snakes under the tattooed skin. I imagined digging my nails into the dips above his ass. Now was not the time to puss out.

He snapped on what looked a goofy fanny pack and we put on the snorkels and fins. I tried to keep up in the choppy water and was totally out of breath by the time we got to a dark crack in the rock.

"You swimming okay with that hand? You'll be able to touch inside," he said and casually swam through the crack.

I treaded water. I read once about the legend of the demigod Māui.

He tried to make all humans immortal by swimming into the vagina of the Goddess of the Night. She crushed him with the obsidian teeth in her snatch and maintained her position at the portal to the underworld. Disney didn't tell you that part, did they?

This was a regular cave though. Definitely not a portal to the underworld. Fingers crossed.

I swam through the narrow entryway and it quickly opened into a natural cathedral. The ceiling was 30 feet high and a hole in the rock sent a shaft of light down into the center of the pool. The water was perfectly clear turquoise and the sunbeam made it look lit from within. Tropical fish darted through the crystal water. I gratefully set my flippers on the pure sand bottom and caught my breath.

"What do you think?" Malakai asked. He was standing near the sunbeam and ripples of light ran over his torso. He was grinning like a proud little boy showing off his pet lizard.

"It's a lot better than the last cave I had to go in."

He waved me over to a shallow area. He put on his snorkel and grabbed a large rock from the bottom. He sat cross legged on the cave floor, snorkel above the water and lava rock holding him down. I did the same and we sat perfectly still except for our long black hair seaweed-waving. After a few minutes the fish swim right up to us and I couldn't help giggling when they started nibbling on my pruney toes.

After a while I got goosebumps and started shivering. Malakai surfaced and helped me out of the water onto a fall of lava rocks. He pulled a bottle of Fiji Bitter and some crackers out of his dry bag. Turns out I was smart not to make fun of his fanny pack.

"Where did you go when you left the island?" I asked.

"Who says I left?"

"Well great white sharks are very rare around here, that tattoo," I pointed to a terribly rendered peace sign on his ankle, "isn't traditional and you speak some Mandarin. So I'm guessing."

"You pay attention, huh?"

I took a long chug of beer and concentrated all my energy on not blushing.

"Yeah I thought I was bigger than this place when I was young and dumb. I was good at rugby and they recruited me for a fancy English boarding school on Viti. It was fun to play with guys who were better than me, put me in my place a bit. Some of the expat kids were really stuck up and cruel to us locals. I got a good education though, whether I liked it or not."

I nodded and kept quiet. Most people try to fill a silence. I've found if you sit and wait long enough the fish come to you.

"When I graduated, I tried out for the All Blacks in New Zealand. They kept me for the bench and I thought I was the man. You have any idea how big of a deal the All Blacks are in this part of the world? They're like the Yankees for you Americans. Anyway, I didn't come home or stay in touch for a long time. Too busy training you know?" He kicked at the peace sign with his other foot. "And getting hammered and doing mad stunts to one up my teammates."

"It was great until I got hurt. Dislocated hip, and the socket broke." He pulled up his board shorts to show me the start of a nasty centipede scar. "I trained and rehabbed and trained. I just couldn't come back at the same level. They cut me. I tried to play in France for a while. I hated it there. The winters were so cold and rainy. I missed my ocean. And my family. So I quit and came back. And everyone has been very forgiving about me thinking I was too good for them. Except Nei Talei. She calls me 'Big Britches' and teases me about it all the time."

"I'm sorry you got hurt." It was all I could think to say.

"I am too. I was getting laid like crazy in New Zealand."

I laughed.

"No, it was probably all for the best. I was never going to be a starter. And I don't belong in a city. This place is my home."

"It's a good home."

"Yes, it is...You want to see the next cavern?"

I looked around for an exit other than the one we'd come through. It was all rock wall.

"The entrance is under water. You swim through a short tunnel and come out the other side." He got a waterproof flashlight out of the pack before resealing it and leaving it on the rocks.

"No thanks," I said quickly. "This is plenty cool for me."

"Come on, it's a tiny swim, maybe eight feet."

He took my hand and practically dragged me to the spot. I ducked under and saw a narrow black hole in the wall. It looked barely big enough for Malakai to fit through. Why? Why did this keep happening? This time I had the option to say no at least.

"I don't like small spaces. I'll pass."

He looked at me with disappointment and questions in his eyes. I hadn't backed down to anything in front of him before.

I wasn't going to tell him why. One person hearing that story on this trip was more than enough.

"You won't see a cave like this anywhere else in the world. It's special to this place. It's special to me."

Agggggggggggggg.

"I'll go if you're right behind me in case I get stuck."

He nodded eagerly and handed me the flashlight. Here we go.

I took a deep inhale and went headfirst into the tunnel. Do not think about the tons of rock above you. Do not think about getting stuck and running out of air. Do not think about-

I popped out on the other side. Ok fine, that was a tiny swim.

This cavern was totally enclosed and pitch black beyond my flashlight beam. Malakai popped up beside me and took the light. He shone it up and I gasped. There were hundreds of colorful stalactites above us. The only sound was the light plinking of drops of water coming off them.

The water must have been even more salinized than the ocean because I could float on my back with zero effort. We floated in silence while Malakai performed a slow tour of the cave ceiling with the light. It was disorienting. We could have easily been floating high in the air, looking down at a series of large rock spires.

Suddenly it was pitch black.

I yelled. Malakai chuckled nearby. I tried to splash in his general direction even though I couldn't see my hands in front of my face, let alone him. I never experienced blindness like that. My heart raced and tracers zoomed across my vision, my brain trying to make up input that wasn't there. I reached my toes for the bottom. Nothing. Control over my claustrophobia was slipping.

Malakai's hands found my waist in the water. I grabbed at him, desperate for something solid and real. I wrapped my arms and legs around him like he was a tree anchoring me in a flood.

He chuckled softly again. I pulled back and smacked him around where his face should be. I think I got his neck.

"That is a bullshit move! Some junior high scary movie...bullshit!"

I didn't let go.

17 IN THE CAVE

Malakai nuzzled my face with his, searching for my mouth in the dark. He found it.

He tasted like bitter ale and seawater. His body radiated heat and it felt amazing against my chilly skin. I guessed he could touch the bottom, because he was able to stay in one place in the slippery water.

He started to untie my bikini top. I stopped him. I only had one and didn't want to lose it. Instead I shifted the wet fabric to the side. He lifted me higher in the water and rubbed his face into my breasts. The little bit of stubble on his chin felt like a cat's tongue as he kissed them.

With no sight and only the sound of dripping water, my sense of touch was on fire. I swear I could feel the raised skin of his tattoos well enough to draw them in my mind. Or maybe I'd just spent enough time side-staring at him to have them memorized.

Malakai nibbled on a nipple and it reminded me of the fish earlier. I giggled. Encouraged, he moved to the other one. I felt him grow rock hard against me through our bathing suits.

I pulled his head up by the silky tangles and kissed him hard, rubbing up and down against him in the water. He moaned into my mouth and whispered something I didn't hear.

"What?" I whispered back. I didn't know why we were being quiet but it felt right.

"I want you," he repeated. "I've wanted you since you showed up with your cat eyes and that ass." He ran his hands over it possessively. "Did you know your shorts have a rip in the back? Right here," he traced a line at the bottom crease. "Driving me mad with that rip."

I did not know about the rip. If it made him take me into this bubble and let me feel like melted wax against him, I didn't care. I made myself slow down my hips. This could be the only time. Better to make it last.

He moved us through the water to a natural shelf in the rock, sitting back onto it so I was straddling him. I dismissed the question of how he found it in the dark and how many other girls had been here with him. I didn't care if there had been a hundred sheep-faced skanks in New Zealand, or even a promised girl in the village across the island. He was mine right now and I was going to take him.

His hips rested right above the water line. I slid down and undid the strings to his board shorts awkwardly in the dark. My mouth found him just fine though. Holy shit. I could barely get two thirds of the way down it. His thighs tensed under my hands and he gripped my hair. He felt the strands between his fingers as I worked up and down, breasts bouncing against his inner thighs. I wanted to see his face but I could tell enough about how he felt from the way he was holding himself back.

He pulled me up and found my mouth roughly. I heard a weirdly familiar crinkling noise.

"You brought a condom!?" I whispered. Presumptuous. And so smart. I stroked him a few times to feel it on him.

"Come here," he answered.

He was inside me in one quick motion. I forgot how full and hungry it made you feel. Like you didn't know a piece of you had been missing. I rocked back and forth on him slowly. He untied the sides of my bikini bottoms and they floated away. Fuck it. I'd wear the ripped shorts if he liked them.

I couldn't tell what was him and what was me. It was all goose bumped skin and wet hair in my mouth and heat where we were connected. After a minute riding him the heat rose all the way up into my cheeks and pulse thudded in my ears. I could feel it building. I wanted to wait for it. My body chose different. The first wave hit hard, and each one of the set hit harder than the last. I pushed against it, knees digging into the rock, trying to get him even deeper into me. As it started to ebb, I realized I had his face pressed so tightly into my chest that he was struggling to breathe.

Malakai didn't wait for me to recover. He lifted me and stood up. With a lot of precision for a blinded person, he pulled me in front of him, facing the wall and spread my legs.

He ran one finger from my front to my back. Paused. Then drove into me with full force. All I could do was hold on to the little holes in the invisible rock as he took me. He wrapped my hair around his one arm and pulled me back toward him, making me arch. The other hand gripped my hip, pulling me down as he thrust up. I don't know how long it lasted. I do know I wasn't a body anymore; I was only a feeling of surrender in the dark.

He took a sharp breath and I could feel him pulse inside me. He rested his heavy head on my shoulder. I turned around and wrapped myself around him again. We floated. After a bit I started shivering again. He rubbed my arms and whispered, "We should go before the tide rises."

You know when you come out of a matinee movie in the afternoon all confused about why the sun is still out? That was me times one hundred leaving the cave. The sun glared into my eyes, I was starving and felt all loose limbed and weak. I almost accepted Malakai's offer of a "dolphin ride" back to the boat hanging onto his shoulders. I swam it myself. I still had my pride, even while bottomless and fuck drunk.

18 IN THE SHOWER

At dinner I went back to side glances. I didn't really know this guy. I didn't know what taking me to that cave meant to him. And I didn't know what was okay for the resort family to know. Better drink beer and not make eye contact.

Malakai didn't ignore me or single me out. He said *bula* and went around making everyone a little happier like usual. As the night wound down, I headed for my tent. I bent down to grab a stick in case that crab was still in my bed when I felt a hand on my ass.

"What the-" I whipped around with the thick branch. Malakai grinned at me in the spotlight of my headlamp.

"Who are you gonna bust up with that?"

"You, if you scare me in the dark one more time."

"Come to bed."

"That's where I'm headed. If a crab isn't snuggled up on my pillow."

"No, my bed."

I looked at him directly. I had left scratch marks on his shoulders. What would people think about me coming in and out of his hut? I didn't want Nei Talei and Sam and Litia to think different about me. Not going to lie, I was also pretty sore. Then I thought about the word "bed".

It was the first time I'd laid on a mattress in two months. With clean, sand-free sheets. It was a cloud from Heaven made of ice cream flavored cocaine. The first thing I did was roll around in it for a few minutes, working my legs against the smooth cotton. The mosquito netting hanging all around made it feel even more like a cocoon for a princess.

"This is the best bed in the entire world," I sighed, rubbing my face into the crisp pillow. Finally, I looked around the rest of the hut. It was a traditional structure with a tall thatched roof. The walls were plain white with decorative *mati* hangings and a shining tile floor. A teak dresser and a chair were the only furniture. Malakai was in the small attached bathroom. I knew they had outdoor showers too. This place was the freakin' Ritz.

I was so excited about the glamour of standard living conditions I forgot to be nervous about what would happen next.

"Did you know you have the best bed in the world?" I gushed to him as he came out.

"You've been living rough for a bit, so I'll take that with a grain of salt. It does look very good with you in it."

He came over and stretched out next to me. Somehow lying next to each other, face to face and fully clothed, felt more intimate than when he'd been inside me in the dark.

"What would make you feel good?" he asked, lightly stroking my hair.

I had a lot of ideas. One came out on top by a lot.

"Can I take a shower?"

"Sure. Can I come too?"

As long as you let me have most of the hot water, buddy.

I'd been washing in the outdoor community shower between the beach and the resort. It was my only option, even though it was only meant for guests to rinse sand and salt off before getting an afternoon beer. Someone had left a bottle of "Steel Courage" Old Spice body wash in there, so I usually smelled like a preteen redneck.

The hut showers had solar heaters to provide a little hot water. I stepped into the stream in Malakai's open-air shower and sighed. It felt so good on all my bumps and bruises and bug bites. I tipped my head up to find my favorite constellations and the smear of the Milky Way in the sky while the hot water ran down my scalp. Sweet Jesus.

He came in to the little cubicle too, filling the small space with his bulk. He let me stay directly under the spray so I didn't complain. He lathered a bar of coconut smelling soap between his meaty hands. He started at my shoulders and worked his way down.

"They aren't that dirty," I laughed when he spent a lengthy amount of time on my breasts.

"Best to be sure. We want you spanking clean," he replied, turning me and giving my butt a fierce little swat.

"Ow!" I yelped.

He shushed me, putting a finger to my lips. I bit it a little. He was right though. I knew how much you could hear everything in the huts. I'd been woken up at 3 a.m.by someone taking a leak every night since I got here. If I didn't want this to be public knowledge at breakfast, we would have to be quiet.

He gently washed my back and was about to get extra personal. I'll handle that myself, please and thank you.

"Your turn," I said, taking the soap. The moon was bright, casting a silver light over everything. I wanted to take my time exploring him. No side eyes.

I started at his shoulders like he did with me. They reminded me of a mountain range. He had those crazy muscles that built guys have, the ones that make a triangle between their shoulder and neck. I tried to remember the anatomical name for them. Then I got to his mounded pecs and stopped trying to think. There was a patch of dark curls across his chest. I followed it down with my soapy hands. He had a little belly on him and I kind of loved it.

I kept going. He was already half hard and it took a second of not-so-gentle washing for him to be lamp post upright. He braced his hands on either side of me against the thin walls, leaning in to the pressure. I wanted to see what we were working with here. My only impression from the dark cave was "big" and "powerful" and "maybe a Sea Demon invading my soul".

Right as I was about to explore more a piercing pain shot up from my right ankle. I couldn't help yelping again. Malakai jumped back and I swatted at my lower leg.

Whatever the fuck had crawled out of the jungle and bit me, I hoped it wasn't poisonous.

19 AND IN THE HUT

The enormous one-clawed crab was scuttling in the shadows, in a battle position, ready to strike again.

"You asshole!" I hissed. "What did I ever do to you?"

Malakai gave him a swift kick out of the stall.

"Where'd he get you?"

The hot water had run out and my ankle stung like hell. Shower Party was over.

"Why don't you rinse off and we'll go in, check it out in the light," I said.

When he came back in I was wrapped in one of his white sheets examining the damage. The pinch was straight across my Achilles. That bastard left a hell of a welt.

"I'm gonna eat that goddamn crab for dinner! Watch your back, Pinchy!" I swore.

Malakai laughed and looked at the mark. He ran his hand up my leg. My skin was normally very smooth and a pretty caramel color. Now it was a dusky bronze, which you could barely see between the scabs from the surfboard leash, bug bites, various scratches and bruises, and now a crab attack wound.

"Is this from today?" He circled around the fresh scrapes on my knees from the cave rock. "You are kind of a mess."

"Why thank you," I replied, curling up in a kittenish pose on the bed and batting my eyelashes. "If you like that, wait till you see the bruising on my dislocated finger."

Yup, still not great at flirting.

"Lay down. I'll help you out." He guided me onto my stomach and pulled the sheet so most of me was exposed.

I didn't know if he meant with like, antiseptic ointment, or with the heaviness I felt between my legs any time he touched me. Either way I wasn't going to argue.

Turns out it was both. He got a big bottle of children's bubbles out from under his bed.

"We're blowing bubbles now?"

"It's coconut oil. We press it ourselves and try to use bottles people leave here to store it. We need containers, and it keeps the trash runs down."

He poured some onto his hands and started at my feet, rubbing firmly as he went. He worked carefully around the sore spots, avoiding the open cuts while rubbing a lot around my scabs.

"Apply this every day and you'll heal without scars. It has Vitamin

E, and it helps collagen production. If I'd been smart enough to have them send me packages of it when I was playing, maybe my face wouldn't be such a disaster now."

I don't even know what I mumbled in reply. Between the nice sheets, warm water and now the natural oil massage, I felt like I was at a fancy spa. This is how it looked in movies about publishing mavins in New York, anyway.

Malakai took his time, working into the sore muscles in my lower back and giving lots of attention to the flesh around my bruised hand.

"Tell me if it hurts," he said, "Getting more blood flow around this will help it heal."

"That's the perfect amount of pressure. How are you so good at this?"

"When you play pro, you get treated like a sacred cow. We had the best masseuses in the Pacific on staff. They taught me a lot about how to take care of my body."

He straddled me, sitting right below my butt. The pressure of his weight stretched my lower back and things that had hurt for so long I didn't even feel them anymore, let go. I felt tears pricking at the backs of my eyes and blinked hard to stop them. Getting a sensual massage from a super-hot Fijian rugby star was nothing to cry about. But he had released toxins from some deep places and I could feel them banging around my nervous system, looking for a way out.

He ran his fingers lightly down the length of my spine.

"You don't have any tattoos. Most backpackers your age do now."

"How old are you?" I non-replied. It suddenly occurred to me he could be a very well-preserved 45-year old. Yikes.

"Thirty-three. How old are you?"

"Twenty-three."

"Huh. You seem older. So why don't you have any tattoos?"

Persistent, this guy.

"My Aunt Mary always said never to get a tattoo. That's how the police identify you."

He chuckled and I could feel the vibrations in my thighs.

"She sounds smart."

I turned over and pulled his arms so he was laying on top of me.

"I don't want to talk about my Aunt Mary."

I kissed him.

Up close, in the light, I could see how scarred his face really was. From a distance (or a side-eye) you only noticed the lines through his eyebrows. At kissing closeness, I could see dozens of white lines running across his temples and down his cheeks. My hand found his thigh and the scar he'd shown me in the first cavern. I traced it up his leg. A full 16 inches of scar tissue, pimpled with little bumps where the staples had been. I kissed him harder.

He pulled the wadded sheet out from between us. I could feel him down the length of my body, coated in a sheen of coconut oil. He grew quickly under the boxer briefs he'd put on after the shower. First the dark, then an evil crab, now these stupid Jockeys were in my way. I pushed him up to kneeling and peeled them down his thighs.

Damn. Alright then.

I stroked him with my good hand, root to tip. It wasn't a short trip. He put his hand over mine and showed me how he liked it handled- rough and a little more toward the tip. Fine by me. After the massage of my life I wanted to make him feel amazing too.

I pulled him toward me and pressed my breasts around it. Slick with oil, he could slide himself back and forth between them with the perfect amount of friction. As he thrusted harder the tip reached my mouth. I gave it a quick lick each time and the white scars stood out on his face as his cheeks darkened. He held himself up with an arm against the wooden headboard and he pulled it so hard each time it started knocking my head. I tasted a hint of sea salt and he suddenly pulled back, breathing hard.

I sat up and kissed him again. He held my hands in one of his so I couldn't touch him. With the other he felt between my legs. It wasn't all coconut oil that was making me slippery. I kind of squeaked.

"Are you ok?" He looked up quickly, searching my eyes.

"Fine. Just a little sore from earlier."

"I'm sorry. We don't have to…"

"I want to. Just be gentle, and don't make it last forever."

He released my hands. They went back to his cock like magnets.

He groaned and pulled me to him, running his lips over my breasts.

"That will not be a problem."

He grabbed a condom from his nightstand.

"When's the last time you were tested?" I asked.

"Got a full physical two months ago when I had to go in for a tetanus shot. Clean and healthy as a horse," he grinned. "What about you?"

"I'm on the shot. And I've never been tested."

"Oh...well then," he shrugged, tearing the wrapper.

"I've only had sex with one other person. We were virgins and monogamous." I tried to say it boldly instead of apologetically. Still. It sounded weird out loud.

"Um...I don't want to sound like an arse but...really?"

"Really. We don't need to use one. I wouldn't lie about this."

Very slowly, I lowered myself onto him. It stung a little on the surface then felt delicious inside.

Malakai held perfectly still, watching me closely. I started to move on him and looked down at us together. His big hand cupped my chin and forced me to look at him directly. His dark almond eyes burned into me. Without breaking eye contact he sat up and wrapped my legs around him. He held my face firmly two inches in front of his own. His air was my air. I wove my fingers into his hair and pulled against it, pushing myself onto him harder.

I could see the struggle in his eyes to control himself. His jaw muscles were clenched hard, creating dark hollows in his already carved face. His broad chest rose and fell between us with shallow breaths. He hadn't moved against me at all. I had total control over the pressure and pace.

I whispered, "I'm fine. Let go."

He rocketed forward, knocking me onto my back. Then he drove into me like a fucking train. His white teeth flashed and he was still locked in to my eyes and I had the crazy thought he might try to eat me alive. It lasted less than 10 seconds and I don't know if I could have taken any more. There was some wild, elemental streak in him that made my mind go blank and my body give way. I usually think loss of control is a weakness. Somehow letting go and riding that surrender with him made me feel powerful too.

We fell asleep right there, wrong ways on the bed. It had been a hell of a day.

20 THE NEW NORMAL

I got up before dawn and crept out of the hut to rake. I think Tukai winked at me. Or a fly landed on his eye. Either way, I was on high alert for harassment or coldness from the resort family. Thankfully it was business as usual. Either they didn't notice or they didn't care.

Malakai grabbed me on my way to my tent again that night. I asked if he was sure he wanted me to stay with him again.

"Do you want to?" he asked.

"Well yes...I didn't know…" I trailed off into silence. He took my hand and led me toward his hut.

We were nose-to-nose with him deep inside me when he growled, "I want you in my bed every night you want to be here. Do you understand me?"

I nodded.

"Say it," he demanded, increasing his pace.

"Say what?" I half laughed.

He looked down. "Say you want to be here every night."

It was my turn to grab his face and demand that he look me in the eye. I arched into him, grabbed his ass as hard as I could and rose to meet each thrust.

"I want to be in your bed Malakai Navakasuasua. See what happens if you try to kick me out." Then I bit the shit out of his lip.

He yelled in pain and half pleasure.

"Shhhh, we're supposed to be quiet!"

"Then keep your teeth off me, woman!" he hissed, but he was grinning and writhing against me as hard as he could.

And then it was the new normal. My hand healed and the wind came back. I surfed every day and usually didn't see him till dinner. He still made the rounds around the tables, making guests feel welcome and joking with the other workers. Then he sat near me to eat. And when the sun went down every night I went to his bed. It got to be where the sunsets weren't only spectacular to watch, they also made me wiggle with anticipation.

One day our paths crossed in the late afternoon. Malakai was carrying a tangled net; I was sitting perfectly still outside my tent.

"What..."

I shushed him and pointed to a wooden crate I had propped up over chunks of coconut. He crouched down next to me. His eyes traveled along the string in my hand to the branch holding up one side of the crate.

"I'm gonna get that motherfucker," I whispered, not taking my eyes off the trap.

He laughed so hard he fell over.

"Shut up! You're gonna scare him off!"

"Who do you think you are, Elmo Fudd? You're not going to catch a rascally rabbit *or* a coconut crab with that thing!"

"It's Elmer Fudd, dummy," I grumbled. Name calling is really immature and rude.

He stopped laughing.

"Let the crab alone. He was here before you, and he'll probably be here after you."

He walked off with his net and I was left to chew on that idea.

It must have stuck with Malakai too because that night he asked the question I'd been avoiding thinking about.

We were on his tile floor. How we got there was a little blurry. All I was sure of was the warm cream feeling in my bones and the growing sore spot on my left knee. My head rested on his chest and he played with my hair.

"How long will you stay?"

"Hmm?"

"You heard me." He shifted so I was looking up into his eyes. I really wanted to tell the truth.

"I don't know."

It wasn't what he was asking. But it was true. I was living how all those shitty self-help books told you to: in the moment, mindfully. When I was surfing I was surfing. When I was eating, I was thinking about how good the simple food tasted and smelled. When I was fucking I wasn't thinking about some movie star or a fancier bed or a porn I saw once. I was in that moment with him.

The problem with that kind of self-centered focus is you forget things that aren't in the moment. Like your dad's birthday. Or when your period was supposed to come. Or the fact that you had a round-the-world ticket and were maybe staying in one tiny part of the world for too long.

"You'll tell me though? When you want to leave? I keep thinking I'll wake up one morning, see that tent gone and know I'll never see you again."

"I'll tell you," I promised. And I meant it.

The next day he was waiting for me on the beach when I dragged Pink Demon out, panting.

"I've got to do some maintenance on the backup generator on the ridge. Want to rinse off and come with me?"

"I kind of wiped myself out today. The waves were almost five feet! I think I have to guard the hammocks from invading pirates."

"The generator building is near the site where they used to do human sacrifices."

"I'll get my sneakers."

"Don't forget my favorite shorts," he called after me.

21 CANNIBALS

Malakai hopped in a battered Jeep I'd seen lurking at the back edge of the property.

"This thing runs?"

"Mostly," he grinned, brushing bugs off the passenger seat. "Buckle up."

The rocky 4x4 track ran tight switchbacks up the steep hill behind the resort. By the time we crested the ridge I was covered in dust and my brain felt like scrambled eggs.

The view from the top of the island was fully was worth it. I pulled up on the roll bars to take in the 360-degree view of the Pacific surrounding us. The smudge of land to the east was Viti Levu, the biggest island. There were a few other green dots to the west, representing the outlying island chains. Otherwise you would have to sail 1,700 miles to reach the next continent (you might hit New Caledonia on the way if you were lucky). My love for the vastness of this ocean pulled at my chest.

"Isn't she beautiful?" Malakai asked.

I nodded, grateful to have someone next to me who saw more than waves too.

"You can take a rest in the shade. It won't take me long. Quick maintenance check to make sure everything is ready for cyclone season."

I stretched out under the palms and tried to picture what a tropical storm would look like blowing in across this open ocean. I didn't like small spaces and I wasn't a huge fan of wind storms either. I closed my eyes and drifted until Malakai woke me up with a kiss.

He pulled me into his lap and we kissed for a long time. It was a little weird to make out with him in broad daylight. We had only ever been together in the dark. His mouth made its way down my neck and tugged at the straps of my tank top. The heat I had started thinking of as "Malakai Fever" built up and a flush crept across my sweaty chest. He took my hand and made me feel his own reaction to me.

"We shouldn't here," I said, pulling his head away from my cleavage.

He groaned, hugging me tighter. "Why not? You feel so good."

"There's ant colonies everywhere," I pointed to holes in the dirt around us. "I'm not trying to get my ass eaten by ants while you get off."

"We can stand up," he offered hopefully. I shook my head, stood up and offered him my hand.

"Come on I want to see the sacrifice site."

He sighed and got up, rearranging himself. I had a feeling he was going to get me back for this at night in our hut. Bring it on buddy. After you show me where the real shit went down.

Malakai led me a little way through the thick brush until we popped out into a clearing. It looked like a natural amphitheater with a stage of rock at one end and a sharp drop down to the resort and the bay at the other. Rough, man-made rock benches ran on either side. I immediately got the chills. This place had some intense juju.

"Four men would pick up the man to be sacrificed, one for each arm and leg. Then they'd run full speed toward the rock wall and smash his skull into it," Malakai said, pointing out the harsh wall of rock at the opposite end.

"Why?"

"Well, sacrifices were done for a lot of reasons. Here, they were mostly done to launch a *drua*. That's a war canoe. They were enormous. Picture a boat that could carry 150 warriors, 100 feet long and with a 70-foot mast. My ancestors built them here and it could take the better part of a decade to build."

I looked down into the bay and tried to picture something that big and destructive floating in the peaceful little hollow.

"Why did they need to kill people to launch a canoe?"

"Sacrifices protected the ship and the warriors on it. When the canoe was ready it had to be rolled to the ocean. They would lay out logs and human bodies to act as the rollers. They would also hang some of the bodies from the mast. After the canoe was at sea, the builders would cook and eat the bodies. There were many special rituals for preparation, like cutting off certain parts and eating the flesh with a special fork instead of your hands."

I knew South Pacific cannibalism rituals weren't a myth. I read once about Ratu Udre Udre, a chief in the 1800's who ate more than 900 people. He kept a box of preserved human meat next to his bed for midnight snacks. Looking at the wall where so many people's lives were ended, my stomach turned a little. Tales of cannibalism seemed a little more darkly sexy from a distance.

I must have looked a little queasy because Malakai led me to a seat facing toward the ocean instead of the wall.

"Don't worry, the last white person we ate was all the way back in 1907," he teased, nibbling on my neck. "That the British knew about, anyway."

I laughed it off. He had shown me a dark thread in the fabric of this paradise that I hadn't noticed before. I couldn't un-see the ghost of the war canoe in my happy little bay.

"We have cannibals where I come from too," I said.

"Really?" He stared at me and waited. He had asked me a lot about myself and where I came from. So far, I hadn't said much.

"My mom was Ojibwe. She used to tell me about the Wendigo, a cannibal giant that lived in the north woods. Wendigos stink of dead flesh and have bare teeth because they ate their own lips off. When it was angry or ate a big meal, it would grow taller than the tallest pine trees. No matter how many men a Wendigo ate, it was always hungry. When I was bad she'd tell me the Wendigo was going to get me."

"That's a good way to scare your kids. It's only a story though."

"Well, there are real cases of something called Wendigo Psychosis, where someone goes nuts and eats people. I read once about a man named

Swift Runner who ate his entire family. When they ran out of food they were only 25 miles from supplies at Hudson Bay. He didn't need to kill or eat all five of them to survive. He did anyway. So maybe Wendigos aren't just a story."

"Damn. What was the word you said your mom was?"

"Ojibwe. It's an American Indian tribe. You know, like the Navajo?"

"Oh yeah, I know about American tribes. I hadn't heard of that one before though."

"It's a small tribe, part of the bigger Algonquin group. Most tribal members live in Michigan or Wisconsin."

"What's Michigan like?"

He must have thought he was on a roll, now that he'd charmed me with tales of eating human faces, and I would tell him anything. Lucky for him this wasn't personal.

"Pretty boring. Up north is dense woods and more interesting landscape. The south is all flat, farms and factories. The winters are terrible. It's grey and cold from November to April. There used to be a lot of snow when I was little. We'd have a couple storms a winter where drifts would be taller than me. Now it's cold without much snow. The lakes are great in the summer though; they actually call them The Great Lakes. There are five of them, and they're like inland seas. We learned in Geography that the whole country of Israel could fit in Lake Michigan. That's how big they are."

Malakai looked out over the ocean and I could see him trying to picture an inland lake that size.

"Are there tides?"

"Yes. Not as big as ocean tides though."

"And it's fresh water?"

"Yep, a tagline for tourists is, 'No Salt, No Sharks'."

He snorted. I got the impression he was categorizing both Wendigos and inland lakes so big they could swallow whole countries as tall tales.

My stomach growled and the sun was sinking in the sky. I suddenly wanted to be far away from this place and this conversation.

"Let's head," I said, walking for the Jeep.

Of course the fucking rust bucket wouldn't start. Malakai grumbled with the universal annoyance of every man when his horse comes up lame. I joined him under the hood.

"Alternator?"

"I replaced that three months ago. Shit, I bet it's the fuel injector. That's one damn thing I haven't replaced. Sorry, I think we'll have to walk back."

"Roll it," I said, heading for the driver's seat.

"What do you mean, roll it?"

"Use those thick ass thighs and push. It's all downhill. If you can get us rolling, I can coast us down."

"You cannot 'coast' that track, honey. It's a 30-degree pitch."

"Watch me, honey." I replied. I opened the driver's door, released the hand brake and started pushing myself. The Jeep started rolling down the hill easily and I hopped in. Malakai stutter stepped with indecision, then ended up chasing me and jumping in.

"Buckle up," I grinned.

We were flying. It had been too long since I'd gotten to do something stupid behind the wheel. I hadn't forgotten the feel though. My brain zoned in on two levels: maneuvering the rocks right in front of me while anticipating the next two turns. The bumps were brutal but I kept it fast enough to skim over some ruts without popping a tire. The hand brake got us around the switchbacks. Malakai gripped the roll bars for dear life as one back tire spun in space over a cliff edge. I giggled. I was riding the line between totally in and out of control.

"Stop!" Malakai yelled toward the bottom. The track sloped upwards here so I pulled the brake and let us lose momentum. We rolled backward to a stop. He looked straight out of the dust-covered windshield, breathing heavy.

"Leave it here. It's actually closer to the parts shed."

"Great!" I chirped, stepping out and stretching.

Malakai got out slowly, took my hand and pushed away a screen of palm fronds on the side of the track

"Want to take a shortcut home, Daredevil?"

The drop was probably 30 feet to the waves crashing into the sheer cliff face below. Adrenaline pumped in my temples. He wouldn't dare me to do it if it wasn't safe.

I was so high on the rush I jumped before I had time to think about not jumping.

Mid-fall I had the sickening realization it was more like 40 feet.

The water had a little more give than concrete and I went in at an angle. I shot down almost to the bottom and struggled against the undertow on the way up. I came up gasping with painful ribs.

"My girl!" Malakai shouted from the cliff top. "Didn't even blink!"

He did a front flip off the edge and barely made a splash on impact. Show off.

He surfaced and swam to me. The water beaded in his eyelashes. He had a booger hanging out of one nostril. I wiped it and flicked it away.

"How'd you learn to drive like that?" he asked. I shut him up with my mouth. The ocean and the body buzz washed away my anxiety about tribal wars and cannibals and travel timelines. He pulled me close and it was just Malakai and me and the sea.

22 SHOULD I STAY OR SHOULD I GO NOW

Our first fight was so stupid. All first fights are stupid. Doesn't matter if you're running out of a nice dinner drunk and furious, or starting World War III at IKEA over tea lights, the first time you yell is the first time the Magic Bubble breaks. It doesn't matter how good you are at getting each other off, the real relationship barometer is how willing you are to fight fair.

I wanted to learn how to carve. Watching Tukai on the beach for hours made me think I had a decent idea of how to do it. All I needed was a good knife.

And stupid Malakai wouldn't lend me one. He had at least five in his tool shed that would work. Instead he said no, "Carving is a man's craft."

If he had any sense in his oversized melon, he would have seen the signs of setting me off: crazy look in eye, earrings coming off, feet planted, weight on the toes, ready for whatever.

Instead of backtracking or hightailing it, this motherfucker tried to explain himself.

"It's tradition! There are traditional women's crafts like weaving *tapa* and *tana*, and then there's traditional men's crafts, like carving. Nei

Talei can show you how to weave if you want a new hobby."

Oh. Hell. No. He caught some fire.

I shook the bugs and sand out of my neglected tent. A five-inch centipede under the pillow tested my dedication. Out of pure stubbornness I stayed in my own bed.

The next day I took a dull kitchen knife and pointedly sat outside the kitchen with a piece of driftwood. I was getting nowhere fast and I wasn't going to admit that to anyone.

Litia came out and sat with me. She watched me determinedly fail at making shapes in the wood.

"So you're back in your tent, aye?"

I guess any ideas I had about Malakai and I being a secret were wrong.

"Yeah. Did you ever learn to carve? It can't only be for men."

"Here, it is. Women weave and men carve. It's not that one can't do the other, it's that we are each specialized in a skill."

I chucked the deformed piece of wood into the brush.

"I don't want to learn to weave," I pouted.

"I don't want to teach you," Litia laughed. "It takes a long time and a lot of patience. Who says you have to learn either?"

I wrestled my thoughts.

"It's not that I have to...it's what you all do. When your hands aren't busy. And something productive comes out. I rake, sure, but then I sleep and surf and eat. I want to help...or do…more."

"I understand. We all want to feel purpose. However, for his entire life, Tukai's purpose has been to carve. When he wasn't farming or raising a family, anyway. That is his purpose. He would find it disrespectful for you to take his purpose, his role as a man. Do you see?"

I thought about when I was 16, the first time I got a paycheck from working at Wendy's. I spent the whole wad on canned goods and was so excited to show my dad when he came home. Look, pantry's full! He took one look, turned around and didn't come back for two days. When he did come home (eyes bloodshot, smelling like pickled shit), he made me promise not to do that again. It was my money, I earned it and I should save it for college.

"I see," I said. The one-clawed coconut crab scuttled out the shadows.

"Pinchy! Litia, how do we kill that thing and eat it?"

"That old one has been terrorizing the island for years. We'll let him go his own way, aye? And you'll find a way to be useful without carving, I promise." She looked me over. "You are a sad sight in those rags. I have plenty of *sulus*, I will bring you one to wear. There's a worn out green one that will match your eyes."

I was gonna go ahead and take that as a compliment.

I am terrible at apologies. I pretty much crept into Malakai's hut and sat on his face. It wasn't elegant. However, by the time we were done I think my meaning was communicated clearly.

"You know it's not that I think you can't handle a knife, right?" he asked after. "It's how things have been done here for a thousand years. It's not my place to try and change it."

"I know." I buried my face in his chest. It did make sense. I just couldn't help wondering what else I wouldn't be allowed to do here. And where he would draw the line between tradition and modern ideas when it came to other things. Female genital mutilation was a tradition was a tradition too, you know?

As I raked the next morning the wind felt different. Urgent, maybe. My low-grade worry felt justified when I passed through the dining area to grab breakfast. The workers were all murmuring to each other and the TV was turned to the news. Usually it broadcast some never-ending dance party happening in South Korea. Or *The Wizard of Oz*. Nei Talei loved her some Judy Garland. Now there was a lot of meteorological diagrams and serious talking heads.

"What's going on?" I asked Sam.

"Tropical depression west of here," he said without taking his eyes off the screen. "They'll update us if it turns into a tropical storm."

I was grateful for all the prep I'd seen around the resort for typhoon season. There was twice the normal amount of bottled water and canned goods stocked in storage and Malakai had been doing preventative maintenance on every structure and system. Still. It was an itty-bitty piece of land in a big ol' ocean. The wind ruffled my anxiety feathers all day until I retreated to our hut early and hid under the covers with a book.

The next morning it was blowing so hard I gave up on raking halfway down the beach. No one was going to be sun worshipping on the

137

sand today. The sky stayed dark grey even after dawn. Everyone, including guests, were gathered around the TV in the dining area. The system had been upgraded to a tropical storm and sustained 40 mph winds were predicted in the next 24 to 48 hours.

I knew the resort had a policy of mandatory evacuation to Viti Levu for cyclone warnings. Evacuations for lower-grade tropical storm evacuations were up to the guest's discretion (sorry, no refunds).

Malakai got up and made the announcement.

"We will take you to Viti this morning if you would like to evacuate. According to the forecast, we should not be out on the water past noon today. It is your choice if you would like to leave or stay. However, if you chose to stay, you will not be able to leave until it is safe to take the boats out again. That will likely be 48 hours from now, although it could be longer. If you have set travel plans, we recommend you leave now to be safe. The first boat will leave in half an hour."

There were a lot of whispered conversations between groups and sour looks. In the end, all of the guests decided to evacuate.

I helped carry luggage from the shore out to the boat. Malakai was working hard to keep it steady in the waves.

"You staying or going?" he called over his shoulder at me.

"Um." It hadn't occurred to me that I would leave with the resort guests. He didn't have time for non-answers.

"There will be room in the second boat. Decide by the time we're back."

23 THE WENDIGO

I watched Malakai expertly pilot the boat through the rolling waves. I hated wind storms. I would be a liability to the resort family if something went wrong (one more body to keep hydrated and fed). I could ride this out at a cozy inland hostel on Viti and come back when the sun was shining. Maybe eat at a different restaurant for the first time in forever, buy some clothes that weren't filthy.

I helped load the second boat too.

"You got a bag?" Malakai asked.

"No." He looked me in the eye for the first time that morning.

"You sure?"

"Yes."

He turned back to his work, shuffling the guests around to balance the boat and yelling at Sam. I caught him smiling before he turned.

The entire time the boat was gone I bounced between the TV and the beach. Nei Talei snapped at me to stay put.

"This is not the first storm they drive boats in! They'll be back soon."

The wind was tossing the palms like a cheerleader's pom poms. I couldn't figure out why my mostly-healed hand was throbbing until I realized the barometric pressure was dropping fast. The ocean was a silvery grey and each wave seemed to break bigger than the last. Finally, I spotted the boat on the horizon.

I waited not-so-patiently as they got the boat out of the water and safely stowed inland. Then I almost tackled Malakai with a ferocious hug. If everyone already knew it didn't matter who saw. He held me tight for a moment.

"I'm glad you're here. I have a lot of prep to do though," he whispered into my hair. "Why don't you get your stuff together and head to the shelter in the main building?"

"Doomsday Prep away," I smiled at him.

After all this time I had never been in the main hotel of the resort. It was even nicer than I imagined. Lots of teak and silk, and a beautiful tile mosaic above the check in desk welcomed guests to "The Garden of Eden". I followed Litia through the hallways to a sturdy metal door. She opened it with a noisy key ring and led me inside. It was a full-size Panic Room, equipped with bunks along the walls, food and water, First Aid equipment, a bathroom and even an overflowing bookshelf. The one thing it didn't have was windows.

She left the door open and I kept it that way when she went back to work. I considering going out to help. Nah. I knew I was mostly in the way when it came to their established routines and responsibilities.

Plus, even in this bunker I could hear the wind picking up and it set my teeth on edge. I cruised the bookshelf out of habit. The entire *Lord of the*

Rings collection was intact. Well that was appropriate. I picked up *The Hobbit* and started at the beginning.

"In a hole in the ground there lived a hobbit. Not a nasty, dirty, wet hole, filled with the ends of worms and an oozy smell, nor yet a dry, bare, sandy hole with nothing in it to sit down on or to eat: it was a hobbit-hole, and that means comfort."

By the time Bilbo left Bag End the wind and waves were throwing a fit. And no one was back yet. A tiny voice in my head asked, "What if they all evacuated without you?"

I was about to go looking when everyone crowded in at once. They were all soaked and excitable. You'd think they were back from a damn water park instead of boarding up windows. The room felt much smaller with 15 people crammed into it. Everyone was getting comfortable, claiming bunks summer camp style. Someone turned the radio to the weather station for updates. Nei Talei busily unpacked bags of snacks from the kitchen.

Oh, what fun, a sleepover! I hope we're not all crushed by debris in the night! I reminded myself I chose to stay.

I found Malakai and stuck to his side. Being near his oversized warmth instantly dialed down my manic worrying. With his tasks taken care of, he looked downright happy to have an excuse to cozy up with all his family and friends. Despite myself I got into the spirit of the Storm Sleepover. Sam was pouring Captain and Cokes with contraband he snagged from the hotel bar. I don't usually drink hard alcohol. The first one tasted great though and I downed two more fast before bed.

I woke up to screaming. A storm was crashing outside and I had no idea where I was. Lights turned on and I was surrounded by strangers.

One was too close behind me in bed. I jumped up and spun around, looking for a way out. I sprinted for the metal door. Someone caught me from behind. I kicked and scratched as hard as I could and they let go. I tried to unbolt the door. It wouldn't move. My heart was pounding so hard it smashed my ribs. Hands closed on my shoulders. I whipped around, ready to attack.

Concerned faces looked back at me. The tallest man said my name.

Like a picture clicking into focus, I came back to reality. The screams stopped.

The panic burned up in a drenching wave of shame.

"I'm sorry," I croaked.

Malakai approached me cautiously. Scratch marks bled down his arm and cheek.

"You're okay. You're safe here. The storm should die down by morning."

I nodded. "I'm sorry."

"Back to bed, everyone," Nei Talei said, turning off the overheads. She patted a doughy hand on my arm as she passed.

Malakai led me back to the bunk with a light hand on my lower back. He was scared to touch me more than that...and that killed me.

"I can sleep on the floor next to you," he offered softly.

"No, I want you close."

I balled myself up on the bed and he curled around me like a protective shell. I could hear everyone else dropping back into sleep around us. My heart was still racing and I knew I wouldn't sleep again until we were out of this place. I assumed Malakai was asleep too. Then after a long while he whispered, "What happened?"

Words came out without my permission.

"There was a tornado in my town. It went right down the main street and crushed 10 people under walls of brick. My mom and I were sheltering in our basement. The chimney collapsed against the door and we couldn't get out for two days. We had plenty of food and water. No booze though. She got by the first day. I had gotten permission to pick out books from the Advanced section of the library. I read *The Hobbit* out loud to her while she puked and shook. She was keeping it together. That night though I could still hear the wind when she woke me up. She said there was a Wendigo in the basement with us. I was terrified. I shone the flashlight all around the room. Nothing. She was seeing things. I turned out the flashlight and she jumped me in the dark."

Malakai's arms tightened around me.

"My dad came back from his run the next day and he and Max, our neighbor, cleared the door. I had a broken arm and some missing teeth. It's okay though, they were still baby teeth. My adult ones grew in the holes."

I stopped.

"She was the Wendigo. Never happy, never full. Eating her own flesh. That's the real shit that goes bump in the night."

Malakai stroked my hair with his broad fingers. I squeezed his hand, silently thanking him for his silence. There wasn't anything to say.

I stared at the wall and listened to the wind until morning. I only knew it was morning because other people woke up and turned on lights. Someone flipped the radio back on and confirmed the storm was blowing south.

While no one spoke to me as we packed up, many people gave me smiles and small pats. Tukai pressed something small and smooth into my hand. I examined the perfectly detailed sea turtle carving and managed a smile for him.

People here had a special way of being. They moved gently around things that were painful. Instead of calling out awkwardness or differences the way Americans feel weirdly compelled to, they flowed around them until the bump or jagged edge was simply gone.

I was still ashamed as hell. I'd released my mind monsters in The Garden of Eden. No more Captain and Cokes, ever.

24 THE BIG BREAK

I spotted the boat with the first load of tourists on the horizon. It had taken a lot of work to clear the resort of downed palms and debris. While I was in the way for specialized tasks, no one minded me doing the backbreaking work of hauling garbage-filled tarps into the interior. Overall though, the place had weathered the storm pretty well.

Now it was time to welcome back the palefaces. I sized up this group from the beach. All guys. Youngish. I didn't need to see them handing boards out to Sam to know they were here to surf. This crew was rocking some strong puka necklaces, dreadlocks and hubris.

Plenty of Jerry's had tried to get with me since Malakai and I started. I would still show them my surf spot and let them buy me beers. Then I'd hustle them back to the resort after we were done. Once in a while one would try to follow me into the dark when I left dinner. That guy would get the picture when he ran face first into Malakai's chest on the dark path.

Litia and Nei Talei were knee deep in the water, welcoming the group with a *meke* dance accompanied with *lali* drums. They did this for every boat of guests and I had no idea how they made it look so sincere every time. Shit, maybe they *were* sincerely happy to see each boat bringing in walking wallets.

Something stopped my train of thought dead. It was the flash of a watch on one of the guy's wrists. My eyes tracked up the obnoxious timepiece to a head of wild curls, bleached at the tips. I blinked hard in the bright sun. Watched him lick the salt spray off his lips.

No mistaking it. Gabe and his long, pink tongue had shown up to the Garden.

I high tailed it to the trees. I needed to sort how I felt...and TBH maybe run a brush through my hair before greeting our new guests.

Gabe was shocked and thrilled to find me here. I answered a lot of questions about Thailand and surfing before I realized he wasn't answering any of my questions. As a Master Deflector, I was annoyed it took me so long to catch on. We were drinking beers in the dining area with his crew; Pete, Adam and Nathaniel. Each one had a dark tan and a man bun trying to distract from their bad teeth.

If I had been worried about Malakai's reaction to my reunion with this guy, I should have saved that emotional energy. He was warm and welcoming to this group as always. The only tension came when I made fun of their identical hairstyles.

"Come off it! It's how we keep it out of our eyes in the surf," Adam said defensively.

"How come you don't have the top knot, Bruv?" Nathaniel asked Malakai. "You people invented it!"

"You're confusing us with the Maori in New Zealand. The tikitiki is their traditional hairstyle, not ours. Bruv." Malakai answered with a smile. Only I noticed the clenched muscles carving out his cheeks.

They discussed the plan for hitting the south break early in the morning.

"You have to come with us!" Gabe said. "I want to see how you've got on."

"No thanks," I immediately replied. "You guys paid for the boat, and the water time. It's not right for workers here to take time from guests."

"Are you like, actually employed at the resort?" Pete asked. I recognized his Scooby Doo face from Bangkok. I didn't like him then either.

I fumbled for the right answer.

"She's part of the family here," Sam answered smoothly for me and he brought another round of beers. Bless you, Young Sam. I was kind of curious what Malakai would have said though.

That night in the hut was urgent. He was inside me before I was done working coconut oil into my curls. He took me from behind, kneeling behind me and drizzling the rest of the oil in the container on my back. It was a little uncomfortably dry and I tried to pull away. He held me tightly in place, working the oil all around me. It didn't take long to get more comfortable. His slippery hand came around the front and petted me tenderly while another hand was rougher with a nipple and his thrusts were pounding. The different pressures scrambled my senses until I stopped feeling them separately and only felt the swelling need.

I took a slightly sweet finger into my mouth and let go. Sometimes I hated having to be quiet and sometimes it made it way hotter to come silently, some part of him or his sheets stuffed in my mouth. I moaned around his finger and bucked back against him. I could feel his thighs shaking with the effort to hold still and let me ride it out. When I was done, I turned around, took as much of him as I could in my mouth and went to town. Looking up at him I could see past his little belly roll to his massive pecs to his hard chin, and the burning look in his eyes as he gave in was so fucking satisfying.

The next morning Gabe convinced me to come out to the break with them. I had been getting a little tired of my spot and felt ready to try bigger waves. If he wanted to cover the gas, that was on him. I had that mix of anxiety, adrenaline and excitement that I had come to associate with bodily injury and some of the best days of my life. I didn't talk much as we sped south.

The waves looked to be about eight feet, a low day for a break that could get up to 20-foot waves in the right conditions. They were plenty loud, fast and big to me. I let all the guys get in the water before I did. Malakai coached me in a low voice without eye contact.

"They come in sets of six. Paddle faster than you're used to and be ready for more speed on the wave. It's a narrow break, so you can get out to the sides pretty quick whenever you need to. I'll be right here with the boat. You've got this, go have fun."

I didn't know which I appreciated more; the fact that he knew I needed a pep talk, or the fact he waited until the guys gone to give it to me. I kissed him hard. Then glanced at Gabe to make sure he wasn't looking. I don't know why it mattered. Fuck it, get in the water.

I let them catch a few, noticing their choices. Then a minute or two of official stalling. Get moving, you weakling.

One two three GO. I paddled as hard as I could and a mass of water rose up underneath me. I popped up perfectly. Then the speed of the wave grabbed Pink Demon and ripped her out from under my feet. The mass crashed over me.

I tried not to fight and let the water whip me around until it was done. I got to the surface in time for a big gulp in the trench. Rode out the next wave underwater and paddled like hell for the side of the break. I made it and tried to catch my breath, answering Malakai's thumbs up with one of my own.

Nathaniel shouted something to me as he paddled by. The words were lost in the crashing. I got the idea the tone wasn't complimentary. Fuck you Austin Powers, with your gnarled butter teeth.

Okay, so that's what Malakai meant by being ready for the speed on the wave. Got it. I paddled in position and grabbed another one. This time I adjusted my weight on the pop up and hung on for the fast drop. It was heaven. I was flying along a crystal wall of water and I had never felt freer. I yelled as loud as I could and the wave swallowed the sound. I ripped out the side, whooping and already looking for the next one.

I rode hard for an hour and was getting shaky. I took a couple passes in the lineup and watched Gabe in the waves. Great abs and a better cutback. My favorite combo.

One last ride and I would call it quits. I almost ate it popping up, then held on and streaked across the wall. Then a big, yellow shape dropped in from the sky. I yelped and tried to cut left. Lost my balance on jelly legs. The wave crashed over me and I submitted to the washing machine again. I tried to spot my board mid-spin. She spotted me first. The pink fiberglass smashed into my chin with a nasty uppercut. I couldn't see anything and I tasted blood. I had no idea which way was up until I felt a pull on my arm.

I gulped air at the surface and choked on sea foam and blood. Gabe held me up as I coughed and pulled me half on his board, paddling quickly to the side of the main swell. Malakai was there immediately, pulling me into the boat. My vision came back in line and the first conscious thought I had was "Ooo he looks mad."

He rubbed my back and held my hair back as I spit up salt water over the side of the boat. When I stopped coughing, he gave me a towel-wrapped ice pack for my lip.

"Anywhere else hurt?"

"No," I rasped. I was wrung out and my jaw throbbed but I was okay. "Pink Demon…"

Gabe had taken my leash off to drag me more quickly and I saw flashes of pink rolling away in the waves.

"No worries, we'll get her later. First let's gather up our guests."

I remembered the last time he had said "guests" with so much disgust. There had been a lot of spit up salt water and blood then too. He drove around to the lineup and whistled to the other three guys. They paddled to the boat and Malakai grabbed Nathaniel's board.

"Woah bruv, we're supposed to be out here for two hours. Times not half up!"

"When someone drops in on another surfer and knocks them out, times up, Bruv. Get in the boat."

I looked for the bright yellow color that flashed right before I fell. It was fucking Pete's rash guard, of course.

"Come on now, let us get another wave or two," Adam whined. Pete at least had the sense to keep quiet. And Gabe, who had seen Malakai's face when I landed in the boat, had even more sense.

"Get in the boat guys. It's time to go."

"What, the girl you fancy gets laid out by a wave and we've all got to go home? That's some bullshit Gabe," Nathaniel chimed in.

"You can hand me your boards now or you can swim back," Malakai said calmly.

They handed boards up to the rack, grumbling. Pete was the last to climb up the ladder. Malakai stopped him with a meaty hand to the chest. Ruh-Roh, Shaggy. I was going to have to tell Nei Talei why we came back from surfing with a dead guest.

He turned to me. "You got anything you want to say to him?"

I kept being surprised at how much Malakai surprised me. And shit yeah, I had something to say. I got in Pete's face and pointed a finger at his chest.

"If you *ever* drop in on me again, I'll eat your dumb dog face for dinner. Got it?"

I smelled the fury on him. But the other guys were laughing and hooting and with Malakai behind me he wasn't going to do anything. He forced a laugh and I tried to smooth over the tension by passing around beers from the boat cooler.

That night nose-to-nose in Malakai's bed I traced the scars on his temples while he gently patted my ripped lip with cocoa butter.

"They're leaving soon," I said.

"Not soon enough. Do you have any idea how much I wanted to destroy that guy? Rip his ugly head off and feed it to the pigs..." he tranced out, no doubt picturing how he would merrily dismember Pete.

"They asked me to come to Nadi with them for a night. To see a DJ."

Malakai snapped out of his fantasy.

"*They* didn't ask you. That one, Gabe, asked you." It was a statement, not a question. I shrugged.

"Do you want to go?"

"Kind of. I haven't worn shoes, let alone been in a club, in months. Sounds kind of fun for one night."

This was the part where the possessive boyfriend says "Fine, go. Just don't expect me to be here when you get back!"

"You should go. You haven't even seen Nadi yet. What club?"

"Club Feenix. Will you come with me?"

He laughed loudly.

"Oh no. Not on your life. I burned through every club in Nadi and

Suva before I was 18. I think I got arrested at Club Feenix once. You're on your own in that scene."

I still felt torn. I played with his hair.

"Who will rake the beach in the morning?"

"That's Sam's job. You showed up and started doing it and he never said anything. He's your second biggest fan on this island."

"You're kidding! That little punk…. You sure you don't mind me going?"

"I trust you," he said simply, and rolled over to sleep. I had trouble falling asleep myself and kept playing with his hair. After a while I wrapped myself around his back and snugged my hand into his crotch. He was dead asleep when he pressed into me and murmured, "I love you."

I didn't fall asleep until dawn.

25 CLUB FEENIX FEAT. DJ KLUBFOOT

The busy streets of Nadi made me dizzy. No sleep and a few hits of a joint on the boat ride didn't help. I stumbled into a salon and a round woman looked me up and down.

"What you need honey?"

"All the things," I replied, sinking into a cracked massage chair.

"Yah, you do," she agreed.

Her name was Ella and she worked me over for hours. I said yes to whatever she suggested and by the end of the afternoon I didn't recognize the girl in the mirror. Granted, I hadn't really looked in a mirror in 10 weeks.

Everything was sharp and shiny, from my nails to my eyebrows to my long, straight hair. It had taken the better part of two hours to blow it out. Ella was incredibly strong in patience and forearms. The whole time she fed me iced green tea and French pastries. I gave her a big hug and a bigger tip and left feeling like a different person.

Absolutely nothing in my pack was worthy of "da club". The one going-out dress I'd packed was musty and crazy wrinkled after being crumpled at the bottom of my pack for months. Surviving on a couple cheap meals and beers a day, I was killing it on my budget. It was time to go shopping.

I bought a new bikini to replace the one I'd destroyed/lost in the cave. It was red, curvy and brief. I checked myself out in the store's full-length mirror and was pretty damn impressed. Months of surfing, raking and hiking had shaved inches off my waist and sculpted my shoulders and back. Butt Check: yup, still back there, still big and still looking fan-fucking-tastic.

A couple new tank tops to replace my ratty regulars. I debated new board shorts then smirked, thinking of Malakai, and left them on the rack. Time for the dress. There was a ridiculous amount of slutty clubwear on the main strip. Nope. Not trying to look like a bedazzled sausage.

Instead I found a perfect Little Black Dress at a consignment store. I didn't spot the Prada label until I took it off, already in love. It was $215, second-hand. The most expensive dress I'd ever bought was my prom dress, a splurge of $89.99 at Fredericks of Hollywood. If you don't think a skeezy lingerie store sells prom dresses, you've never been to Flint, Michigan. I plunked down a credit card and left wearing it. Light, silver heels were a no-brainer.

"You look all tarted up," Adam commented when I met them in the hotel lobby. For a second all the confidence and fabulousness I'd felt getting ready burst. I wanted to shout, "It's not for you guys, it's for me!" Instead I tossed my hair, smirked at him and went to the bar, where a group of middle-aged businessmen almost fell over themselves to make room for me.

I heard Gabe whisper to Adam, "Knock it off or I seriously will cut you out of this run."

What run? I grabbed my beer and joined them; ears perked for anything else that seemed weird. I could have been that I was having mini-culture shock being back in a city with these mostly-strangers...but I was catching some tense vibes from his crew. They fidgeted a lot and were too quick to laugh or not quick enough. Probably on some pills.

I decided to ignore the Goon Squad and focus on Gabe. He didn't look too bad cleaned up either. Black button down, fitted jeans, not covered in sand. Same curly eyelashes and mismatched eyes. Same mouth. We chatted and downed beers and both pretended he wasn't sneaking peeks at my cleavage.

By the time we left for the club I had a solid buzz going and had to concentrate on walking in the high heels. I had no shame taking Gabe's arm when he offered. It's not like something was going to happen with him. I had my own room and wasn't a skank.

"What DJ are we seeing?"

"DJ Klubfoot."

I almost fell over laughing.

"No, really, what DJ?"

"I'm not kidding. He's huge in Norway."

Absurd name or not, DJ Klubfoot brought the noise. I hadn't danced like I meant it since the Cairns clubs with Felicia. It took less than three songs before the heels were off and I was in the groove. Gabe actually knew how to move and we owned that dance floor.

We took a break for more beers. Gabe slung his arm around me on the couch like in Bangkok. I slid a couple inches away.

"Is Malakai your boyfriend?" he asked outright.

Something kept me from an immediate yes. Maybe it was the word "boyfriend". Malakai was a man-ass-man. There wasn't any boy there. Also, we had never put names on anything between us, it just was.

Pete snorted. "Give it up Gabe, she's obviously gone native. That asshole almost gutted me for making a mistake in the water. I should have told him his cheesy Ray Bans were a mistake."

I cringed. Malakai's 15-year-old Ray Bans *were* cheesy. I had thought about getting him new sunglasses while shopping because they bugged me so much. If I had asked him about it I'm sure he would have said they still worked fine, so why should he get new ones?

"Let's dance some more," I said to Gabe, wanting to work out the greasy feeling of agreeing with Pete. He was busy in his phone.

"I'm good for a minute. We gotta figure out our travel times tomorrow. You go ahead."

Fine then, it's not like we were on a date.

I found a gorgeous girl on the dance floor with an ironic fanny pack and a sense of rhythm. She and I had a blast and I barely noticed when the guys joined us. They passed around fresh beers and tried to move in on my lady friend. When that didn't work, they started chatting up a group of blonds.

Her name was Nita, she was from Chicago and she wanted to get into nursing school. She looked like a black Tinkerbell, felt warm and familiar and I was glad when she agreed to come back to our hotel. The pack on blondes came too. This time I held Nita's arm on the wobbly walk back. Aunt Mary said it was always acceptable to remove your shoes to dance, however it was never acceptable to walk barefoot on the street.

The dance party kept going in the guy's multi-room suite. It was a way nicer room than mine and I wondered again how they were financing this extended "vacay". I'd asked Gabe a couple times and gotten brush-off answers. I also didn't know how they had financed the pile of coke that appeared on the coffee table. I wasn't above taking some though.

Nita kissed me first. We'd been grinding and touching for hours and it didn't feel wrong. She tasted like fake strawberry with a bite of coke backwash. The guys whooping sounded far away from our spot on the couch. My head spun; low with the beer buzz, high with the coke.

My torn lip hurt and I didn't mind her biting it. Her skin was even softer than mine. It's not cheating if it's with a girl, right?

"Let's go outside," I wasn't trying to put on a show. Like my Prada, whatever was going to happen, it wasn't for any guy's benefit.

26 TEMPTATION

The suite had a bomb ass deck with an ocean view and a hot tub. I turned on the jets, then twisted my silky hair up and presented my zipper to Nita. She slowly unzipped my dress and I got in the hot tub real sensual-like in my bra and underwear. I knew she was looking.

She splashed in and came right over to straddle me. Cute boyshort cut undies and nothing else. She was built like a fairy that did CrossFit, bird bones covered with tight muscles. In the watery hot tub lights her skin looked like chocolate silk.

We kissed for a long time. A warm, liquid heat was building between us. We moved together, synchronized to a beat we could both feel. There was something about being with a woman that felt less certain than being with a man. Things built and disappeared, flashed and then hid. It was like trying to fuck quicksilver.

"Hello ladies."

My head snapped out of our embrace. Gabe grinned wickedly from across the hot tub.

Oh no, no no no. You are not invited to this party. *Persona non grata.* Get your Sideshow Bob head on out of this tub.

Apparently, Nita didn't feel the same way. She slid right on over and welcomed him with a long lick to his neck. He grinned and kissed her neck in return.

A bolt of white-hot jealousy cramped my gut. I didn't know which one I was jealous of. Or why. All I knew was I hadn't felt like that since the 7th grade dance when Gina Montoya danced too close with Diego to "Lollipop". My heart beat in my throat and I wanted to fight and it wasn't only the coke. Fuck it.

He tasted like I remembered. I couldn't tell which legs were mine and which were Nita's. We wrapped around him from each side, two vines slowly choking him. He had plenty of attention for both of us. She and I kissed again, breasts bumping, while he rubbed our low backs.

"You are so beautiful together," he whispered.

Nita brought his mouth to her blackberry nipple. My turn to watch. His shoulders had gotten more built since the last time. Flashes of his pink tongue gave me prickles from the base of my skull all the way down.

He reached for me and pulled me onto his lap, facing away. Nita straddled me again. I could feel him underneath me and her on top of me. No matter which way I tried to wiggle away there was only more pressure. Gabe nibbled along the cord of my neck while Nita teased my nipples. I throbbed so hard it hurt. I needed it. My hand reached around and pulled his cock out of his boxers. I wanted to rub on it so bad. A couple pumps up and down and I would explode. It was right there.

A parrotfinch squawked loudly at the coming dawn. It was the sound that woke me up every morning on the island, telling me it was time to untangle myself from Malakai and start raking.

I froze.

"What's wrong?" Gabe asked softly while his fingers searched me from behind.

I didn't answer. I firmly set Nita's tiny ass off to the side and got out.

"Where are you going?" she asked in a pouty voice.

I ran past the half-naked tangle of bodies in the living room, bounced off the locked door to the hallway bathroom, and locked myself into one of the bedroom baths before I could breathe again. I felt filthy and was shaking violently. Making sure the door was locked, I pulled back the shower curtain and went to turn on the hot water. WTF had I done. WTF was I thinking…

…And WTF was in that duffel bag?

27 CONTRABAND

An expensively heavy duffel sat partly open on the shower floor. It was stuffed with individually vacuum-sealed packages of...more drugs? Nope, not unless this cocaine had dark brown scales. I ripped my hand back out and willed the fuzzy buzz to go away. It's ok, they're all dead, whatever they are. I dug through the bag, trying to figure out what the hell these guys were into.

Then I found it.

Even bundled in layers of plastic wrap I knew what it was.

I marched out of the bathroom, stopping only to throw on a stinking t-shirt from the bedroom floor, back to the hot tub.

Gabe had Nita bent over the side of the tub. His eyes were closed, head tossed back, grinding on her as hard as he could.

I wound up and hit him across the head. The ivory tusk and his cheekbone met with a satisfying crunch.

He bellowed and swung around. Nita looked up and yelled too, "Bitch are you crazy?" She at least had the sense to scramble out of the way.

Gabe grabbed for the tusk. I held it out of reach. He was half out of the tub, panting, still rock hard, with blood gushing down one side of his face. Dawn broke over the east horizon. I could see him perfectly clear.

"Your dick looks like the Pillsbury Doughboy when you're soft."

He looked horrified. I bashed his head again with the tusk and he crumpled over onto the decking.

"Get out of here before anyone wakes up," I told Nita, tossing her clothes at her. I ran back to get the duffel and grabbed someone's passport off a nightstand for good measure. I was almost out the door when I remembered my Prada. Shit shit shit. Someone in the living room was stirring. I danced at the door. God*dammit* my butt looked so good in that dress.

I threw the duffel in the hall and sprinted back through the suite. Scooped the dress off a canvas chair, kicked Gabe in the back one more time for good measure and almost made it back to the door.

Pete stumbled out of a bedroom and blocked the hallway.

"Whacher doing?" Being wasted didn't keep him from being a naturally suspicious bastard.

I sized him up. He was 6'4 and a meaty 220. I had left the tusk in the duffle. It was only me, pantsless in a Bob Marley t-shirt, vs. the Hulk.

I blinked up at him.

"Um...well...it's a little embarrassing...Gabe and I ran out of condoms."

Add little shrug. Fidget adorably. Try to look well-banged.

"I'm gonna see if the front desk sells them."

"Heh! I knew it. Girls like you will fuck as soon as the boyfriend is out for a cig."

I pushed past him and managed to close the door gently. Nita was nowhere in sight. I grabbed the duffel, tore through my room packing like the devil was after me, and made it to the street before I started crying.

28 THREE EQUALLY SHITTY CHOICES

The overgrown tree screened me from people strolling through the park. I hugged my knees and stared at the black bag at my feet. My first instinct had been to hide. The park was public enough that if they found me I could make a scene, and the wide green leaves gave enough shelter for my animal brain feel safe and be able to function.

Okay, list the things you know.

1. Gabe and Co. were trafficking endangered animals.

2. Endangered animal trafficking was run by international crime syndicates.

3. Endangered animals are a huge market in China for traditional medicines.

4. One time, I read about a Chinese crime boss named Wan Kuok-koi. They called him Broken Tooth Koi, and he ran the 14K Triad in Macau. He started bloody battles with the other Triads in Macau for territory and couldn't use his two middle fingers caused they'd been hacked by meat

cleavers. He finally went to jail after car bombing the police chief.

5. Shut up, that's not helpful.

6. None of them knew my full name. Shit, Gabe maybe saw it on my passport when I first got to Bangkok. Possible, still unlikely.

7. The bag at my feet probably represented hundreds of thousands of dollars of merchandise. Those guys were on the line for it.

8. I had Nathaniel Cunningham's passport. Whether he wanted to run to his boss to solve this problem, or away from him, Nathaniel would need this little book to get out of the country.

9. The first place these guys would look for me was the resort.

Those are the facts. What are your options?

I could throw the bag into the ocean, get on a plane to another continent, never look back.

I could run back to Malakai, hide under the covers and hope to hell he can scare off whoever comes looking for me.

I could go to the cops. Hand over the evidence and make a documented statement against international smugglers. With my real name.

Those were not pretty options. Option 1 meant I'd never see my resort family again. For the rest of his life, Malakai would think I had left him without any warning, after promising I wouldn't. That thought made me want to puke. They would be safe though.

Option 2 sounded best. But could I really stay under the covers while Broken Tooth Koi beat up Nei Talei? Maybe no one would come and it would all be okay.

Option 3 sucked balls. I hate the cops. I don't care if they're Fiji cops or Flint cops or freakin' Chip n Dale's Rescue Rangers. A narc is a narc, and they are never looking out for you. I would be on record here. I'd establish a paper trail, and maybe even have to testify. How did I go from seeing DJ Klubfoot to standing trial against the Chinese Mafia in 12 hours!? Fuck. On the other hand, if the cops got Gabe and the guys and I stayed out of it...everything could go back to how it should be.

Something rustled behind me in the bushes. I jumped like a flea, landing on all fours outside the tree screen. A little grey bird cocked its head at me, impressed it had caused such a reaction.

I had to move. Choose an option and move.

The ocean smelled like equal parts gas and salt on the docks. I was soaked in sweat from carrying my pack and the heavy duffel. I wondered where the next flight out would take me.

The bag wobbled on the pier railing. I looked west toward my island. I could barely see the dark green smudge on the horizon. Don't be selfish. Don't ruin their paradise with your oil spill of a life. Let go of the bag.

29 WILD THINGS

Goosebumps covered my arms as the police boat sped toward the shore. The officer behind me cut the engine and we coasted into the shallows. I spotted Sam cleaning up the beach. The change in his posture said he wasn't a big fan of the cops either. Sorry Sam.

The Officer Kikau anchored the boat and I splashed to shore. The group was gathering now. I remembered the disgust and fear I felt every time the cops brought my mom home. I'd let him tell Nei Talei the details.

"Where's Malakai?" I asked Sam.

"Generator maintenance."

I dropped my pack on the sand and started running up the steep track. I hadn't slept for three days or eaten anything besides some stale Ritz crackers from the police station vending machine. Somehow, I had enough left in the tank to make it to the top of the ridge.

I shouted his name at the top of my lungs when I got to the clearing. Then I sat down in the dirt, fully on Empty. The sunset was gorgeously bloody. I was so spent I couldn't absorb it.

He came running out of the building and spotted me on the

ground.

"What's wrong? Are you okay?"

He sat next to me and ran his hands over me, looking for a physical reason I was shaking all over.

I grabbed his face between my hands and pulled it to mine. His skin shone like bright copper in the setting sunlight. I looked into his dark eyes. They felt like home.

"I did something bad. Or good. I don't know. I did a lot of things. I couldn't leave and not tell you."

"You're leaving?"

The dart of pain that passed through his eyes pierced me.

"No. Unless you want me to after you hear the whole story."

He pulled me into his lap and kissed me.

"You're not going anywhere."

***

There were a few scattered tourists risking it during tropical storm season. They kept to themselves that night and no one tried to engage them. The resort family all sat together and talked in low voices. I couldn't get enough of the comforting rice dishes and Litia kept refilling my plate.

"So, they have the men in custody?" Malakai asked. I let Nei Talei answer. She had still been talking to Officer Kikau when we had come down from the ridge.

"Yes, they hadn't left the hotel. He said they were packing up though. If she had waited longer, they probably would have been gone."

I ate my rice and pork and nodded.

"The police have plenty of evidence to build a case based on what they found. They haven't pressed charges yet though," Nei Talei continued.

"What happens if they don't charge them? If they let them go?" Litia asked.

"They might come here looking for me. They for sure know I called the cops." The rice stuck in my throat. I didn't look up at them as I chugged water. Malakai rubbed my back lightly. That was about as close as we got to PDA in front of the family.

"Let them come to our island," laughed Sam. "They wouldn't make it to the beach."

"I'm not so much worried about those guys. I'm worried about their bosses. Lots of crime syndicates are involved in wildlife smuggling," I said.

"The Yakuza isn't going to come to Fiji to investigate one lost duffle bag," Sam replied.

"It's more likely a Chinese Triad. The market for endangered animals is huge in China," I replied.

Malakai spoke softly.

"Have you considered this was a one-time time deal? Or they are low-level smugglers with no connections? Maybe you've seen too many

American movies about gangs. I think it will all be fine."

I bounced between relief and outrage. I was *not* being dramatic. Thinking back on Gabe's behavior in Bangkok I knew he was carrying a payload then too. And my experience with gangs wasn't from Hollywood. It was so tempting to believe him. "It will all be fine." What a lovely thing to believe.

I nodded and yawned.

"Go to bed," Nei Talei said immediately. "This is enough talk for today. If there is more to know, Kikau will tell us. He is my *tavale.*"

Even though I had given up trying to understand their crazy complicated system of kinship, I did know that meant if there was anything to know, officially or unofficially, we would hear about it.

Malakai and I walked silently down the dark path until a large shadow on the ground blocked our way.

"Pinchy!"

I approached the giant coconut crab and he snapped at me evilly.

"Missed you too, buddy."

Malakai swatted him out of the way with a quick foot and he let us pass.

I beelined for our bed. It felt as good as the first night I got to sleep in the cool sheets. I couldn't go to sleep yet though. Not until the rest of the story was out.

I watched Malakai walk toward the bed in his boxer briefs. Damn.

That was a man. He carefully brushed any grains of sand off his feet before getting into bed, all toothpaste breath and damp hair.

He held me close. I shifted so I was looking at the wall. I'd been weak today. Made selfish choices. That stopped here.

"I hooked up with a girl. Last night. We were in the hot tub after the club. And then Gabe got in. And we all made out some. Then I stopped and got out."

He stopped stroking my hair.

"You leave me for one day and you have a threesome?"

I cringed. He shook a little behind me. Fuck, was he crying? I flipped over.

He was laughing. Dick.

"Why are you laughing?! It was terrible and I feel terrible and I'm a terrible person and... stop laughing!" I smacked him with the pillow.

He grabbed it from me and rolled over on me, pinning my arms down.

"You're not a terrible person. You're 23. I knew that asshole would try to get with you. And I figured it was better to let you decide what you wanted to do."

"You were *testing* me?"

"No. I was letting you go and seeing if you'd come back. It's what you do with wild creatures. Chaining them up won't ever make them happy."

I chewed on that for a minute. Diego would have lost his goddamn mind if I'd told him I'd made out with someone else. Let alone two someone else's at the same time. It was kind of the same as when Malakai hadn't punched Pete after he wiped me out. He let me fight my own battle. I wanted to be the kind of girl who wanted that. Who didn't need a man to stand up for her, who didn't need to be owned in order to feel wanted. And still some stupid part of me wished Malakai had fucking destroyed Pete, and even wished he was crying over my mistake instead of laughing. Fucking patriarchy has claws in deep.

"Was she cute?"

"Huh?" his question startled me out of my muddle. "Who?"

"The girl you made out with."

"She was adorable," I said dryly. "But not your type."

"You know, you're not my type either. I typically go for a leggy blond."

"How very basic of you."

"One time, at a training camp in South Africa there were these two best friends, could have been twins..."

I wiggled an arm out and started tickling him. He chuckled and tried to trap me back down.

"I'll twin you good," I threatened, biting his ear.

He kissed me hard. The heat built immediately. I broke away and looked him in the eye.

"I'm sorry I did that. Really. I'm not a cheater."

"Tell me why you stopped and got out."

I guessed "because I heard a bird" wasn't the answer he was after.

"Because I love you."

His grin could have cracked the stone planes of his face. He took the Claddagh ring off my right ring finger, flipped it and put it back on with the heart facing my hand. I wondered how he knew the ancient Irish way to change my status to "In a Relationship".

But then he pressed me to him so hard it hurt and I didn't have the breath to ask.

Later, when Malakai slid in to me, I heard him moan my name. It sounded like "I love you too."

That night a long dream pressed heavy on me. It was all guilt and heat and chasing. Hands kept reaching and pulling at me no matter how fast I ran. They were all colors and sizes. One pair with star tattoos on the wrists kept coming back. They were Diego's hands.

I finally stopped running and let them touch me. They were hands without a face and they ran over me gently. It was so real I felt the rough edges of callous catch on my skin. They were tender and familiar and I leaned into the feeling. Diego's hands stroked me with building intensity and I began to throb. I was about to turn around and surrender to the hands when one whipped up and slapped me hard across the face. My head snapped and my cheek stung and I wrenched away. Running again, hard, until I woke up covered in sweat.

30 A SHELTER FOR PINCHY

The TV showed looping footage of people up to their necks in swirling water. Young boys navigated debris on homemade rafts, picking up as many people as the bamboo could keep afloat. One young mother held her bundled baby on her head and stretched to keep her chin above water, calling desperately to the boys on the rafts.

"The Solomon Islands continue to experience devastating floods in the wake of this tropical cyclone. Initial fatality counts are nearing the 100 mark without reports from many of the inland villages," the TV anchor stated.

Malakai gave the evacuation speech again to all the gathered guests in the dining area. This time no one muttered. It had been raining for five days straight and they were all ready to get somewhere their clothes could dry out.

Unlike the gross calm a while ago, I liked the rain. It was fun to surf in and it meant more time with Malakai during the day.

He joined me out in the waves when he got back from the run to Viti. No new guests came with him. Nei Talei said everyone had cancelled reservations for the next two weeks. More waves for us!

This time we weren't showing off for each other. We were dancing with each other and our ocean. After a fall I practiced holding my breath. I needed to be able to stay under for a minute or more if I wanted to tackle the bigger waves at the south break.

I gazed up through my waving seaweed hair. The rain textured the water's surface while the force of a wave shaped it into a fluid mountain. I could spot a sea turtle gliding toward the open ocean. Watching her front flippers beating through the water was hypnotizing. The shushing heartbeat of the water slowed me down and erased the past and the future. I was only here, now, with the sting of salt in my eyes and the dark shape of Malakai streaking above me with silent speed.

We sat on our boards waiting for the next set. I shivered in the rain.

"We gotta get you a wetsuit," Malakai said.

"Nah. I'd only need it a couple days a year here. Promise me a hot shower later and I'll be good."

Malakai looked at the horizon.

"This storm's gonna be bad. Much worse than last time. I think you should head to Viti."

"No way! I won't freak out, I swear."

It almost seemed like that night in the shelter happened to another person. It felt far away and not like, funny, but...absurd or something. I would stay sober as Aunt Mary at a sentencing hearing, and as long as I was near Malakai I knew I would be in control.

"I'm not worried about your claustrophobia. I'm worried about the building collapsing."

I pictured the heavy metal walls tucked inside the sturdy hotel.

"It's going to be that bad?" I asked.

"Set's up," he replied and started paddling.

On our way back, we saw Sam sitting with Tukai. Someone had propped a faded beach umbrella over him to keep the rain off. Malakai waved me ahead and joined their quiet conversation.

I rifled through the junk pile behind the kitchen looking for just the right box.

Malakai found me putting on the finishing touches a while later.

"What is that thing?" he asked, looking at the reinforced crate I had nailed to the side of our hut. I was filling it with mangoes.

"Crab Shelter. For Pinchy to weather the storm."

"Lose the fruit, it'll attract ants. I'm glad you're not trying to kill our local mascot anymore," he laughed. "Come on, we're taking the boat out."

"What? You promised me a hot shower! I'm freezing. And it's getting dark."

"I promised you no such thing, woman. Buck up and put on my slicker. We're going out."

I shook so hard my joints hurt the entire boat ride. By the time Malakai found the hidden buoy (even he had trouble spotting it in the fading light) the last thing in the world I wanted was to get back in the water.

"I've seen your damn cave," I grumbled, tossing back the last of my beer from the boat cooler. "Litia was making *kokoda* for dinner. Why-"

He stripped his raincoat off me and tossed me overboard. Right as I surfaced and got the water out of my eyes, he cannonballed next to me. I impatiently wiped them again and waited for his head to come up. Then I spat and entire mouthful of seawater into his face. Eat me you bossy son of a cannibal.

Compared to the rain and wind the water actually felt toasty. Not that I would admit it. The swim to the mouth of the cave warmed me up too. Malakai waited for me there.

"You know, when I brought you here the first time I didn't know if I was going to kiss you or not."

"You brought a *condom*. I think you were pretty confident."

"I always bring a condom when I go somewhere with an American woman. It's a safety precaution."

That got a splash to the face. He pulled me close to him while we treaded water.

"No, I couldn't tell if you liked me or hated me. You had been here for weeks and I didn't know anything about you. You were a confusing mystery with a world class ass."

"So, what made you think you could kiss me then?" I asked, bobbing even closer.

"I'd already fallen for a stranger. I owed it to myself to see if she'd let me in."

I grabbed the back of his head and kissed him as hard as I could. We both started to sink. I laughed and swam for the dark passageway.

A strange blue light was coming from the chamber ahead.

"Close your eyes," Malakai commanded. He took my hand and led me forward. I searched blindly until my toes hit sand and I could stand up.

"Okay... open them."

I blinked hard, trying to process what I was seeing. The cave was dark and the water was...glowing somehow. Like a galaxy of blue stars lived in the sea water. I looked down and saw they were on me too, thousands of tiny points of light outlining the curves of my body. I ran a hand through the water and it created a tracer effect. The smallest motion created a trail of even brighter light behind it. Either I was dreaming or I was tripping balls.

31 BIOLUMINESCENT DINOFLAGELLATES

"What is this?" I asked Malakai. In the darkness the only way I could see him was the pinpricks of light clinging to his body.

"Bioluminescent dinoflagellates."

"Come again?"

"Tiny organisms that glow. Tukai told me they sometimes show up in protected water along the shoreline before a big storm. Do you like it?"

I took a full spin with my arms outstretched in the water. Swirls of light followed me, creating a full ball gown skirt made of stars.

"It's...unbelievable," I laughed.

Also, unbelievably, the clouds must have parted for the first time in a week because a bright moonbeam suddenly shot down from the hole in the cave's roof.

Malakai looked up at it and cocked his head listening. "Wind must be picking up."

I watched him, lit from above in the silvery moonlight and from below by the blue organisms. Before I knew him, I thought he looked like a

God of War. Standing waist deep in the glowing water with the light cutting hard across his built torso and sharp jaw he did look dangerously powerful. Then he smiled at me and held out his hand and he was transformed into something better than a god; a loyal, humble, hardworking man who wanted to fly side by side with me instead of clipping my wings.

I joined him in the moonlight. He unhooked my bikini top with a sharp snap. I tossed it on the lava rock pile in the corner. Didn't want to lose the new one either.

The blue dots freckled my cleavage. He traced the curve of my breasts with a fingertip. Goosebumps broke out over every inch of my skin and my nipples pricked.

"You look like a mermaid, you know that?" Malakai whispered. "I used to daydream about mermaids all the time. Before I knew what that feeling was, I would get it when I thought about women who lived in the ocean with long hair and bare breasts."

He tickled my nipple with one of my dark curls, then took my hand and made me feel him through his board shorts. He was so hot I wondered if he had a temperature. I untied his shorts and set him free. Every time I saw him that hard it made me wet and a little scared.

"In legends mermaids drown poor sailors trying to find a port in the storm," I said, brushing it lightly with my fingers.

"I'll take my chances."

He pulled my shorts down so roughly the worn fabric tore apart. No more little rip to tease him with. Oh well. Teasing time was over. He lifted me up and greedily sucked on my hard nipples. He tried to enter me. I pulled away.

"Wait."

I took a big breath and ducked under. Let's see how all that breath-holding practice was working.

I took him deep in my mouth underwater. Wrapping my legs around his ankles I could stay in place and suck him for as long as my breath held. I started counting, then opened my eyes and wondered at the tiny blue lights stuck everywhere between us. Malakai's tree trunk legs were tensed against my all-out assault on his cock. My lungs burned but I made it to 47 before he pulled me up. I could have kept going. Something about swallowing him made me ache places other than my jaw.

"God you are good at that," he groaned. "Lay back."

I floated on my back. I could see the real stars shining in the hole in the roof. I had missed them over the past week.

Malakai's tongue interrupted my search for the Southern Cross. He lifted my hips just enough out of the water to lick me where it counted. Once. Twice. Three times. Then he stayed there and made a meal of it. I had to work to keep my head above water and to keep breathing. When he slowly put a wide thumb into me, I couldn't handle it. I gasped, choked on sea water and had to stand up.

We stood a few feet apart, breathing heavily. The water around us was bright blue from all the...agitation.

"This is how I'll picture you," he said, almost to himself, as he ate me with his eyes.

"I'm not going anywhere," I promised. Fuck the rest of the world. I wanted to stay here.

He picked me up and I wrapped my legs around him. I started to come the second he pushed inside me. We forced ourselves to be slow. It still built fast. Pushing off his giant shoulders in the salt water, I could lift myself almost entirely off him before slowly sliding back down. His fingers dug into my hips as he tried to keep me pressed to him. I fought against him to pull away and come back. He roared in pleasure and frustration. That look was back in his eye, the one that made me feel like I had suddenly come nose-to-nose with a tiger in tall grass. My stomach dropped and I stopped fighting for control.

Malakai pushed into me with all his strength. I didn't have to stay quiet in our cave. My screams bounced around the close rock walls as the tightness broke and I dissolved around him. He doubled his grip on my ass and held his breath as he got close. I pulled his face to mine and we locked eyes. We were two wild creatures chasing each other in a galaxy of blue stars.

32 TROPICAL CYCLONE ANA

I woke up sore and lost. My hands searched for Malakai in the bed. The sheets were empty and cold. I sat up and saw him moving quickly around the room, packing both our things. The rain was back, pounding the roof of the hut and the wind screamed. Something hit the side of the hut with a bang and I jumped.

"Is it time for the shelter?"

"It's time," he replied without looking at me.

"Come back to bed, just for a minute. We might not get to make out for a while."

"No, please get dressed. And wear your warmest layers."

Ok Bossypants. I don't like to snuggle after either.

I pulled on leggings and a hoodie. Malakai had already cleared out my drawers and he handed me my pack, along with a plastic rain poncho.

"Put this on. Don't leave anything behind, there could be serious flooding." He walked me through the kitchen where Nei Talei and Litia were busily packing supplies. Sam was shuttling bags of food back and forth to the hotel shelter.

"Surfer Girl!" Nei Talei called over her shoulder, "You take this." She handed me a hefty old rice bag and gave me a quick kiss on the cheek. I looked around for something else to carry on the way to the hotel. Litia surprised me with a big hug from behind. What was with these ladies? They were not the kissy-huggy type. Guess I didn't blame them, the blasts of wind had me weird and edgy too.

I followed Malakai back out into the driving rain. Instead of heading on the path to the hotel, he pulled me toward the beach.

"What are we doing?" I yelled over the wind.

Then I saw the boat.

A volunteer Coast Guard vessel was anchored outside the reef and a bright orange skiff was headed for shore.

I didn't know what was happening. A sick, cold panic rolled through my guts.

"Malakai!" I shouted, grabbing his arm, "What the hell?"

He finally looked at me.

"You're getting evacuated. This could be a Category 4 cyclone. It's too dangerous for you to be here."

I hated the "official announcement" tone in his voice.

"If it's that dangerous why are you staying? Why isn't everyone evacuating?"

"This is my home. The others feel the same way and I need to be here for them. I left them once and I'm not leaving them again."

The skiff was getting close to shore despite the waves. I looked around desperately, like there was someone else to take my side or another answer lying on the beach. Instead I saw Sam bringing Pink Demon to the shoreline. He at least had the courtesy to look ashamed.

"No! You can't make me leave!"

Anger broke through the cold front he had been giving me all morning.

"Yes, I can. You think you're the only one who can be stubborn?" he yelled, "I will not have you stay here and be trapped and miserable in that shelter for days, trying to act cool while fighting the whole way to stay sane. That's the best-case scenario by the way! The worst is much, much uglier. I will not be forced to choose between you and Tukai if it comes to the last mouthful of rice. I will not."

"You are not my keeper!" I shouted back. "I choose where I go- and I choose to stay!"

Sam waded out to the skiff and passed my pack, board and Nei Talei's bag of food to the men in yellow rain slicks. The storm had tilted my world at a steep angle and I was scrabbling with my fingernails to hang on.

Malakai tried to kiss me and I ducked him. I made a break for the line of palms.

He was on me in a second. He threw me over his shoulder and marched to the breakers. I kicked and fought and ended up in the boat anyway.

"Stop making this harder. It's for the best. We'll see each other soon, I promise."

Enough people had left me in my life for those words to take the fight out of me.

"Liar," I whispered with the misery of a child who knows they're being abandoned.

"Look at me." He was soaked with rain and waves and his hard chin quivered a little. "I love you and I'll see you soon. Promise."

A wave almost upended the boat and the men yelled at Malakai. Time was up.

"Be safe."

It was all I could say. He nodded and slapped the boat twice. We swung around into the crashing surf and sped out of the bay. I couldn't breathe right.

It was hairy getting onto the larger boat and, even though I kind of hated them, I gave the volunteers a sincere thank you for risking their necks.

There was a cozy cabin inside. Instead I plopped down on the windy, soaked deck. I wanted to watch my island as long as I could. How could he say he loved me and still send me away? Was he secretly madder about Gabe than he was letting on? I didn't think he was a game player like that. Then again, I hadn't thought I'd go from last night's soul-melding in the cave to being banished from the Garden. My head spun while my stomach churned from the choppy waves.

As the boat headed north, I could barely make out the white smudge of the hotel on the green shoreline. The steep ridge above it seemed to ripple oddly for a second. I rubbed the rain out of my eyes and looked again.

Like a woman dropping her coat, all the dirt and trees shrugged off the rock. Every tree on the hillside came down in a single wave of destruction. The crashing was loud enough to bring officers running out onto the deck.

The slide formed a wave of earth when it hit flat ground. The little white building by the shore was swallowed up as it ran out to the ocean, turning the bay into a dark brown disaster.

I screamed. The wind seemed to pick up the sound and carry it out of me in a long stream of pain and disbelief. I didn't realize I was trying to climb the railing until hands pulled me back. The noise kept coming out of me until one of the hands slapped me. It stopped and I looked into the dark brown eyes hovering over me.

"I need to go back," I gasped.

"That is not possible," the stranger replied.

I closed my eyes and tried to make it a dream. When I opened them, the hillside was still bare, the dark mud had spread further out to sea and the devastation was real.

PART THREE:

THE CITY

33 THE PARK BENCH

My park bench was living room, waiting room, restaurant and bar. Sometimes other people tried to sit on it too. Good thing I can eat a falafel sandwich so aggressively. They wouldn't last long and I could spread back out. Kindle in hand, head on daypack, occasional beer in brown paper bag. I was set.

I had spent the last 28 days on my park bench outside the Fiji High Commission in Wellington, New Zealand. I had a room nearby that was more for pooping than for sleeping. I hadn't slept more than an hour or two to at a time. I would catnap on my bench during the day and read in between little spurts of sleep at night. I drew the line at pooping in a public park however. I was traumatized, but I wasn't a chicken head.

The nice receptionist at the Commission, Barbara, had told me a hundred times I didn't need to sit out here. They had my cell and she would personally call me if they had any news of a Malakai Navakasuasua, or any other names I gave them. I tried to go sightseeing one day and it felt totally pointless. Fuck this bright blue river. Fuck a sea bird. Fuck a Hobbit. I needed to know if my people were alive or not. Being on the bench meant I was there for them, ready and waiting.

Yeah, I read *Waiting for Gadot* once. Leave it at that.

They named the cyclone Ana. Should have named her Cunty McCunterson. Hundreds of people had died from flooding, landslides and rough seas. I saw Fijians entering and leaving the building all day. Sometimes they came out glowing and rushed off to what I hoped was a joyful reunion. Other times they came out looking gut punched. One time a Gut Punch came and sat next to me on the bench. I made room for her.

She had long grey hair and friendly padding around the middle. She kept putting her hands on her knees as if she was going to get up. Never quite got the momentum though. I offered her a package of SweetTarts and she ate them slowly. When it got dark, I asked if she had a place to stay. She nodded and didn't move. I didn't know what to do besides leave her there with the rest of my candy. She was gone along with the wrappers in the morning.

Day 29 was a game changer. I was reading *The One*, totally caught up in the fantasy that you could be DNA matched with your soul mate. Never mind the horror of the storyline where the detective is matched up with a serial killer, what if your soulmate was a guy who wore Adidas slides and socks out of the house?!

I barely noticed when someone sat next to me. They tossed some crackers to the pigeons. I looked up, about to go on a rant about Sky Rats and the Bubonic Plague.

Diego calmly looked back at me.

"Hi Charlie."

Here's the thing. I sure didn't kill Aunt Mary for her estate. The truth is she didn't have any money. After everything was said and done I actually owed the funeral home $3,000 and the State of Michigan $7,000 in back taxes. I didn't have $10,000.

So, I stole it from Diego's Uncle Lou. Along with another $40,000. Uncle Lou had a legit auto repair shop and a not-at-all-legit chop shop. His garage was so insulated with bricks of cash, I figured he wouldn't notice some missing until after I was gone.

I guess he had noticed.

34 THE HIGH COMMISSION

"How did you...what are you doing here?" I asked Diego.

He gave me a long look.

"Nice to see you too, *mi sol.*"

I looked right back at him. If he was here to shake me down let him be the one to say it. Plus it was so weird to see someone I knew in the flesh. It was proof my old world and this world were actually on the same planet. His hair was shorter. It looked good on him.

"You used our old credit card at a grocery store around the corner."

Fuuuuuuck. I was in such a haze when I first landed here, I made a couple dumb mistakes, including forgetting to pay for a meal and getting chased down the street by a sushi chef with a filet knife. I couldn't believe I'd used an emergency backup card to buy candy. So stupid.

We stared at each other. His ears stuck out more noticeably with the buzz cut. A bad fight had given his nose a drunken lean. His left canine had come in crooked. One time his cousin said he looked like a "broke ass Enrique Iglesias" and I fell out laughing. It was true, and to me, the rough edges only made him hotter.

It occurred to me that we hadn't been apart for more than a day or two since we were 13. I had been gone seven months. Almost enough time to grow a new person. Or be a different person.

"You're dark," he said, reaching a tentative finger to stroke my bronze forearm.

The jade circle on my wrist jumped as I flinched from his touch.

He pulled his hand back.

I looked down at my legs to avoid his eyes. Dark, muscled and scuffed from hard work and hard play. There were light spots on my knees where I had scabbed them riding Malakai in our cave. My changes weren't only skin deep.

"I still can't believe you left me that way. No idea you were alive or dead."

I couldn't meet his eyes. A glimpse of the star tattoos on each wrist made me squirm, remembering my dream.

"You owe my family a lot of money, *mi sol*. For a few weeks I told myself you'd be back any day. You freaked out and would come to your senses soon. Then Thanksgiving rolled around and Uncle Lou told me to stop being a fucking chump and start trying to track you down."

I could see it so clearly the smell of canned cranberry sauce tanged in my nose. The pile of little cousins in front of the TV after the meal. The plastic laid down over the high-traffic areas of the carpet to keep it nice. Cigarette smoke pouring out from under Uncle Lou's walrus mustache after the meal. Taking deep satisfaction in the promise of pecan pie and shaming the shit out of his favorite nephew. Uncle Lou didn't hit him anymore. He was satisfied by controlling him with a toxic yoke of guilt and shame.

It wasn't that I hadn't ever thought of Diego since I'd been gone. It was that I hadn't thought about what my leaving had done to him. A deep well of guilt opened up and I raced to slam a lid over the top.

I lunged forward and kissed him. My charge landed somewhere near his nose. He pulled back and grabbed my face.

"Not that easy. It's not that easy," he hissed, staring me down. I knew his eyes better than my own. Usually when he looked at me, they were the liquid warm of fresh coffee. Right now they were scalding.

I answered his fury with an "I'm sorry". Only with my eyes. Somewhere around high school graduation we had stopped needing to say things to hear each other.

His pupils widened and the hard line between his eyebrows melted.

I knew what would happen when he broke and I didn't try to stop it. It would have been like trying to stop a car crash after the tires left the road.

Diego's lips had always fit to mine just right. They were hot and chapped and familiar. The way he kissed me was part punishment and part homecoming. I let him grab my arms and pull me against him. He couldn't have left Flint too long ago- his shirt reeked the off-brand fabric softener his family always used. That smell was so tangled up in my brain with sex it might as well have been a cattle prod to the clit.

I let muscle memory take over. My hands snaked to their place at the nape of his neck. I was used to feeling baby soft curls there before he had buzzed them off. The stubble was slick with his sweat. His hands slid down the back of my skirt, hungry for the curves of my ass.

We could have been back on the bench outside Dairy Queen at

home, except for the sharp tang of lemonwood tree and nasal New Zealand accents floating in the air. One called out, "Get a room, there are kids around!"

We came up for air. His eyes darted around and landed on the thick shrubbery. I gave him a look and shook my head. I had a better terrible idea.

The second-floor bathroom in the Fiji High Commission was always spotless and empty. I pulled Diego inside and locked the door.

We came together with a fury. His mouth was back on mine before I could say anything smart assed. He kissed me hard and lifted me onto the creaky sink. His hands slid back down my skirt and his thumbs dug deep into my ass cheeks. I pulled his shirt off and greedily ate his neck.

I forgot how it was to be with someone who knows you. And for all his faults, Diego knew me better than anyone. We had gotten each other off for a decade and each knew exactly what the other wanted. The game was whether you gave it to them right away or made them beg.

Neither of us had patience for games now. He only took his hands off me long enough to unbuckle his shorts. They hit the old tile with a thud and it was only thin cotton between us. He pulled impatiently at my thong, finally giving up and ripping the fabric out of his way.

A loud knock on the door made us both jump.

"Occupied!" I squeaked.

"Please conclude your business and exit the bathroom," a familiar voice said. "There has been a security alert issued for all foreign embassies. We are evacuating for everyone's safety."

I've said it before and I'll say it again. Fuck you, ISIS.

I realized we had been ignoring the sound of hundreds of footsteps moving toward the ground floor. I moved to get off the sink. Diego held me tightly in place.

I told him we had to go with my eyes. He shook his head and rubbed against me. I gave him a "Really?" eyebrow raise and he heaved a sigh of defeat.

"Coming!" I yelled at the door.

"I wish," he grumbled, arranging himself back into his shorts. I desperately looked around for another way out. Window? Nope. Sealed shut with a hundred years of government paint jobs. Shit.

I opened the door slowly, hoping the voice would have moved on down the hall.

No such luck. There was my friend, the nice receptionist Barbara, with a Safety Warden hat perched on top of her steel wool curls. Determined to confirm all restrooms and offices were evacuated.

One time we were fully hooking up in Diego's room before we realized his little cousin had been hiding in his closet, sneaking peeks at his *Playboy*. 12-year-old Ernesto stared at me, looked down at the magazine, looked back up at me...and winked. It was mortifying.

This was worse.

I slunk out with Diego on my heels. I couldn't meet Barbara's eyes. She let me get to the end of the hallway before she said, "A word, please, my dear?"

I nodded at Diego to wait and turned back. Shame crept up my neck in hot wires. It wasn't that she caught me fucking in a government bathroom. It was that I had told her all about Malakai and the island. She had patted my hand and fed me strong English Breakfast tea and news every morning for a month.

I forced myself to meet her deep-set green eyes. The crinkles around them got deeper when she gave bad news.

"Did you hear something?"

"No. Nothing. And frankly, my dear, that's not good. I think...I think if they were alive, we would know it by now."

Streams of people pushed past us in the hallway. We were alone in a bubble of truth. I knew this without her saying it...and she'd probably been trying to find a way to say it for a while.

I nodded at her. The balloon of hope I carried around had lost a little air every day I hadn't heard anything. Now it popped and I quickly swallowed the ripped plastic pieces. Maybe I could digest them with enough time.

"I'm sorry for your loss. I truly am. Still, you can't live on a park bench for the rest of your life."

I nodded again. It was too hard to talk around the lump in my throat.

"Whoever...whatever that is," she waved vaguely in Diego's direction, "It's probably for the best."

Whooo, Barbara, that situation is not "for the best." But I feel you on the rest.

I gave her a fierce hug. She was comfortingly squishy under her fleece vest.

"I have to get moving. I have your email and of course I'll let you know if I hear anything," she said.

Something hit the floor between us. I looked down and saw my torn zebra-print thong on the shining wood planks. She picked it up, pressed it in my hand and gave me a final pat.

"Best of luck to you, my dear."

35 A FAIRLY DECENT PROPOSAL

The wind whipped through Lambton Harbor as we walked south. Locals were meeting for lunch in fancy boat shoes. We were strangers in a strange land.

"Why are they all wearing pastels?" Diego grumbled, as a group of 20-something guys passed us in a rainbow of Polo shirts. "Easter egg-looking motherfuckers."

"Tell me what you really think about your first time out of the country," I laughed.

He took in the beautiful vista; blue bay dotted with white sailboats, neat wooden houses climbing up the green face of Mount Victoria.

"I don't know...it's cool how they designed the wharf structure to make it more fluid for earthquakes."

"Christ, you are such an engineer."

We walked in silence a while. I wasn't used to silence being awkward between us.

"So how is school going?"

"We're talking about school now?" he teased, "I didn't think we decided whether or not I was going to hog tie you and throw you on a direct flight to Detroit."

"I figure if you chose fucking over fighting, I'm pretty safe."

"For now, *mi sol*," he smirked. "School's fine. My advisor has my back and I'll be done sooner than I thought."

In Diego-speak that meant he was still at the top of his competitive graduate class.

"I bet you'll be the first guy to graduate at the top of University of Michigan's masters engineering program with a juvie record and eight-pack abs," I laughed. "Your semester's almost over, huh? It's weird with it being fall here I forgot-"

"The Crows know about what you did to your Aunt Mary," he interrupted.

I shut up. Cozy Catchup Time was over.

I pictured the three mean old ladies that made up Aunt Mary's ride-or-die crew. Edie. Sharon. Georgine. Each one more pickled and vicious than the last. When I got my period for the first time they took me out to Olive Gardens and told the cute busboy I could have his baby once I was off the rag. Life had ground these women down and the stumps that were left gave zero fucks. And they knew I had done in one of their own.

"Would they go to the cops?"

"They might. Edie's been talking all around town about you 'getting what you deserve'."

I looked out over the forest of expensive boats. They all had cheesy names; "The Wet Dream," "Nauti Bouy," "Ship Faced". I wondered what problems fancy boat people dealt with...and kinda hoped it was more than impotence.

I lost it.

"FUCK! Fuck fuck fuck, what am I going to do, Diego? It will take me forever to make that money back and even if I show up back there and try to get straight The Crows are gonna get me sent to county."

I paced back and forth, pulses of nausea and cold fear rolling through my guts.

Diego captured my flapping arms and pulled me in tight. His heart beat against my cheek and I tried to calm down, matching my gasps with the steady rhythm of his chest.

It was how he held me when I'd hop the back fence between our houses and sneak in his window in the middle of the night. When shit was going down at home and nothing felt real even though it was all too real. The first time he'd held me this way his chest was thin and hairless. Now I could feel the broad, smooth stretches of muscle. We'd grown up. And we were always going to be scared kids.

He stroked my hair and waited until my breathing matched his.

"I get why you left. You gotta know it was an accident though. I only meant to hold my hand up, to say, 'Enough!' you know? I didn't realize you were that close behind me. I wouldn't hit you on purpose. You gotta know that."

I made a neutral sound, nuzzling my face into his heartbeat.

"How much is left from the $40,000 you took?"

I did some quick mental math.

"I still have about $20,000."

"Here's what we're gonna do. Uncle Lou wants to buy your lot. He can take out the fence, knock down the house and build a work barn. He said if you sell to him, he'll call it even. Then it's only another couple months till I've got my masters and I'll be making real money. We can move anywhere you want; Detroit, Chicago, even Atlanta. Never go through another winter."

He stroked my hair back from my temple softly. "Come home with me."

"What about The Crows?" I whispered, still hiding in the safety of his soft plaid shirt.

"If you pay Uncle Lou back and your part of the family, you'll have our protection. They know better than to really mess up a Rodriguez. I mean, I can't promise they won't spit on you in the cereal aisle at Meijer's but…"

The cogs clicked in place. I looked up into his eyes.

"You want to get married?"

36 RETREAT AND DEFEAT

Flight 657 blew through the sunrise as it sped east. The sun bounced off the skin of the Pacific and back into my miniature window. Diego slept hard in the middle seat. I watched his nostrils flutter and remembered how closely I'd watched Gabe sleep on the first day of my trip. I'd barely made it five months on my own. Guess I wasn't cut out for trying to be more than what I was.

I hadn't said yes and I hadn't said no to Diego's semi-proposal. I'd hugged him, the wind whipping my curls around us in the salty wharf air. When he went off to check out of his hostel I did some manic Googling of New Zealand work permits and licensing. I couldn't work there as a nurse without re-licensing and all the temporary work permit jobs paid minimum wage. It would take me a decade to save up enough to pay Uncle Lou back.

I could have ghosted Diego and gotten on a plane headed to Dubai or Denmark or Durbin. I could have, except the fight seemed to have been drained out of me. It was time to admit to myself Aunt Mary was dead. Malakai was dead. And I owed a dangerous man $20,000.

I took the Claddagh off my finger. The skin under it was pale and crinkled. I turned the worn silver circle and replaced it with the heart facing up.

The adventure was over.

I watched the shifting texture of the open ocean. It was so different from where the water met the land. The waves rolled instead of crashed, silently gathering power as they crawled across the hemisphere. I tried to imagine exactly how each one would break when it finally met land.

Diego had given me a look when the airline clerk rang up the oversize baggage charge for the Pink Demon. Sorry pal, you want me to come home, my Ocean Baby comes with me. Even if she only sits in a garage, a sweet memory crusted in dried out wax.

Diego's hand sprawled open on the arm rest. I examined the scars in the bright light. This small ridge happened his second week at Uncle Lou's shop. Clamp slipped. The jagged tear on the thumb from when he tried to jump the chain link fence at the 10th St. pool. Same pool his little cousin Starr drowned in last summer. He got the star tattoos on his wrists right after, and not long after that one shot through the night air and broke us apart.

I hadn't thought about that night much since I'd left. It was a closed door in my head I didn't want to knock on.

We'd been fighting about moving to Ann Arbor. Diego was driving two hours round trip every day he had class. I was sure I could find a job there. It has arboretums and book stores and I don't even know…maybe poetry slams or some culture-y shit. Aunt Mary was circling the drain and it was taking everything I had to keep us afloat. The only silver lining was that she was the last reason I had to stay in Flint.

We had shared a couple pitchers at Duke's and were walking home. The tone went from Fun Banter to Battle Stations in a single block. We shouted at each other in the yellow cone of a streetlight, fall leaves blowing around our feet. Diego was right about the rent being expensive. I knew what the real problem was, though.

"You're scared to leave home! What are you, 12? Grow up, you little pussy ass bitch."

He flinched. I knew I'd taken it too far. I am not my best self after five Miller Lights.

He turned and walked away into the dark.

I followed him.

"Hey listen-"

He turned quickly with his hand up. The star on his wrist zoomed out of the darkness and connected with my cheekbone. I stumbled backward and sat in the wet leaves. Tears stung my eyes and the blow rang around my brain, loudly banging on all the other doors I had shut and spray painted with a red X. Do not enter.

Diego was saying something and trying to help me up. I shook him off and ran.

The next time I saw him was on the park bench, across the world and upside down from where we started. I had no idea where we went from here.

37 HOME IS WHERE THE HEART IS

Looking out the car window at Detroit Metro, I couldn't help noticing the number of obese people. After months away it was shocking to see a person the size of two Thai men taped together. A huge woman rolled by on an Amigo scooter, smoking while oxygen tanks blew O2 right above the Camel's red cherry. Home of the brave, for real.

I also gaped at the amount of concrete spread horizon to horizon as we skirted the city and headed north to Flint. My South Pacific island didn't have a single paved road, and even New Zealand's capital city didn't have highways with 12 lanes of traffic.

It was as if Michigan stopped building cars to drive around cities and started building cities around cars. We hit one of the long tunnels where the concrete arteries met, orange lights melding into a blur as we sped through at 80 mph. On a 10th grade field trip we'd decided these tunnels transported you into a *Star Wars* chase scene.

Diego shouted, "Punch it Chewy, get us out of here!"

I made a loud Chewbacca noise. We giggled.

It felt good to break the awkward silence that hummed between us the entire trip home. I clung onto the thread of normality and ran my hands over Sally's butterscotch leather interior.

"Remember when I suggested you lease a Prius when you started commuting to Ann Arbor?"

"I said I'd sooner let you give me a DIY vasectomy," he replied grimly.

Sally was a '69 Chevy Impala SS in steel blue. Uncle Lou "got" her for Diego's 16th birthday and not a single week had passed since that he hadn't lovingly bathed and waxed her. I checked the backseat- yup, the Navajo blanket was still there, neatly folded over the seat.

Senior year I'd skip gym, pop Sally's lock and read, snuggled under that blanket. Diego was always be happy to find me there, sleepy and dreamy and ready to be kissed. If I had to be back in this over-processed landscape at least I was rolling over it in Sally's comforting embrace.

And Thank Lady God it was spring here. If it was rusty, raw February with steel skies and grimy snowbanks everywhere I might have tucked and rolled at the first Halo Burger. At least the trees sprouting in the abandoned factory parking lots had a haze of green leaf buds on them.

I watched the boarded-up houses roll by as we made our way into the bombed-out core of our neighborhood. Ah, The Vehicle City. There is one cop for every 1,000 residents and the average response time to a high-priority 911 call is an hour. That means if someone breaks in your house and shoots you in the gut, you can watch a *Friends* re-run, microwave two Hot Pockets, do a 20-minute workout routine on YouTube, and still have time to paint your nails before the police show up. It's pretty much the Wild West, with crackheads rolling down the street instead of tumbleweeds.

Hard to judge my hometown too harshly when I committed one of the 45 annual homicides. Neighborhood Rule #1: Don't judge and don't drink the tap water.

Diego pulled up in front of Uncle Lou's run-down Victorian. The house had been the jewel of the neighborhood...in 1886. It was still grand under all sorts of flaking skin and odd bulges. Kinda how I imagined Judi Dench looked naked.

We sat in silence.

"You hungry? I can run to KFC's, or I'm sure there's a tray of something in the fridge. You know there's always plenty of food around here."

"Thanks. I'm ok now though. I need to crash out."

He nodded, rubbing his hand roughly across his stubble.

"I feel so weird. I'm not sure if I need to sleep for two days or stay awake for two days," he said.

"That's jet lag. When you go in you should drink a beer in the shower and try to sleep."

"You're...not coming in with me? Where are you gonna stay?"

"My house."

"Uncle Lou's up north, you don't need to worry about running in to him. And if you don't remember, your house is empty without power or water."

I'd made up my mind on the drive in. Diego and I hadn't really touched since the fireworks in the consulate's bathroom. I wasn't sure about...well, about anything with us. I didn't want logistics, habit or simple horniness to decide if or when we were back together.

"I've got a headlamp," I said, getting out of the car. "See you tomorrow?"

He followed and handed me the board and backpack.

"I'll be out early for class and probably won't be home till late. Gonna have a lot of makeup work to do."

"Right," I said, trying to ignore the twist of guilt in my throat. Sorry you had to interrupt your final semester of grad school to track down your traitorous girlfriend on another continent.

He held out some car keys. "You'll need some wheels now that you're home."

I backed up a few steps.

"You know I don't take things from people," I protested.

"You don't take things from people?" he repeated, cocking his crooked right eyebrow.

I actually blushed at that.

"You know what I mean. I don't take handouts."

"Calm down, it's a '91 Buick Uncle Lou's had sitting around. I know better now than to trust you with Sally, *mi sol.*"

That was fair. Sting-y, but fair.

We eyed each other up, looking for a sign the other would back down.

"The bus line to the library got shut down," he said, jingling the keys.

Dammit he knew me well. I only had four books left on my Kindle. I took the keys.

"Thanks," I said not super gratefully. "I'll give it back when I get back on my feet."

He grinned at me. That goofy ass canine tooth making him look all wolfish.

"Yeah you better, I know where you sleep."

He stepped toward me and cautiously pushed a strand of hair behind my ear. We looked at each other in the glow of the orange porchlight. Mayflies zigzagged through the humid air between us.

Back in his natural habitat, he looked less exotic than he had on my Wellington park bench. His familiar, warm brown eyes crinkled into a half-smile. He leaned in and kissed me on the forehead.

"I'm glad you're here. Get some rest."

He headed for the front door, his little dumpling butt and carved calves looking cute in his Carhartt shorts. Yeah. Better not to share a bed tonight.

I walked around the block to avoid hopping the back fence with a surfboard. On the corner a scrubby toddler was using the soft top of a Lincoln as a trampoline. I jumped a mile when the car started and peeled out. The kid tumbled down the back like a Slinky going downstairs and bounced off the cracked pavement.

I held my breath and resisted the urge to run over to him. Neighborhood Rule #2: Keep your nose in your own business if you like it on your face. Eventually he shook his shaggy head and ambled off into the night.

A few overgrown lots down the block, there it was. My palace. The plywood in all the windows made the 1950's two-story look blind, a pirate with patches on both eyes. You don't fool me, old man. I know you've seen some shit behind those walls.

I dug the house key from an interior pocket in my backpack. It always felt funny when my hand would brush that key while rifling through my pack in some dark hostel room. Like an astronaut finding a daisy tucked in his pack on Mars. That key belonged to a different person on a different planet.

I walked up the crumbling concrete stoop. Someone had been using the half-walled front porch as a squatter toilet. I was surprised to see Aunt Mary's cheery Hobby Lobby doormat hadn't been stolen.

"Home is where the heart is," it declared in hot pink cursive. I swallowed the golf ball in my throat and went in.

38 SHOWER NEGOTIATIONS

I got an air mattress and some groceries the next day. Then I didn't leave the house for a week. My mind shut up when I cleaned, so I cleaned every inch of the place, shaking out spiders and uselessly scrubbing the grungy grout. I read by my headlamp at night and went through the entire *Girl with a Dragon Tattoo* series again. Reading about a sociopath who extracts brutal revenge on her enemies made me a regular old fuckup in comparison. God bless the Swedes and their obsession with our heart of darkness.

I avoided sleeping as much as I could. Every time I closed my eyes, I'd fall into these thick chowder sleeps where I dreamed about chasing Malakai through the waves and woke up throbbing and sobbing. It was fucking pathetic. Plus, the crinkling of the air mattress drove me crazy.

When I started talking to the spiders, I realized if I didn't leave the house I was in danger going full *Grey Gardens*. I was out of peanut butter and beer and if I didn't shower soon I wasn't going to be allowed back into society. I'd called to get the power and water turned back on but considering the level of go-get-em Sheila in the Utilities department showed on the phone, it could still be a minute.

I'd barely seen Diego since I was back. Guess I didn't need to be too worried about him trying to creep into my room at night and make sweet love to me. He texted he'd be around more this weekend. What the hell, I'd get cleaned up for the occasion. I didn't have shit else to do.

I looked through the kitchen window at Uncle Lou's house. In spite of neighborhood protocol, it wasn't ever locked. Between his sons and their kids and the cousins and random shop employees, there was always someone home. And if a stranger walked in looking to cause trouble, anyone from the four rottweilers to the vicious four-year old Valentina would mess them up. Even if I wasn't necessarily a welcome house guest, I wasn't a stranger. Fuck it.

The hot water felt amazing on my back as I scrubbed the rings of ground-in dirt from my heels. I was sure there was enough water to get clean, shave my legs *and* armpits. Luxury.

The old door creaked open. Crap. You'd think I'd remember to lock the door after the hostel where an old goat from Greenland tried to wash my back.

"Someone's in here," I called. "*Ocupado.*"

"It's my bathroom. I don't care if it's *ocupado.*"

I froze with one arm lifted above my head. The curtain was too thick to show the outline of the intruder. I didn't need to see him to know though.

Uncle Lou was back.

Plastic clinked against porcelain. Was he...no. No. He was probably sitting on the closed seat so we could have a cozy little chat.

"Thanks for the $20K back," he said cheerfully.

"You're welcome," I replied, lowering my arm inch by inch.

Dummy, he's not a T-Rex. He knows you're here whether or not you're making quick movements.

"I'm glad you're looking after my house. Activity keeps the squatters away. You're kind of moving chairs around the deck of the Titanic though. You know I'm gonna bulldoze it when you sell, right?"

He let out a soft grunt. I closed my eyes and concentrated on the hot water on my shoulders. His rheumatism was probably acting up. Yup, rheumatism. There was no other explanation for that noise.

"I know," I said.

"Well sweetheart, here's something else you should know. He didn't sleep or eat for weeks, when you left. I made all his favorites: mole, chicharróns, even roasted a whole pig in the backyard so he could have the ribs. He'd only chug those nasty energy drinks."

I kept my eyes closed and visualized a full suit of armor covering my naked body. Clank. There went the visor into place.

"You messed him up good."

The smell hit my nostrils with a burning clarity. This wasn't happening. I was back on my beach, about to paddle out to an even swell. Tra la la la.

"You know the saddest part? He tried to convince me you hadn't taken the money. For weeks, he insisted it was a random break in. He really believed it too. I finally had to show him the CCTV footage. He needed to know even though it damn near broke my heart to do it. Needed stop thinking you were some kind of angel."

I found my voice somewhere deep inside the armor.

"He's always known I'm no angel."

Uncle Lou laughed and farted.

"True. He hadn't pegged you as someone who steals from family, though. I tried to explain to him your family's garbage. No loyalty. No one teaching you right from wrong. Even your pious little aunt was scamming Social Security for years, cashing your mom's checks."

My voice died again. What could I say? Aunt Mary sure did use those checks to buy groceries.

This OG talking to me about right and wrong was rich. I guess he did live by a strict moral code, just not the Michigan Penal Code. In Uncle Lou's world stealing from family was an executable offense. Almost as bad as snitching or hosting a party without enough food.

The toilet paper stand clinked. The hot water was running out. Oh well. I'd stand in here for days under cold spray before I'd reach out and ask this man for a towel.

"I want you to sign the property over, and then I want you gone," he said, flushing and finally getting to the point. "My boy is graduating soon with a world of opportunity in front of him. He doesn't need his trashy high school sweetheart holding him back. You've got a rock where your heart should be and you obviously don't love him. So, let's talk about the paperwork."

I felt sick. My knees gave out and I sunk to the floor of the tub. Eyes still closed, head in my hands, I raised my thick voice over the running water in the sink.

"I'll sign it over. Tell me how."

"My real estate guy will draw up the papers. I'll tell him to get a move on it. Last thing we want is for you to hang around long enough to get pregnant. And in case you have any ideas about selling to anyone else, take one look at the market around here and you'll be on your knees thanking me for this offer."

I nodded into my hands.

"Sweetheart?"

"Yes!" I half shouted, shivering in the cold spray. "I'm in. I want this to be done too."

"Then you'll get the hell out of our lives life, yeah? I don't think he cares about you anymore. Better safe than sorry though. Bad habits can be hard to kick."

"He asked me to marry him," I shot back, a flame of defiance shooting up out of my shame puddle.

"Then he's not as smart as I thought. It's time he learned that people don't change."

He finally left, purposefully not closing the door behind him. He hadn't washed his hands. I snagged a towel and snapped off the spray. Big drops circled down my curls, landing with little cold thuds on my thighs.

I hated my house. Everything from the basement door to the green bathtub to the walnut staircase was infected with some terrible memory. So why did I want to tell Uncle Lou to go fuck his offer in the earhole?

39 GOODWILL

I muttered a rant about materialism and American consumerism to myself as I swung the Buick into a Goodwill parking lot. I had really enjoyed cutting all my worldly possessions down to fit in a backpack. It made me feel light and free. The last thing in the world I wanted was to spend the little money I had left on clothes. I guess everyone needs some "pants" though.

This was the Goodwill where I ditched the entire contents of our old house here before I took off. Everything except the box I found in the basement marked "Vicki's stuff" in my dad's sloppy handwriting. I was tempted (real tempted) to go through it. I didn't though. Decided whatever junk my mom left behind wasn't worth my time.

I gave it to my dad after the funeral, along with a couple other boxes of papers and family heirlooms, including a velvet painting of Ty Cobb as Jesus in "The Last Supper." His new wife Tiffany had probably chucked it all anyway.

I thought about asking to stay with my dad and getting a nursing job in Kentucky to save up the money I owed Uncle Lou. Wouldn't have to deal with The Crows or this Flint bullshit. Then I remembered how Tiffany had a dead tooth and always stank of hot dogs. And how her 16-year old son always passed by me too close while wearing sweatpants. And how one time I read about a Kentucky man who was held at gunpoint and forced to eat his own beard in a dispute over a riding mower. And, you know, the fact that my dad never asked me to stay there.

Nah, I'll risk the lead poisoning in my hometown, thanks.

At the front of the store a rack of "1960s Klassics" stopped me in my tracks. No summer wardrobe is complete without a blood red leather trench coat, right? I swung it over my arm for safekeeping. I quickly clicked through the dashikis and swing dresses until a baby pink suit stopped me cold.

I checked the label. There wasn't one. It was for sure Aunt Mary's handmade church suit. It shouldn't have shocked me. I was the one who left all our shit in the alley behind this place. That logic didn't stop the floor from swaying weirdly under my numb feet.

My entire life Aunt Mary never missed a Sunday rally in this suit. When she got her license revoked, I took her every week. Thankfully she didn't want me to go in with her. Said I was so naughty I might bring the Lord's lightning down from heaven and she didn't want to get caught in the crossfire.

Eventually Edie smashed up her Cadillac too, so I'd pick her up on the way. Sweet Baby Jesus help me if I was five minutes late. Edie would slide into the backseat yapping at me, reeking of Ponds cold cream and crotch.

I'd read in the car while they acted out the piety play. They'd both ride in the backseat on the way home, making it easier to gossip in low tones. As if I gave a crap if Mimi Hancock's granddaughter had an abortion. When we got home Aunt Mary always ferreted a stale donut hole out of her purse for me. One time I jokingly made the sign of the cross before I popped it in my mouth.

"Don't do that," she snapped, sharper than usual. "I don't need you to believe. I do need you to respect my belief."

I sure hadn't respected her Classic Two-Piece Church Suit. I wondered what part of the Bible told all old women they needed to dress for mass as if they were selling Jesus life insurance. Goodwill wanted $15 for this handmade vintage gem. It was a green tag discount day. I gently bent the plastic fastener, worked the yellow price tag off and swapped on a $5 green tag. There was no way I could leave it behind a second time.

I walked out with a bag full of green-tag jeans and tops and one old lady suit, Size -0. As I dug through to make sure the sleepwalking clerk bagged everything, I paused to hold the door for someone coming in.

She stopped at the threshold. I looked up into Georgine's skinny, sour face.

Fuck me, did the church suit conjure her here with The Pope Signal?

She glared at me and worked her underbite back and forth.

"You're back, eh?" she spit.

"Yeah. I'm back." I resisted the urge to straighten her crooked wig.

"Your skin's too dark."

"Nice to see you too, Miz Georgine," I muttered, trying to scoot around her.

Her clawed hand grabbed the suit draped over my arm.

"Did you pawn Mary's good suit?" she shrieked.

"No...that's not how Goodwill works..." I tried to explain.

"You vile girl. Give me that."

We had a pitiful tug of war over the pink knit for a couple seconds.

"Fine!" I said, letting go. "You keep it." I stalked off toward the car.

"You shoulda stayed gone, sweetheart," she shouted after me.

I glanced back when I got to the car. She hadn't moved. Her bright purple sweat suit glowed against the fluorescent poster boards in the store windows. I swear even the kittens on the front of her pilled sweatshirt were mean mugging me.

Well, The Crows knew I was home. They always said the city was big but the neighborhood was small. I should have known it wouldn't take long for them to sniff me out. What I didn't know was what they were gonna do about it.

40 BIG DOG, LITTLE DOG

I watched Diego's cousin Chewy stick an entire chicken wing in his mouth, chew and suck aggressively, and then spit the clean bones back out.

"You want another High Life, honey?" the Applebee's waitress asked, twinkling her glitter-spattered eyelashes at Diego.

"No thanks, I'm driving," he smiled back at her.

"I'd take another. A tall boy, please," I called uselessly after her retreating green polo.

"So I got allowed into the pen pal program for good behavior, then Tanya starts writing me and right away we hit it off. She's a reptile lover too."

He squeezed the skinny redhead's freckled hand. She leaned in to him.

"It's so good to see him on the outside," she gushed, stroking the strap of facial hair attempting to mark out his wobbly jawline.

"You know, I almost lost her right before I got out. It would have killed me to never have gotten to be with her."

"Were you sick?" I asked Tanya.

"Oh yeah, real bad. I got salmonella-induced blood poisoning. The runs were so bad I was down to 98 pounds and they had to keep me on fluids at the hospital."

She leaned toward me conspiratorially.

"Never share a Capri Sun with your pet turtle."

I stopped eating the wings and clutched Diego's thigh under the table to keep the giggles in. It was rock solid under the worn jeans and twitched a little at my touch. I let go quickly.

The waitress came back with two more Mudslides for Chewy and Tanya, and the check. Diego must have slipped her his card at some point. He signed the bill and grabbed his coat.

"Great seeing you guys, we gotta roll."

"You didn't have to do that," Chewy said, but he looked relieved.

"Welcome home, man. The family's glad to have you back."

I rolled my eyes when Diego and Chewy exchanged an A-frame man hug with a lot of back slapping. That's right guys, gotta make sure you don't get your balls anywhere near each other or you might turn gay for each other. Even though you're cousins.

Still it was sweet of Diego to cover their tab.

I bumped his shoulder with mine as we walked toward Sally in the purple twilight.

"'Let's go out', you said, 'It'll be fun' you said. Next thing I know, I've got second-hand turtle salmonella!"

He laughed his ridiculous laugh. It actually sounded how comic books wrote out laughter, "heeheeheehee," and it always made me laugh harder.

"You want to have some real fun?" he asked, twirling his car keys.

He gave me that crooked smile and hitched his low-slung jeans up on his narrow hips. I thought about Uncle Lou saying he hadn't been eating. His belt was on the tightest hole and his favorite 501's still sagged on him. His big eyes had a spark of mischief in them. I missed that spark.

"Yeah," I nodded. "Yeah, I do want to have some fun with you,"

"Dukes?"

"Yeah, Dukes."

A low holler greeted us in the dark, skunky hole.

"Hey Diego…. what- Chuckle Bear! Where you been CB?"

The bartender flipped his hinged bar top and hustled over with his oversized meat paws reaching for me.

"Hey Duke," I wheezed, as he picked me up and shook me in a smothering hug. "Missed you too."

He grabbed my glass mug from the hooks on the ceiling and flipped the Miller Light tap, angling a plastic pitcher under it expertly.

"Can we get some barrels? I don't have mine on me."

Duke slid the bar's beat up dart set over the polished wood.

"Your dad know you're home?" he asked casually. Duke and my dad went way back, back to when kids played tackle football and people had jobs. He and my dad had pierced my ears in this bar, each one stabbing a tiny lobe at the same time. Even though they were likely drunker than skunks the holes were perfectly even and they never got infected.

"Sure does," I lied easily. "He'll probably come up from Kentucky to see me soon."

"Mmmhmm," he replied, eyeing me closely. Duke was sharp as shit behind those droopy eyes. "Well when he does, tell him to stop by and have one on me. Cheap bastard."

"Will do," I chirped and kissed him on the cheek. He passed the perfectly poured pitcher and our two mugs across the bar. I grabbed them and we headed for the board.

"Diego," he called from behind me, "You keep CB from causing trouble, yeah?"

"I try, Duke, I try," Diego threw back at him.

We warmed up by throwing a few rounds without keeping score.

One of my tosses hit the wire and Diego had to jump as the bounce back narrowly missed his Adidas shell-toes.

"Dang, you're rusty," he teased.

"Give me a minute and two beers, and I'll whoop your ass per usual," I shot back.

He turned to look at me dead on. A charge bounced between us. He raised a long-fingered hand and lightly traced the puff of my bottom lip.

"I like per usual between us," he said quietly. We looked at each other for a long beat and I was sure he was going to kiss me. And I was surprised at how bad I wanted him to.

Instead he took the darts from my hand and nailed all three throws into the bullseye.

Oh, I get it, your ego needs me to be the one to make the move. Well enjoy the wait, punk. I tossed a dart low on purpose and took my time bending over to pull it out of the plywood in my cutoffs. And enjoy the

225

view.

"Y'all gonna play or what? We got next."

We turned to see an odd pair of dudes. They were opposites in every way: white and black, skinny and fat, tall and short. Which made it even stranger that they had matching outfits: Big Dog t-shirts and spanking new Jordans. Looking good, players.

"What do you think, baby, you wanna play or you want to hang?" I asked Diego, my voice going up a few notes.

That twinkle was in his eyes and his full lips parted into a broad smile. Duke eyed us closely from the bar, lips pursing.

"I'll play if you want to play, *mami*. You guys want to do doubles instead of waiting?"

"I'm not very good," I apologized to the Bigger Dog.

He smirked at the bar-issued darts in my hand and unzipped his custom set.

"We'll take it easy on you, baby."

We played 301 first. I missed a lot of close ones.

"I should slow down on the beers," I giggled, chugging the last of my third Miller Light. I could feel the alcohol pulling me into the Delightfully Overconfident Zone.

Diego was encouraging. Instead of getting frustrated, he stood behind me and showed me how to square up my shoulders more. The Little Dog sighed with annoyance when Diego took his time standing there, pressing a little into my ass and running light fingers over my arm to guide it into position.

I finally nailed the wedge I had been aiming for.

"You did it!" Diego cheered.

Bigger Dog hit three triples in a row and won the game. "Didn't get the hang of it soon enough though, baby," he mocked.

I decided not to comment on his disrespectful tone or his inability to stop scratching his dick every 20 seconds. We were playing the long game.

"That was fun! How about Cricket next?" I asked the Dogs. "And let's make it interesting. $100 to the winner."

They hesitated.

"You guys don't go out without some cash, right?" Diego asked lightly. "I'm sure you've got a hundo between you."

"We got more than that," scoffed Little Dog, "We're over doubles though. Y'all play and we'll get next."

"That's a sweet chain," I said in an admiring tone. "Is that a blinged out Pokémon? I bet that's worth $100."

Little Dog's hand snapped to the thick chain around his thick neck. The chain was real even if the colored crystal chips on the pendant were worthless.

"I don't gamble with Pikachu."

I shrugged, turned and threw a dart way wide of the board.

"Come on Diego, they don't want to play. Let's throw some and leave 'em alone."

They looked at each other, exchanging the quick non-verbal shorthand of a long-married couple.

"Let's see your cash," Big Dog demanded.

Diego pulled five crisp $20's out of his wallet. Always prepared, this guy.

He set the cash on the sticky high top and raised a cocky eyebrow at the Dogs.

Big Dog nudged his pal and he reluctantly pulled off the chain, plopping it on top of the cash.

I motioned to Duke to bring another pitcher. He glared at me while flipping the tap. This shit made me thirsty.

"You throw first," Diego nodded to Big Dog.

He hit a double 20.

"Good one!" I said perkily, then hit a triple 20. "Oooh, lucky me!"

On each turn after that either Diego or I hit triples, until I only had to get a bullseye and double bullseye to win. When we passed each other we high fived and followed the swing around to smack each other on the ass.

That's when I took a breather and started scoring points on the numbers still left open.

Little Dog swore as his attempt at a triple 15 bounced off the board. Beads of sweat were starting to line the deep creases on his neck, reflecting the blue neon of the bar signs.

You better sweat motherfucker. My dad was a four-time Southeast Michigan Dart Club Champion and I'd been throwing since I could be trusted not to put my eye out. You don't get your own mug at Duke's by dogging it on Dart Night.

Time to nail the casket. I hit a single and a double bullseye, and tossed the extra dart on the 19 they still hadn't closed...just to make my point.

"Pay up, Big Dog," I laughed, swiping the chain and the cash off the table. "Pikachu's got a new master."

"Fuck you, little bitch ass hustler!" Little Dog grabbed for the chain in my fist.

Diego was there before I could blink.

"We won, son. Don't get ugly."

Big Dog manned up behind his partner and it was most definitely about to get uglier than fresh roadkill in here. I worked the warm metal around in my hand so the sharp little ears of the metal charm were between my knuckles.

"Fuck you too, spic. Give me my chain back!" Little Dog shouted.

My right hand flew straight out from my shoulder and connected with his doughy cheekbone. The guy's own Pikachu sliced his skin open, leaving two deep gashes across his face. Oh, the sting of betrayal.

He screamed and Big Dog jumped Diego, knocking over the high top and landing on top of him.

Before they had a chance to do more than swap a couple glancing punches, Duke pulled the double barrel out from behind the bar.

Both Dogs froze at the sound of the round being chambered.

"Out. Now," Duke said, casually leveling the two gaping muzzles at their chests.

They scampered double time. I couldn't stop laughing, even though my hand was throbbing badly.

"Godammit CB, I told you not to start shit in here!" Duke grumbled, carefully replacing the safety. "Get on out of here before they come back with some friends."

I pulled Diego off the ground and looped the bloody chain over my neck. Spoils of war.

"We're out, we're out," I promised Duke, "Sorry."

"You ain't sorry," he grumbled.

"And you're not really mad," I countered. "Gotta keep this place from going soft or the regulars will get bored."

I blew kisses to the row of sour, drunk mushrooms growing from the bar stools and they all raised their mugs to me.

Diego and I hustled to the car, keeping an eye on the shadows for any signs of movement.

We couldn't stop giggling as he sped us off into the night. My pulse raced and my skin itched. I wanted to throw another punch or jump in a lake or...

Diego stopped at a red light. I looked at his chiseled profile in the red glow. I was unbuckled and straddling him in a second.

He inhaled sharply as I bit his neck and grabbed him through the worn denim. Fine, you win, I caved first. But let's see if you can drive while I do this...

41 BACK IN THE SALLY AGAIN

Diego lasted three blocks before he swore and peeled Sally into an empty bank parking lot. I couldn't get enough of the taste of his neck; sweat and stubble stung my tongue as I tried to gulp him. The soft cotton of his jeans pulled against my Goodwill cutoffs as I pushed against him. I wanted to make everything between us disappear and swallow him whole.

He didn't take his eyes off the road or hands off the wheel until we came to a full stop. He carefully turned off the engine before turning his attention to me.

When he did it was with the force of two battle lines clashing at full charge. He grabbed my face and met my mouth with his. Both of us gasped for air in the split seconds our mouths parted. Our bodies ached to connect that airless way everywhere.

His hand fumbled with my shorts while I tried to unbuckle his seat belt. We laughed into each other's mouths and untangled, moving to the back seat with practiced precision. There wasn't a lot more room there. Good thing we knew what to do with the space we had.

I unbuckled his belt and yanked the too-big jeans down to his knees. I paused a second to feel him from shaft to tip. He pulsed in my hand, a tiny bit of moisture gleaming on the tip in the streetlights. Hello there, Old Pal. I'm happy to see you again too.

Diego scrabbled at my button-front shorts, grunting in frustration. I leaned back and undid the buttons neatly, no thanks to his interference. When I wiggled out of them, he gathered my black satin underwear in a fist and pulled on them roughly. The motion of the fabric against me almost made me melt on the spot.

Everything that had felt dead for weeks was rushing out in big gobs of sensation. I could taste the early summer humidity on Diego's skin, hear the light patter of moths bumping into the windows, smell the car's vintage leather and most of all I could feel the need radiating out from my center all the way to the tips of my hair.

Diego slid a long finger around the underwear and pulled me toward him, the beckoning motion moving heavy inside me.

"*Mi sol*," he whispered, "You are burning up."

He brought my face close to his and bit my bottom lip. The way he was teasing me with his fingers and the satin fabric was new and different and brain-scrambling. It occurred to me for the first time that he might have been with someone else too. The thought, "I will kill that bitch," blazed through my head. Guess I'm kind of a hypocritical dick like that.

The sensation got so intense couldn't take it anymore and tried to pull away. He grabbed my waist and held me put.

"You stay there. You stay right there and let me see you come for me."

He leaned me back between the seats and kept pulling at the soaked fabric and I did exactly what he told me.

Before the shaking swells could stop he spun me around and entered me in a single thrust. My nails dug into the leather of the front seats while he moved me back and forth from his clenched grip on the satin.

What was between us was chemical and complicated. But all the history and hurt and love shrank down to a long, slow burn as he pushed me away and pulled me back, over and over until we both yelled into the close night air.

***

I woke up in the morning to the strange, sweet awareness of another body wrapped around mine. Diego's long limbs snaked over me, trapping me in a net of hard, brown muscles. I felt amazing and I had to pee so bad. I nudged his prickly chin gently out from the hollow of my shoulder. Kissed his sleep-puffed lips even though he had cat breath and a little collection of white spit in one corner of his mouth. He instinctively squeezed me tighter, moaning a low, "No. You stay,"

I arched into the stiffness growing against my lower back.

"Did you know every time you let morning wood go to waste, a fairy dies?" he whispered, still not opening his eyes.

"Don't worry I'll be right back. And we'll save the fairies."

He grumbled and rolled over. My knees were useless as marshmallows as I banged my way awkwardly down the hall. After a shudder-worthy piss I dumped water into the toilet to "flush" and took a long look in the mirror.

Between the wild tangles, unplucked brows and the bloody Pikachu around my neck, I was a goddamn mess. I also looked awake for the first time in a while. I promised myself I'd clean up my act, starting today. No more dressing like a homeless ghost. Definitely brushing my teeth with some sort of regularity.

I climbed back onto the uneasy sea of the air mattress and curled around Diego's broad back, hand snaking around the front.

He leaned into the pressure, sighing.

"I want to ask you something," he said to the wall.

Oh man. I wanted to have morning sex, not a confessional.

"Hmmmm?" I increased the pace.

"I have my capstone presentation today. In Ann Arbor. It's kind of a thing…the Big Three all send reps to scout the graduating talent. If your project's any good you should get some job offers…"

He was trying and failing to sound casual, either because this was a huge deal to him, or because he had his hand over mine now and was pushing hard against us.

"There's a nice reception after at the Hilton. Maybe we could get a room, stay the night. Cele- celebrate," he breathed.

"Stay at the Hilton? Fancy. Oh, do you think I'll see you getting all academic on electric battery technology and be overcome with throbbing need to suck your cock?"

He lifted his head and glared at me over his shoulder.

"You can be really mean sometimes, you know that?"

Well shit. It was a joke. This obviously mattered to him, and he wanted me to be his date.

I rolled him over and straddled him. Scooted down so I was close enough that my breath tickled his balls.

"Say 'drive shaft'."

"Drive shaft," he whispered huskily.

"Oh yeah baby, you know I like it," I purred, licking in him long strokes. "Say 'death of the combustion engine'."

"Death of the- shit, *mi sol*, stop talking!" he gasped, digging his fingers into my tangled mess of hair.

"Fine. I'll come with you."

42 *SEHNSUCHT*

If I was going to be Diego's arm candy for his big night, I needed to make good on my promise to get cleaned up. After he left to practice his presentation, I evaluated the situation; it took one try at getting a brush through my hair to diagnose myself Officially Busted.

I wished I could walk into that fabulous Fijian salon and have my burly Fairy Godmother make everything pretty while I nibbled on pastries. Instead my broke ass sneaked over the back fence into Uncle Lou's house. I was at least going to need running water to fix myself up, and between the six girl cousins there had to be a straight iron or two.

I checked myself out in the glass storefronts as I clacked my way through downtown Ann Arbor. All things considered; I was proud of my work. No fairy godmother or twittering birds had showed up to make me beautiful. A three-legged mouse did run through the bathroom though, and I think he wished me well.

Cousin Mikey had an electric razor and I'd taken the bold move of shaving half my head. A knotty dreadlock had formed above my right ear and no amount of combing was getting it straightened out. Zoe Kravitz was on the cover of a magazine in the bathroom with a half-shaved head and it looked amazing on her. As a general rule, thinking what looks good on Zoe Kravitz will also look good on you is poor judgement. Luckily in this case it worked out.

I also shaved off all my pubic hair. I almost felt bad using the razor Mikey put on his face to shave my taint. Then I remembered how glamorous I had felt in my shiny silver prom dress with a matching silver wrap. Until Diego and I were taking pictures and he called down the stairs, "Baby girl, why you dressed like a damn baked potato?"

Fuck you Cousin Mikey, I'll get all the nooks and crannies and I won't rinse this thing off.

Now in the storefronts I could see the little black Prada was doing its expert-tailoring thing on my curves. Red lipstick, my jade bracelet and a Payless splurge on some spike pumps later, I looked classy and a little edgy. Good enough to make Diego look good, anyway.

I paused outside a used bookstore and had a pang of that weird/nice/sad feeling I always got on college campuses. After I dropped Diego off here the first time, I Googled a long string of feelings words came up with "*sehnsucht*." It's German for longing or yearning for ideal alternative experiences. The brick buildings, the grassy quads, the atmosphere of higher purpose. Crawling with people younger than me, so confident in a future full of suits and respect and 401K's that they were free to walk around ratty pajama pants for now. It all made me feel real *sehnsucht-y*.

I found the right ballroom in the Hilton and slid in back, right in time for Diego to go last. He was handsome and a little too skinny for his suit and tie as he introduced himself. His tone and body language were confident. Only I would have noticed the small tick of rubbing his thumb and index finger together that showed he was nervous. Once he got into the flow of information the tick stopped and his voice became more animated.

The technical stuff was Greek to me and I could still tell he was killing it. The assembled crowd of Standard Middle-Aged White Dudes nodded along and whispered to each other. I got the sense they thought the complicated diagrams on Diego's PowerPoint slides were disruptive; worthy of longer conversations and academic poking and prodding.

He wrapped up and hearty applause clattered around the room. A ferrety professor invited us all to join the department at the rooftop bar. I hung awkwardly by the door as Diego chatted with colleagues and wrapped cords. The anemic blond girl who went before him was way too eager to help, chattering away and laughing too loudly at his responses. Easy honey, he's clever, not hilarious. I relied on the armor of my Prada to not feel totally out of place.

Finally, he spotted me and hurried over.

"Hi! How did it sound from the back? You look amazing!" He was glowing, obviously relieved to cross the finish line of a marathon academic challenge.

"Wonderful. You sounded wonderful. I'm proud of you," I smiled at him. I wanted to make a joke about his collar sticking up in back and decided to keep my mouth shut. This was his moment and he had shone and none of the guys with cell phone holders on their belts would hold a fashion faux pas against him. Instead I kissed him on the cheek and carefully tucked the crisp white fabric back into his suit coat.

"Let's get drunk," he grinned.

The rooftop had a Golden Hour glow and a stiff signature cocktail that Diego gulped quickly. I chose white wine over beer because, you know, classiness.

He downed a few more drinks while fielding dozens of conversations with the recruiters from GM, Ford and Chrysler. All of them gave him business cards and I knew they were really interested in hiring him when they started shit talking each other: "Bill from Ford cheats at golf. Call me first."

Diego kept checking that I had a drink and wasn't too bored by the tech talk.

"It could be worse. Fantasy baseball is starting soon," I assured him, squeezing his hand.

The truth was I was enjoying myself. The sweet, cool wine was my favorite varietal: *Chateau Gratis*. The men were polite to me and I understood that being on Diego's arm was helping him make a good impression. No one knew I was an aunt-killing, unemployed embezzler from a shady family. Maybe you didn't have to go all the way around the world to start a new version of yourself.

The crowd thinned as the sun sank behind the green treetops of the Arboretum. Diego wrapped his arms around me from behind and whispered in my ear, "Let's go downstairs."

His breath was laced with bourbon and bitters and the start of stubble on his cheek reminded me of the close prickles I'd felt all day between my legs. No one was near us and I was facing the deck wall, so I guided his hand under the front of my skirt. His fingertips met the close shave and froze.

"Did you only shave half of that too?" he whispered in my ear.

"Oh, you're funny," I replied, "I didn't know I was dating George Lopez."

"We're dating now? I thought I asked you to marry me."

There it was. The conversation that I'd been avoiding since Lambton Harbor. I knew I hadn't answered him and he knew I hadn't answered him and I guess it was dumb to think we could pull hustles and have sexy sex and pretend it never happened. I turned and looked at him. The setting sun flooded his brown eyes so they glowed dark amber.

The skinny blond girl eyed us soddenly from the bar. She obviously had a crush on Diego and I could see how we looked to her in the golden light. A beautiful mixed-race couple who fit together perfectly. The kind that appeared on the cover of IUD brochures and made you think, "Dang, if that thing falls out, they'll have some gorgeous babies."

She probably didn't even know the half of Diego's goodness. He was the kind of guy who actually had an answer to the question, "What's your five-year plan?" While the rest of us were rolling joints with our disappointing report cards at high school graduation parties, he already knew he'd be here today, finishing his graduate degree exactly six years later. I knew his plan for the next five years included love, marriage and a baby in a baby carriage. What I didn't know was how I felt about all that. Thinking about all the overly-choreographed Facebook announcements alone was exhausting.

"Uncle Lou told me to pay him back and leave you alone," I said. "According to him, you're too good for me, College Boy."

We both knew that was a stall.

"He doesn't control my life," Diego protested.

We both knew that wasn't exactly true. I could read the tension in every line of his long body and knew I owed it to him to be honest.

"I'm not ready now. When I was...gone, there was someone-"

"I don't want to know," he interrupted me sharply. "I mean, I already know, and I don't want details. You chose to come home with me, and that's what matters."

Well darling, the fact that I was in a state of traumatic shock and owed your thug uncle $20,000 maybe had something to do with that choice. Still, I was here now. And there were worse outcomes in life than marrying your super-hot best friend.

"Let me get things settled with the house and Uncle Lou, okay? I don't want to be worried about rat poison in my *tres leches* cake at our engagement party."

"You've had the papers for a week," Diego pointed out, frowning into the sunset. "Why haven't you signed them?"

Great question. I was going to. I had to. I should feel lucky I could get out of grand larceny that easy. Somehow though, every time I picked up a pen and approached the stack of legal documents, I found something else that needed doing first. The bum poop wasn't going to hose itself off the front porch, after all.

"I'll do it when we're back tomorrow," I said, wrapping my arms around his waist.

He kissed the top of my head and held me close.

"That's all the answer I'm getting tonight, huh?"

"Come on," I said, "There's a floor downstairs that needs your suit on it."

43 LET'S PLAY

When Diego came out of the bathroom, I grabbed him by the tie and backed him onto the low couch in the sitting area. The wide view of the city lights and the night sky made the small room feel more intimate so I left the tan curtains open. If people on the street could see us, you're welcome.

I slowly took off my dress and climbed on him, the wool of the couch scratching at my knees and the wool of his suit itching my thighs. He wrapped his hand around my neck and pulled me to his mouth. I always knew he wanted me badly when he kissed as if he was drowning.

I was unzipping his pants when he stopped me.

"I got you something," he said reaching over the armrest for his laptop bag.

"You're the one graduating," I protested. "And I didn't get you anything."

He shrugged and handed me a narrow black box. I was relieved it wasn't a ring box.

I untied the satin ribbon and found a long string of dark pearls nestled in velvet. I held it up and even in the dim light the surface of each pearl shone with the quicksilver colors of an oil slick.

He took them out of my hand and looped them over my head, carefully pulling my curls out so the pearls ran right next to my skin, from collarbone, down the twin slopes of my breasts in the thin lace bra, dripping past my navel.

"They're beautiful," I whispered, moving a little to see the light play across them. They felt cold against my chest and the little hairs around my belly button stood on end as they brushed my stomach.

Diego twirled the strand around one finger and pulled me back to him.

"You're beautiful, *mi sol*. And dark. They match you," he whispered into my mouth.

We pulled and unbuttoned until that stupid wool suit was around his ankles. I ran my hands over and over his smooth abs, loving the way his flesh rippled under the tight, tawny skin. I traced the two deep cuts ran from his hips to the top of his boxers. A clinical voice in my head labelled them *transversus abdominis*. Shut up Brain, all you need to know right now is they're a physiological billboard shouting "sexy parts this way!"

He rolled me onto my back on the couch and kneeled before me, peeling off my thin boyshorts. The Payless heels stayed on.

I was more than ready to have him inside me and pulled his hips encouragingly. He shook his head and took the pearls off my neck.

With a Big Bad Wolf grin, he wrapped the black beads around and around his index finger. He carefully pooled the rest of the pearls on my stomach, where they shifted and slithered around with every shallow breath, like a cool snake bedding down in my groin.

The pearled finger entered me inch by inch. I could feel the texture of the small globes against me as my hips rocked back and forth, side to side. A low whooshing started deep in my ears and I closed my eyes to concentrate on the building pressure system between my legs.

Diego hooked my leg over his shoulder and slid his tongue along the back of my knee. I bucked up from the couch as if I'd been shocked. He gave a low laugh and pinned my hips to the scratchy fabric, twirling his finger in a slow circle.

"Not yet. Do you want to play?"

Oh shit. Playing wasn't a good idea. We'd said that to each other many times. Not a good idea. We promised each other we'd stop years ago.

"Yes," I gasped.

He pulled the pearls out of me and put them back around my neck. I winced as he pulled the two strands in opposite directions, trapping my shallow breaths at my throat. He pulled the other leg onto his shoulder and entered me roughly.

The whooshing in my ears became deafening and physical panic mixed with desire flooded my senses. My body pulsed along with Diego's thudding rhythm, from my swollen feet in the pinching shoes to the backs of my eyeballs. I surrendered to the high and let the euphoria wash through me.

Right before I passed out, he let go of the pearls and air flooded my lungs. I gulped it as my body shook and released in massive quakes of relief. Diego sped up, head thrown back, long bumpy throat exposed.

"No," I croaked. Shaking, I stopped him and forced him back under me on the couch. Every muscle in his arms tensed as he braced himself between the two arm rests of the couch. I slipped him into me and rocked slowly.

I pulled his cheap red necktie back around his neck and tightened the knot under his Adam's apple.

"It's your turn to play."

44 5-YEAR PLANS

Diego threw on his house shorts to answer the door for room service. The kid delivering the cheeseburgers could have been a cousin. He took in Diego's tattoos and my painted toes sticking out of the expensive bedspread as he pocketed the tip, then stuck his knuckles out for a bump. The gesture clearly said, "Good on you for getting on the other side of this door, bro. Wish I was in your shoes."

Diego grabbed two beers from the mini-fridge, settled the plates between us on the bed and we dug in. I was starving and he scraped his fries onto my plate after I inhaled my own, ignoring the scratchy soreness in my throat.

"The graduation ceremony is here next week. You'll come?" he asked between chomps of burger.

"Sure. You know I'm proud of you, right? It's one thing to get a master's degree. It's another to get one in a field that's crazy marketable. You did good."

He gave me a close-lipped grin around a mouthful of food. Between the juicy meat, recent orgasm and hard-won praise, he looked pretty damn satisfied with himself.

"Your mom gonna come for graduation?"

The light in his eyes dimmed. He took his time chewing and swallowing.

"Nah. She was here around New Year's so won't be back for a while."

I could count on my fingers the number of times I'd seen Lisa Rodriguez in the flesh. She was 17 when she got pregnant with Diego. Lisa got her GED, had the baby and enlisted in the United States Army the day she turned 18. She left Diego with her brother Lou and his first wife, checking in once a year or so between deployments.

Diego got his smarts and drive from Lisa. She had risen through the Army ranks over her 220 years and was now some sort of big shot in Arlington. I'm sure at this point in her career she could take time to come see Diego more often.

She doesn't.

"You know, I thought you…uh…visiting me in New Zealand was the first time you left the country. I forgot you went to live with her in Germany after juvie."

Diego grimaced.

"Ugh. Yeah. I wouldn't call living on a shitty base an international experience though. I only got to be around other Army brats and the food was gross fake-American slop. And any fantasies I had about Lisa and I adventuring around Europe together got cut pretty short when she chose to leave me alone my first weekend there to go drinking at Oktoberfest with her platoon."

Ouch. I had forgotten that part too. Even though Uncle Lou was manipulative, calculating and a straight up criminal, he had always been there. In our world having one adult who showed up for you was half the battle.

"We're not ready to have babies, you know that right?" I blurted.

Diego half choked and started coughing into a napkin.

"Where did that come from? You aren't…? You said you were on the shot."

"No! No. It's not that. It's…you keep talking about all this future stuff…and I don't know…Neither of us have any idea how that looks. We're not exactly PTA material, all up on educational crafts and shit."

Diego stole back a handful of fries and took a swing of his Heineken.

"I'm pretty responsible these days, even if I'm not be versed in the Montessori Method. In case you hadn't noticed."

"You weren't that responsible at Duke's the other night," I countered with a smirk.

He tickled one of my bare feet poking out of the crisp sheets. I laughed and hid it away.

"That's only because you're a bad influence! I would be a great dad. Best in the business. Never miss a Brownies meeting. You'll see. Later though. I'm not ready now either, ok? So you don't need to fuss yourself."

"I'll fuss you, Mr. Responsible," I grumbled under my breath, finishing my beer.

He stacked our empty plates and placed them neatly on the glass coffee table. He looked around, stretching his long arms over his head. The crazy fan muscles across his ribs stood out in sharp relief.

"I like how they decorated this place. Maybe our apartment can look this nice."

I studied the bland neutrals and natural textures of the generically modern hotel room.

"You like this? I guess if you want to live inside a Lands End turtleneck."

"Is it so wrong to want some furniture that doesn't come pre-stained with Spaghetti-Oh's?"

"No, it's not wrong. Bring that narrow ass back to bed and tell me more about this magical beige apartment. I want to know where exactly it's located."

He took a flying leap back into the king bed and tackled me onto my back. I laughed and swatted him with a feather pillow. He started kissing my sore neck. His stubble felt so good I didn't mind that he reeked of ketchup.

"Where ever I get the best job offer, I guess. And wherever you get into PA school."

Huh what? I shoved him off so I could look into his eyes.

"What do you mean?"

"I mean we can afford for you to go to physician assistant school. If you still want to. You'd be a really great PA, I know you would."

Out of nowhere hot tears pricked at the back of my eyeballs. A while ago I had enrolled at Mott Community College to start the pre-requisites, I needed to apply for a PA program. When Aunt Mary's diagnosis came back, I drove straight from the doctor to the registrar to drop the classes. I allowed myself the 17 minutes it took to make that drive to feel sorry for myself.

"I would be great at it," I said, smothering the weepy feeling with bravado. "My post-graduate grades will kick your post-graduate grade's . asses."

Diego snorted, "I give you two weeks of organic chemistry before you come begging for me to help you study."

I pulled his face to mine and kissed him hard. He explored my mouth with his tongue and I felt him growing against me through the sheet.

I pulled away. "You're serious, right? About everything?"

He looked exasperated. Exasperated and horny.

"Yes Charlie, I'm serious. I don't want to trap you in Uncle Lou's house and knock you up. I want us to build something together; to build a better life than the one we were handed. We don't have to get married tomorrow. I only need you to say you're in- and you're not going to run off again."

At the moment, full and a little buzzed and wrapped in nice sheets and with a creeping tightness growing between my legs, I probably would have said yes to joining a white supremacist cult if it meant he'd take those shorts off. Saying yes to security and a higher education was a no-brainer.

"I'm in," I said, pulling his mouth to my darkening nipple. "Now fuck me like you're paying for my college."

45 A LAKE HURON BAPTISM

It was 4:00 a.m. and I couldn't sleep. It had been three days since we stayed in Ann Arbor and I hadn't signed the real estate papers. I wanted be done with it...and I couldn't help thinking it was a deal with the devil. I could picture Uncle Lou perfectly as Ursula the Sea Witch, rolls bulging out of a black dress and enticing me to sign a scroll that gave him control over my voice for the rest of my life.

I gave up trying to sleep and got in the car. I had missed driving and I kinda fell in love with the Buick wagon. I forgave him for driving looser than a damn boat with 30 degrees of play in the wheel because he had a V8 that could get up to speed in a second. I named him Woody in honor of his wood grain panels and urban cowboy attitude.

I parked at Dunkin' and had one foot out of the car before I realized how fucking stupid I was being. When my dad got moved to third shift, he cut off the lead-filled butt of a pool cue and carved a solid grip into the wood. He kept it handy by the driver's seat for when someone tried to jack his car at 5 a.m. shift change. I didn't even have a hefty flashlight in the vehicle. I locked the car door and pulled into the drive thru for two large coffees.

Woody seemed to have a mind of his own this morning as he

nosed onto I-69 East. A grey blur grew on the horizon and a strong wind seemed to blow the dawn toward my bug-splattered windshield. If I squinted, I could mistake the mounds of white clouds in the distance for mountains. I could imagine I was in a rugged landscape primed for adventure instead of farmland primed for a fresh manure application.

I kept glancing at the second cup of coffee. I was alone, miles from anyone who thought they knew me. It was safe.

"This is where I had my first track meet," I said out loud to Malakai. "The rich suburb kids kept taunting us about having to lock their bus so we didn't steal their phones."

I kept up the narration all the way to the coast at Lexington.

"You didn't believe me about the Great Lakes. You thought I was pulling your leg. Well, take a look at this!" I yelled happily as the street curved and revealed the first glimpse of inland sea.

I parked in the first row of a public beach lot. It was deserted at 6:00 a.m. on a blustery May morning. The stretch of fine, tan sand was untouched except for the cross hatches of seagull tracks. The wind whipped the silver water into whitecaps all the way to the dark blue line of the horizon.

"See? Pretty fucking majestic. It's kind of different than the Pacific though, right? I mean, you know Canada is only 60 miles that way even if you can't see it. When we looked out at the horizon from the top of our island it was 1,600 miles to the next continent. I guess your sense of awe is relative to the level of fucked you'd be if you got lost in the middle of the water."

I studied the wave pattern for a while and watched a charter boat cut a quick diagonal, headed for deep waters.

"Lake trout, brown trout, perch, walleye, really nice salmon at the right time of the year," I answered out loud in the empty car. "We could rent a boat sometime and see how your master spearfishing skills translate to lake fishing. It takes a light hand to hook a perch."

I took a sip of the second coffee cup. It was cold and my anxious stomach complained about adding more caffeine. A crack started somewhere deep in my middle and spread quickly in a series of sharp fractures all the way to my eyeballs. They stung with lack of sleep and salty tears. I gave one loud, gaspy, animal sob and stuffed my knuckles in my mouth. I let it be ugly for a while.

A car entered the lot and my bloodshot eyes glanced in the rearview mirror to make sure I was alone. A flash of pink caught my eye through the teary blur.

I hadn't been able to find anywhere in all the empty rooms to keep the Pink Demon. She looked uncomfortable everywhere in my house. So, I popped down Woody's back seats, wrapped her in an old sheet and shoved her in the long trunk. She made for a good excuse to not give people rides. You know Cousin Lisa, I totally *would* take you and your three screaming kids to the Walmart, except I have this surfboard in my car, so…

The swells were three or four feet and breaking consistently at a sandbar about 20 feet offshore. I was very quickly getting a wild hair up my ass.

The cold radiated out of the grey and brown pebbles that lined the shore. My feet weren't wet yet and they were already starting to go numb. I got that buggy jitter, where you're bursting to run as fast as you can either toward something or away from something. The board was a heavy and comforting anchor tucked under my right arm.

"Promise me you'll never, ever, go into a break you don't know alone, okay True Blue?" Shane's voice echoed in my head.

The lake was pulling me in with each reaching and receding wave. Sorry Shane. Guess you shouldn't have given me this badass board that made me feel invincible.

The dark green water burned with more fire than ice. My hands burned as they paddled in and out. My back arched on the board, skin fighting to stay away from scorching splashes. I couldn't feel past my elbows by the time I made it to the break. I gasped as my feet dug into the water, egg beating to spin the Pink Demon into position.

These waves were rowdier than the regular Pacific swells. Undisciplined and disorganized, they jammed together and broke jaggedly. I seesawed on their backs for a moment, shivering. If I took a dunk I might not survive the cold shock response. I read one time about Alaskan fisherman and how most men overboard die because a full immersion in 40-degree water shocks the shit out of your system. You gasp, you take in water, you can't move your arms and legs. You're dead in two minutes. Better not wipe out, then.

My brick-heavy hands pulled the water, the bright nose of Pink Demon sliced through the rippled surface, a hefty wave rolled under me. I timed the apex and popped up. My frozen toes tried to grip the wax and find the sweet spot of balance. I overcorrected down the face of the wave and almost nosedived, stomach swooping sickly as my legs fought for control.

There it was. Half a world away, the freedom of flying across water was the same. Piercing joy burst through my chest and I had to remember to breathe. For six glorious seconds I was free, a wild beast sprung loose from an underwater prison. I let out a loud, furious scream from somewhere deep. It sailed away toward the rushing white puffs of cloud.

The wave petered out and I concentrated on staying upright most of the way to shore. I hopped off in the shallows and ran the last few feet.

I gasped on the sand, laughing and trying to slap my dead hands together to get the blood flowing.

"That was the dumbest thing I've ever seen," a calm voice said behind me. I spun around and saw a lanky teenager watching me. He looked like a grown-up version of Bart Simpson. "Your feet gotta have frostbite."

Sure enough, I looked down at my toes and didn't recognize them. They'd gone past blue to a stark white. I started to stand up.

"No!" he hollered. "You shouldn't walk on them. Stay there."

He hustled to a bait shop near the boardwalk. My mouth tanged with old penny and I realized I was convulsing so hard I'd bitten my tongue. Shit. I also remembered reading that getting out of the water didn't equal being safe from hypothermia. The heart can have trouble calibrating and you can suffer "post-rescue collapse," a.k.a a heart attack. Maybe this hadn't been such a good idea.

The bait shop employee came running back with an armful of stuff. He started pulling my soaked t-shirt over my head.

"Hey!" I protested.

"You need the wet stuff off, idiot. Ain't no one around at this hour."

I stopped struggling and helped him get my leggings off as best I could without functioning hands. He wrapped warm, wet towels around my hands and feet, one of those spaceman tin foil blankets around my trunk, and then another fleece blanket around that.

Eventually, the convulsions became shakes and the shakes became shivers. When he refreshed the warm towels, I could wiggle my toes again on command. Red hot wires of pain shot up my shins though.

"Worth the ride?" he asked sarcastically, checking my pulse.

"Totally worth the ride," I answered thickly. My tongue was swelling badly where I'd bitten it.

"You'd make a good nurse," I said, "How does a bait shop kid know how to treat hypothermia?"

He snorted, tossing his flat brown hair.

"I'm training to be a Rear Admiral in the Coast Guard. Not a nurse."

I resisted digging in to the very heavily suggested idea that nursing was for girls and towing drunk fishermen back to shore was for boys. The title of "Rear Admiral" was also pretty fair game.

"You should be okay to walk now. Come on to the shop, there's some dry stuff you can put on."

It turned out dry stuff meant a "Whitey's Bait and Tackle" t-shirt, size XXL, and a pair of his old basketball shorts. Still, it was better than hanging out naked when the Billy Bobs started coming in for Styrofoam cartons of worms.

I grabbed a hoodie from the car and checked my phone. Diego had texted asking where I was. You don't want to know, bae.

I scrolled my Gmail out of habit. An email from

barbara.brown@nzconsulate.govt.nz stopped my heart. I skimmed as fast as my eyeballs could move.

Hello! I hope you are well.

I debated about sending you a note, as there is no conclusive news. However, we have seen a government report that a group from the Mamanuca Islands were recently accounted for on the mainland. There have been very few survivors from those islands so this was a noteworthy cause for celebration. Of course, I have requested the names, however I have not heard anything further.

I don't want you to get your hopes up. There are many small villages on the islands. Still, I felt you had a right to know. Especially since they've starting issuing visas again.

Be in touch if you want to discuss. Best wishes,

Barbara Brown

Holy...holy motherfucker...motherfucking...

The kid ran out from the bait shop.

"Hey, if you're taking off you need to pay for the t-shirt!"

I horse collared him into a hug, bouncing up and down.

"He's alive!"

My teenage savior untangled himself from my stranglehold. "Who's alive?"

"I *know* he's one of the survivors. I can feel it. Malakai's alive!"

Someone shouted from the shop, "Sam! Why isn't the cooler stocked?"

"Your name is Sam?" I gasped.

"Yeah?"

"It's a sign. A sign from the universe!" I hugged him again, rocking back and forth.

His hands tentatively landed on my waist and worked around to the upper ass. I'd allow it, this kid maybe saved my life and was definitely a good omen.

"So... you gonna pay for that t-shirt?"

I let go and dug a $20 out of my wallet.

"Can I keep the shorts or are you going to make me drive home in my thong?"

He blushed under the spray of acne.

"You can have 'em."

I stood on my tiptoes and kissed his cheek. "You'll make a banging Rear Admiral someday, Sam."

My feet stung and my mind raced as I piloted Woody 90 mph toward Flint.

I'd sign the paperwork for Uncle Lou and he'd be off my back. I still didn't feel right about giving him the land...what else could I do though?

I wouldn't leave Diego without explaining in person. I wouldn't do that to him twice.

He also wouldn't take me back twice. Too much pride. I'd be the same way. If I went to Fiji and Malakai was dead, or I never found anything...I'd be alone.

Alone wasn't the worst thing I could think of being. I voice texted

Diego to meet me when he was back from class.

I had hung the little sea turtle Tukai carved for me from the rearview mirror. I pulled it down and traced the intricate pattern on the shell with my fingertips. The wood was warm from the sun. My mind calmed and I concentrated on one truth: somehow, some way, I was going back to Fiji.

I looked in the rearview at the pink fins sticking up over the seat.

"We're going home, baby," I whispered to the Pink Demon. "We're going home and we're gonna find him."

There was just one thing I needed to do in Flint before I left for good.

46 WHISPERING PINES

I pulled up to the back entrance of Whispering Pines hospice center. The low cinderblock building looked depressingly the same. The landscaping was nice at least. The Rotary Club came and planted annuals each spring. As if offerings of petunias would ward off death and allow them to spend eternity as Active Seniors.

Shonda and Pat were smoking at the picnic table out back. Shonda had new Dora the Explorer scrubs. Spicy.

"Hey girls," I said waving.

"Hey Charlie!" they called in unison.

"Where you been? You have a baby?"

"No, I didn't have a baby Pat."

"Wasting the width of them hips," Shonda muttered as I passed.

I chose to respond with a standard, "You have a blessed day ladies."

The second I stepped through the automatic doors the soft murmurs in the halls, the beeping of the machines and the stink of rotting flowers all closed in around me. I felt the weight of the endless shifts I spent here and a red-hot dread of punching that time clock again.

Each bland beep of my pin code would signal another day that was the same as the last, performing routines that delayed death without ever outsmarting it. Over and over until it was my turn to get in bed and give up. I fought the urge to turn, run and not stop running until I was on another continent.

Edie was sleeping in her darkened room. I checked the chart at the foot of her bed. It confirmed what I could smell. It wasn't long now.

I sat and took her hand. Force of habit more than empathy. Between her disintegrating chin and withered frame, she didn't look super threatening. But there's a special breed of nasty that can break you without lifting a finger. We grew a lot of that breed in Flint.

Her eyes opened and she examined my half-shaved head.

"You look like shit, Charlene," she rasped.

She knew I hated my real name and made a point to always call me by it.

"You smell like shit, Edie. How's the pain?"

"They've got me on the good junk. I still hurt under the high," she sighed.

"Yeah I bet. You're gonna die soon."

"If the Lord sees fit to take me, who am I to argue?"

I needed to get out of this place.

"Are you going to tell the cops?" I asked.

"About what?" she drawled.

"Don't play with me Edie. I can tell them to back your meds off."

"I heard you were selling Mary's house to the Mexicans. I bet you got some good cash for it. My niece got out of county and could use some help getting back on her feet."

She couldn't waft her own farts and she was still trying to blackmail me!

"Say I get her set up in an apartment. How do I know you won't still turn me in?

"I'll be dead soon, according to you."

"Sharon or Georgine could make me too," I countered.

Cornered, she changed tracks. "How'd you do it? How'd you kill her?"

"How do you know I killed her?"

I had been wondering how the Crows had known since New Zealand.

"Open that shade," she barked. "I'm not in the funeral parlor yet."

I sighed and let in a stream of bright spring light. It caught in the thousand wrinkles across her knit blanket and thin skin and sparked the bright silver hairs on her chin.

She looked out the window at the lush, diagonal-mown lawn instead of me.

"She asked me to do it too. I knew something was up when she tried to give me that ring." She turned her head and nodded to the silver ring on my right hand. My fingers curled around it instinctively.

"That was mine first, you know. Your Uncle Brian was my

sweetheart in high school. He gave me his mother's Claddagh as a promise."

I sat holding my breath. I had no idea. Every time I thought these old broads were shallow, they went and revealed a new deep trench.

"*I* broke it off with *him*, so you know. Most reliable and predictable man I ever met, and boring as a stump. A year later your aunt asked if I minded if they went out. I said I didn't. Lord knows I did though! Who goes out with their best friend's discard?"

Her jaw worked back and forth, happily chewing the cud of this 60-year old insult.

"Well you know they ended up married and she got my Claddagh. Bad deal for Mary in the end, what with him being sterile and dropping dead of the brain bleed at 36. Bless his heart."

I shifted impatiently and waited. If there was one thing I'd learned in these rooms, it was how to let someone tell a story in their own time.

"Even though we never spoke of it, your aunt knew how I felt. When she tried to give me the ring I asked why. She said in return for a favor. I thought she wanted me to run out for some McDonalds. Instead she asked me to feed her a Clorox cocktail. I about fell off the settee."

She turned to me with a superior glare, "And I said no, because murder is a mortal sin."

"Fucking your cousin is a mortal sin. That didn't stop you and Terry."

"What is it you kids say now? 'Love is love'," she shrugged. "Now there was a wonderfully unpredictable man. Anyway, two days later she's dead and you show up to her funeral wearing my Claddagh. I'm not stupid.

So I'm going to ask you again- how'd you kill my Mary?"

I eyed up the old snakeskin molting away in her deathbed. Fuck it, why not tell her the truth?

"She went without drugs for months. If I unplugged your dripline right now, you'd ask me to put a pillow over your face in 20 minutes. Bet."

At different points I begged Aunt Mary to let me give her morphine. Cannabis edibles. Fucking extra-strength Tylenol. Anything. She didn't want it. She said she would never forget what "the drugs" did to my mother and she wasn't going to spend her last days giving in to her worst enemy. I tried to explain the difference between weed cookies and street methamphetamines to her. No luck.

"She was getting close to needing full-time care. We couldn't get on top of the pain. It was eating her. She was so skinny her knees were wider than her thighs. She was fighting it with everything she had and she was losing."

I could picture her in our avocado green bathtub. Naked, bald and wasted, scowling at the mildewed grout we could never get clean. At the beginning the warm water helped. Then one time I put her in and she sank right under the water. I hadn't realized she couldn't hold her head up. I got her above the surface and she cocked her head at me, water streaming down her cracked face. She said I could let go; it wouldn't bother her none.

"She brought it up a few different times. I asked why she didn't do it herself and she said suicide was a sin. So, she kept bugging me. I always said no."

"Damn straight, and you should have kept saying no!" Edie spat.

"You want to hear how it happened or not?"

She simmered down.

"Now that I think it about it, it was probably the day after you told her no. We argued about moving her to this facility, then I went to Walgreens for Pedialyte and her smokes.

When I got back, she was in a pile at the bottom of the stairs…I stopped the head wound from bleeding first. Then I checked the rest of her. I thought she was lying on some broken china; maybe her tea cup shattered in the fall. Nope. It was her tibia coming out of her shin."

I ignored Edie's uncomfortable shiver.

"She said, 'There now, time to put the horse out of its misery. It's the kind thing to do, Charlie.'"

Whenever I saw that piece of bone -grey, wet, jagged- in my mind, I pictured her at the top of the stairs. I still can't believe she had the strength to drag herself out of bed and down the hall. The strength to look down at those sharp walnut ridges and throw herself into the pain. I don't think she realized how easily the fall could have killed her. Instead, it went exactly according to plan. She was to die sober, in her own house, by my hand. What a stubborn bitch.

"I gave up. I went and got a hypodermic of saline from my kit. Pulled the plunger back a hair and let in a tiny air bubble."

What happened next was between Aunt Mary and me. I took her in my arms at the bottom of the stairs. She screamed once. Everything in our dingy front hall stood out in microscopic detail from the scuffs on the linoleum to a fat black spider that dipped in and out of an old Nike. I avoided looking at her leg and studied the map of blue veins in her stick arm. I placed the needle then stopped as the point dimpled her skin.

"Free me Charlie," she whispered. "Set me free and I'll set you free. Go somewhere far from here. You don't even know who you are yet and you're already starting to rot."

She worked the Claddagh ring off her shaking hand and slid it on my ring finger. The cheap silver was warm and it fit perfectly.

The needle went in textbook. I petted her sweat soaked temple and she hummed something pretty while we waited.

Edie coughed impatiently. I came back to her ugly mug. I stood up, shaking off the flesh memory of Aunt Mary's clammy temple. The feeling of squishing the black spider with my bare foot. I had thought he was the only witness.

"That's how I killed her. It was the right thing to do, and you know it. You were too chicken shit to do it yourself. So, if you're going to do something about it, go ahead."

Edie glared up at me, bared a flash of stained denture and tried to sit up. I could actually feel her physical frustration at not being able to get up and whup my ass. She gave up and fell against her greasy pillow.

"Mary wouldn't want me to make trouble for you. I won't rat, and neither will the other girls. For her sake. I don't want any of our angels in Heaven to know she helped herself along. Or anyone in the parish, for that matter."

I looked at her for a long time. She was telling the truth.

"Thanks. Bye then Edie, enjoy the time you have left."

I turned to go. The need to leave this place and never come back rose up, burning in my throat.

"Hey Charlene, Mary never wanted to tell you this. But I will."

I turned back at the door. Bring it Edie. I am free. I'm going back to Fiji and will do whatever it takes to find Malakai, whether he's alive or dead. I'm too free for anything you can say to hurt me.

"Tell me what?"

"Your mom's still alive. Somewhere south of the border. Mary got letters with funny stamps from her."

Well…fuck.

47 WHY DO YOU SMELL LIKE BAIT SHOP?

My mind was still trying to absorb the idea that my mom was alive as I peeled into the gravel drive of my battered house. I kept trying to imagine where she was and how she hadn't managed to poison herself to death yet. She wasn't dead and hadn't tried to get in touch, which meant she wasn't the least bit interested in whether I was dead or alive.

Fuck her. I folded the idea of her into a neat square and tucked it away for now.

I raced up the walnut stairs and spun around my old room stuffing my pack. Kindle. Journal. Passport. All the same as last fall except this time I had a badass little black Prada and a surfboard for additional firepower.

I dumped the pack in the kitchen, plugged in my phone and spooned out some peanut butter. I was starving. There was no way in hell I was risking getting stopped at Uncle Lou's for some cold enchiladas.

"What's up?" Diego asked, sauntering in the screen door.

He slipped his arms around my neck. The insides of his biceps flexed hard on my shoulders and his lips brushed my neck.

"Whew- you kind of stink, *mi sol.* Why do you smell like bait?"

Crap.

Maybe I should have left him a note too. This wasn't going to be easy.

He froze. I looked up at him over my shoulder and followed his eyes.

My pack bulged in the corner, as incriminating as a stack of empty booze bottles.

"What's that for?"

His casual voice was too casual. I could feel something twitching in his sharp jaw against my cheek. I turned in his arms.

"I'm going. I will sign the property over right now. I'm sorry, I have to go."

His big brown eyes widened and I saw the panic scurry back and forth between them.

"What the hell? You can't leave. You said you were in. I'm almost done and we're gonna move and-"

"I know…" I started.

He clamped his hand over my mouth. No fucking thank you, dude. I tried to pull away but he tightened his python grip on my shoulders.

"You can't leave. You said you'd stay here. You said…Listen, you need me Charlie. We both know you need me."

He backed us across the kitchen. I fought to free my mouth, peeling my lips back and biting his stifling fingers.

Diego yelled and let go.

"What are you *doing?*" I gasped at him. "You don't touch me that way. Ever."

He looked down, chest rising and falling quickly under the deep V of his white t-shirt.

"I know. I don't...I can't..." He looked up at me, and his eyes were filled with tears.

"I'm sorry Charlie."

And he reached behind me, opened the basement door, pushed me in and locked it from the outside.

48 GIN AND ELEPHANTS

I was still holding the jar of Jif. The basement stank of mildew and wet concrete. I stood and stared at the peeling paint on the wooden door. I jiggled the knob uselessly and started laughing.

I had forgotten that. How sometimes I laughed when I was terrified.

I could hear Diego breathing hard on the other side of the door.

"Okay, funny joke. Now let me out."

No one was joking around. But I hoped if I gave him an out, he might take it before this went too far.

"You can't leave. You need me," he repeated. There were tears in his voice.

The tingling panic was brewing. I needed to ignore the warning sirens in my head and stay in control.

I tried to make my voice sweet and soothing, warm milk for a scared toddler.

"You know I hate it down here. If you love me, let me out. I won't be mad."

"I do love you!" he cried. "No one else loves you the way I love you, and no one ever will."

Then I heard the footsteps. The rapid-fire retreat of his Timberland boots across the linoleum. The slam of the screen door.

"Diego!"

Nothing.

"Diego you motherfucker come back here and let me out fucking right now!"

The white paint flaked off in sheets as I banged my fists into the oak door.

I could only hear a drip in the kitchen sink.

Oh good. The city finally got the water turned back on.

I screamed at the top of my lungs, punching and kicking the door.

Finally, exhausted and bruised, I turned and slid down to sit on the top step.

It was a completely average basement. I told myself to examine the boring details. To focus on the dull functionality of this unremarkable room. Cinder block walls formed the house foundation. Tiny glass block windows at ground level let in weak light. The ancient furnace kept the pipes from freezing. This was a utility space, a place you chucked old sports equipment and washed out paint brushes.

One time I read a *Flint Journal* article about a woman my age who drowned in a basement just a couple blocks away. She didn't even live in the house; she was just stopping by to feed her friend's cat. A spring storm overwhelmed the sewer system and water started coming up from the floor drain. A river formed outside the basement door and she couldn't force it open. The neighbors in the duplex heard her pounding but didn't realize what the sound meant until it was too late. After that, every time I saw a cat wandering the neighborhood I wondered if it was the one whose kitty litter had floated around the girl's head while she choked on filthy runoff.

This basement was not a tomb. It was *not* a tomb.

I forced myself down the stairs. Clinging to the locked door wasn't going to save me.

I needed to stay calm. Assess the situation. Think.

First things first. There was no Wendigo hiding behind the furnace. Confirmed.

I didn't know how long I would be stuck. What supplies did I have? I looked around the bare room and cursed my thoroughness in clearing out the entire house.

A cardboard box in the corner only held the last of the paperwork from Aunt Mary's passing. No one tells you how many fucking forms are required when someone dies. You'd think the Grim Reaper's last job was at the DMV.

The utility sink spat thick brown water. I let it run until it went clear. At least I wasn't going to die of thirst down here.

The single overhead bulb turned on when I flicked the switch. Knowing I wouldn't be alone in the dark when night came sparked a shamefully violent pang of relief.

The cupboard under the stairs was empty. Except...as I turned to go the overhead light reflected off something stuffed between the wood framing and pink fiberglass insulation. I reached in gently, shivering at the sensation of a thousand micro spikes of glass scratching my hand.

It was a freezer bag with a Zippo, a half pack of Marlboro Reds and a fifth of Gilbey's gin. I thought I had found all of my mom's Easter Egg stashes around the house. Must have missed this one. Too bad she wasn't addicted to dehydrated rations.

So I had a half-jar of Jif peanut butter and water. It takes 45-60 days to starve to death. Stay calm, my Rational Brain told me. There's nothing to be scared of. You only have to exist until your Loony Tunes boyfriend comes to his senses.

That worked for about four hours. Without a book to distract me I was quickly getting bored with myself and the same carousel of thoughts.

How in the hell would I find Malakai once I got to Nadi? How much fucking longer would I be down here? What exact sound would Diego make when I stomped his 'nads?

I paced the perimeter of the basement to shake off the chill that came with the twilight.

The overhead bulb winked off the bottle of gin every time I came around the furnace. I hated gin. The combination of Marlboro Reds and Gilbey's made my mom reek of pine and tar. It's hard to feel coddled when your mom smells worse than a lumberjack. The last thing I needed to do was get drunk.

The Zippo still worked. I lit a Red and coughed my eyes out. The head rush was unreal though. I closed my eyes and enjoyed the dizzy wave. I cracked the red cap and chased the smoke with burning pine. It wasn't as bad as I remembered. The warmth in my belly was a nice contrast to the damp concrete under my ass. Fuck it, let's do this. The only way I was going to sleep tonight was to black out.

I was watching the elephants at the zoo. One was washing himself, using his dryer tube trunk to reach around and spray his back. I had never seen an elephant in person before.

I couldn't look away. They were magical walking boulders decorated with odd combinations of Mr. Potato Head accessories. One used the pink tip of its trunk to carefully gather the hay spread over the ground. He shaped it into a neat pile before popping it into his triangular mouth.

A man in a tan uniform asked me where my grownup was. The zoo is closing, he said. I realized my shadow was long, that I was hungry and that I had no idea how long I'd been watching the elephants.

She's in the bathroom, I said.

Why don't you come with me to find her, he said, reaching for my hand.

I didn't take it.

She said to wait here, I said. I'm not supposed to go places with strangers.

He smiled and yellow teeth split the wiry grey hairs. No one I knew had a beard. I wanted to touch it so I stuffed my hands in my pockets.

You're a smart young lady, he said. Why don't you wait on that bench, so we know where you are when we find your mom?

After a while he brought me some peanuts and a hot dog. I asked if it was true that elephants only ate peanuts, how they did in my circus book. He said they ate lots of things, they could remember lots of things and they could even hear through their feet.

Sirens blasted behind us. It was funny to see an ambulance driving on the zoo's footpaths. Was there was a sick crocodile that needed to go to

275

the hospital?

The man followed the ambulance. When he was gone, I threw away the rest of the hot dog. My stomach hurt.

The elephants went inside. I picked at the peeling Minnie Mouse on my t-shirt. I was antsy and had to go pee. I walked toward the bathrooms and the ambulance.

Men in blue outfits pushed a stretcher out of the hut-shaped bathroom. Her turquoise rings swung limp off the side. My favorite was the heart-shaped one.

Her striped sweater was covered in throw up. They had put something over her mouth. I was embarrassed that her pants were down. Her skinny copper knees knocked together as they bumped over the stone path.

She needs to be on her side, I said. No one heard me. I ran up to the men in blue.

She needs to be on her side, I said louder. She can choke if she's not on her side.

They looked at me funny.

I said it again, louder. Put her on her side!

They ignored me and rushed to load her into the ambulance. I started to get in. One of the men grabbed my arm to stop me.

That's my mom, I said. Let me in!

The zoo man put his hands on my shoulders and turned me toward him.

You need to stay here, honey, he said. The police will take care of you.

I saw two officers walking fast around Orangutan Island.

Never let the cops come in the house, I said softly.

The ambulance was starting to pull away. I pushed the zoo man away and ran after it as fast as I could, flat sandals slapping the stones. I needed to stay with her. They didn't know how to take care of her. I ignored the heartbeat in my ears, the burning in my chest. She could die without me.

I reached for the silver handle. Hands grabbed me from behind.

I screamed and kicked and clawed. I felt the wiry beard against the back of my neck and heard him gasp when I opened up his finger with my teeth.

The cops came and held me down on the ground. My cheekbone scraped against the wet goose shit on the pavers.

Calm down, the lady cop said, crouching down. We're here to help you.

I turned my head so I could look into her piggy blue eyes.

Liar, I said, You're taking her away. And I spit in her face.

Her heavy black boot came down on my neck.

I saw the zoo man yelling and the ambulance driving away. All I could hear was the heartbeat in my ears and the long, sharp animal cry coming out of my mouth.

The cry echoed around the cinderblock walls of the basement. It poured out without needing a breath behind it. The pitch black pressed against my eyes. My head banged into the concrete floor in a steady drum beat. Thick streams of piney fluid heaved out of my stomach and streamed out of my mouth and nose.

There wasn't anything to hang on to. There wasn't a way out of the box. There was only the terror, eating me from the inside.

49 A TINY, FIERCE SPECK OF LIFE

A dull light creeped through the glass blocks. I sat in the corner farthest from my vomit puddle. Something about knocking my head against the wall in a steady beat was comforting. I timed it with the pounding rhythm in my head.

When Aunt Mary picked me up from the zoo, she said we could see my mom in a couple days. That was 16 years ago. I didn't know if it was better or worse that she had chosen to never come home.

I should get up. Drink some water. Wash the piss off my legs.

Instead I was frozen, wedged between the furnace and the clammy wall. It felt safer here. The two hard surfaces were holding me together. Without them I might turn into a lighter kind of matter and evaporate.

In another 12 hours the dark would come again. The old light bulb must have burned out at some point last night. Diego would come back before then, right? He was messed up, confused and hurt, not a psychopath.

I guess I had known deep down we couldn't be together forever as grownups. We were broken in too many of the same places, bonded in our shared anger and fear instead of joy. Two war buddies who relied on each other to survive, then had awkwardly quiet breakfasts together for the rest of our lives, searching for something we had in common besides the will to go on.

Even if he wasn't going to be my baby daddy, I didn't want him to find me this shattered. I should be raging, lit with fury and ready to kick his ass when he finally unlocked that door.

I tried to work up some nice, invigorating rage. Instead all I felt was an empty buzzing. Under the buzz was the darkness that had had spilled out last night and taken over. My head hurt where I was bumping it into the wall and I couldn't stop. Maybe if I stopped the dark would come back and I'd go somewhere else I never wanted to go again.

I closed my eyes and tried to make myself move something, anything, in a positive direction forward.

Nothing moved. Hot tears gathered behind my eyelids and a familiar voice in my head whispered, "You're going to die down here."

My pulse sped and small whining noises matched the rhythm of my head against the wall.

A different voice answered out of nowhere.

"Breathe with me."

I tried to tune in as if the voice were a radio frequency, hoping to catch the low tones echoing between static. My breathing slowed and I concentrated as hard as I could.

"We're out past the break. It's a still morning. We go under and you can hear the thousands of broken shells tinkling in the shallows. The current pulls your hair back and forth, rocking you.

The ocean floor gives away ahead of us and it's only blue beyond that. Possibilities for thousands of miles. There's no walls. No limits. You're a tiny, fierce speck of life on the edge of infinity. You are free."

I opened my eyes, half expecting to see a meaty, tattooed arm wrapped around my shoulder.

I was alone. But I wasn't scared. The darkness and the fear had scattered.

That's right cockroaches, you better fucking run. I am a fierce speck of life on the edge of infinity and I am free.

I wiggled out from behind the furnace and stripped off my piss-soaked jeans. And my tank top. And my bra and undies. I needed to get clean everywhere.

After a whore's bath in the utility sink, I started pacing the room again. There was a way out. It was a drafty basement, not Azkaban.

Breaking the windows wouldn't do me any good, even if I could shatter the four-inch thick glass block without severing a finger. The windows were too narrow to fit my head through, let alone my ass.

I could break down the door. It was old as hell, maybe it would crack.

45 minutes of bashing and swearing proved that oak could get really old without getting any less strong.

I was not defeated. I was out of ideas.

My finger dug a deep trench in the jar of Jif while I sat and thought.

My eyes landed on the box of paperwork. Nothing else to read. So I started flipping through the pile of official documents.

One stopped me cold. It was the house insurance contract. A little memory popped open and I saw my dad and Aunt Mary arguing over the premium. Aunt Mary wanted to pay for more coverage, my dad wanted to buy a new motorcycle.

Georgine's son's house had burned to the ground (don't sleep and smoke, kids) and insurance wouldn't cover a penny because there wasn't conclusive evidence from the fire department that he hadn't started the fire on purpose.

With the rash of abandoned buildings and arsons in the city, Allscam and Scam Farm all the other insurance agencies had added arson clauses. Unless you paid for the extra coverage.

Aunt Mary won the argument. There was a guaranteed full payout if this house burned to the ground. In this market that wasn't a ton of money...it was more than $20,000, though.

And I was the primary beneficiary.

50 BURN THIS BITCH DOWN

Was piss a fire accelerant or a...de-ccelerant? I studied my soaked jeans and left them at the bottom of the stairs. Better safe than sorry. Which was kind of a funny thing to say when you were starting a fire in a locked room.

I carefully tucked the insurance policy into my bra and crumpled the rest of the old paperwork under the door. I soaked my tank top and tied it around my face, bandit-style. I knew the smoke would kill me before the flames could.

The Zippo felt pretty full, so I risked pouring some of the fluid on the door around the lock. Not too much or it wouldn't light. What else did I know about starting a fire? Not shit. Dammit I shouldn't have written Jack London off as vaguely racist.

Nothing left to do except flick the miniature wheel.

I hesitated and looked around the basement from the stairs. Would the fire burn away the foundation of terror and abandonment and claustrophobia that had been laid here? Was my mom's lighter a ticket to freedom or an invitation for a suicide mission?

Only one way to find out, I guess.

My shallow breathing and shaking hands needed to get in line with the plan. I closed my eyes and took some deep breaths. Imagine you're under the waves, held down by currents you can't control. Hold your breath and don't panic. You will find the sunlight soon.

I flicked the wheel and held the little yellow flame to the paper. It caught and started eating a tax bill. The blue flames climbed up the lighter fluid on the door and spread across the old oak. The smoke was already stinging my eyes. I fanned the flames with papers and lit the crumpled balls stuffed in the crack.

The smoke was pouring off the door in thick clouds. The smell of burning paint was choking. I gagged and coughed, searing pain ripping down my throat. I tried to control the spasms and touched the flame a few more places before retreating down the stairs for cleaner air.

Come on bitch, burn!

The edges of the paper curled bright red and quickly went out. It would have died completely if the lighter fluid hadn't helped the baby flames spread. Every second the smoke crept further down the stairs. I kept backing up until the cool cinderblocks hit my bare back. I pulled the jeans onto my arms, leaving my hands tucked in the wet fabric.

The coughs racked my ribs uncontrollably and tears streamed out of my eyes. I needed to wait until the door was burned enough to break down. I couldn't wait so long that I passed out from smoke inhalation.

Cold terror flooded my veins and tried to override the plan. My instincts wanted me to fling my body at the door, trapped-bird style. It's too strong still, cautioned my rational brain. I rocked back and forth on the balls of my feet, synapses pinging between reflex and control.

Finally, the coughing was so intense I could barely draw a breath between the hacking. My head spun and black spots popped in front of my eyes.

Now. Go.

I ran up the stairs and slammed my denim-covered shoulder into the solid oak. It shuttered and I heard a crack. My feet itched to kick at the barrier with all the power of my legs. I held myself back, not wanting second-degree burns on my only means of running away.

I slammed into the door again, weaker this time. It didn't go anywhere. The dizzying blackness was crowding more of my vision and burning blisters were rising on my bare skin. Panic rose in my throat against the coughs. One more shot. Take one more shot.

I backed down a couple stairs and glared through the grey haze at the flaming door. Sprinted as fast as I could and dropped my left shoulder into the blaze right below the doorknob.

Something made a sharp pop. Was it my shoulder coming out of socket, or the door breaking? When I shoved at the door, I heard it again, even though I couldn't see anything.

I pushed as hard as I could at the popping spot. The heat seared my hands through the denim. The door cracked and I shoved with everything I had. A gap opened in the wood and I could see daylight. I reached a hand through and unlatched the door from the outside.

I poured onto the kitchen floor in a cloud of smoke. Coughing and gasping, I crawled as fast as I could away from the flames.

Safe against the kitchen cabinets, I stripped off the smoldering denim and ripped the scorched tank top off my face. Cold water from the faucet felt amazing sliding down my burning throat between hacking coughs. I crawled to my pack, ripped the phone charger out of the wall and pulled myself up to standing.

The flames weren't travelling off the door, even though smoke was filling the kitchen. My eyes landed on the ancient General Electric gas stove. I flipped all the burners to ignition and heard the gas hissing out. Then I ran like hell.

I didn't realize I was running down the sidewalk in my bra and underwear until honks and whistles from a passing Dodge snapped me back to reality. I dove for the safety of Woody and slammed the door behind me. Panting and shaking I keyed the ignition and hit 55 mph before I got to the corner.

A huge BOOM shook all the windows in the old wagon. I saw pillowy plumes of black smoke rising over the green maple trees in the rearview mirror. I didn't turn my head or slow down.

I thought about driving all over the city until I tracked Diego down and punched him in the mouth. Nope, gotta focus.

I could be on a plane to Fiji in a few hours. It would take months to get the insurance payment, but the money would come eventually and true to my word, I'd pay Uncle Lou back then. In the meantime, if you want me Rodriguez Clan, come fucking find me.

51 REARVIEW MIRROR VS. WINDSHIELD

It's weird how airports make people seem more important. I mean, if you saw this shlubby businessman on a bus you would think he was a loser. In an airport though? He could be Director of Disguise for the CIA, off to expertly apply a beard to a spy in Berlin. Sure, the air is stale, the food is terrible and the carpet probably has Ebola. It's still a magical portal to your Next Big Thing.

I sat across from the Detroit Metro ticketing counters watching the ants march through the turnstiles. It cost $120 for a commuter flight to Lexington, Kentucky. It cost $3,200 for a same day flight to Nadi, Fiji.

I could be to Lexington by noon, to my dad's new house by 2:00, and by 2:30 I could find out where the fuck my mom had been hiding for 16 years. Maybe 2:15 if I used a butcher knife.

He knew where she was. Somehow, I knew that for certain. I imagined balling up the ocean of fury I felt into a tiny marble and holding it tight in my chest. I could hold it there until I got to Kentucky and release it, watching with glee as it set fire to all the secrets my dad had tried to keep hidden.

Or I could take the 20-hour trip to Nadi. Land disoriented in a strange city, with no idea where to start looking for Malakai. The island nation was still a disaster according to the Red Cross website. I wasn't going to get any help from the overwhelmed government in finding one missing person. I wasn't even sure if the roads out of the capital were open.

I spun the Claddagh around my ring finger. What if, after months, of looking, I found out he died the moment I left him? Or worse, what if I never found anything, and spent the rest of my life half hoping to see him in every airport?

I closed my eyes and tried to visit him. He was straddling his board in the turquoise shallows. Flipper feet working below the water to stay in one place. I waded out into the clear water and got on, facing him. His trunks rode up the tree trunk thighs, exposing a strip of lighter brown skin and the start of his centipede scar. He reached out and pulled me into a fierce and gentle bear hug. The pads of his thick fingers were pruned and the little ridges caught the fine hairs at the base of my spine as he stroked my bare back. I shivered a little and he squeezed me so the heat from his chest radiated across my skin.

Beads of saltwater ran from his messy hair down the tattooed hills of his shoulders. I pulled a slick piece of kelp out of the dark tangle. He caught my hand and kissed the palm, bringing it to his face. I traced fingertips over the crisscross scars on his temples.

He leaned forward and rested his forehead on mine. His dark eyes were hungry and sad.

My whole body was tingling, except my legs. They were dissolving into nothing in the bathtub water of the lagoon. Whatever part of me that wasn't touching him wasn't needed.

I could feel him growing under me and pushed off the roughly waxed board to wiggle even closer. The little waves seesawed us up and down as our mouths met and we tasted the need that brewed between us.

Thunk!

My eyes snapped open. An angry traveler had thrown her suitcase into the chair next to mine. I tried to act casual, avoid eye contact and control my breathing. No, no, I definitely wasn't mentally masturbating on this public bench at a metropolitan airport.

"Stupid cancelled flight," she muttered, kicking the bench leg. "Is yours cancelled too?"

I looked up at the digital signs scrolling departures. Which flight was mine?

Aunt Mary always said, "There's a reason your windshield is bigger than your rearview mirror. You gotta look at where you're going, not where you've been."

My past was over, whether I chased it or not. It would be there whenever I was ready to face it. My future was somewhere so far west of here it started in a new day. I spotted the departure listing for Nadi via Los Angeles and hoisted my backpack.

"Mine's right on time," I said to the stranger.

52 MS. QUINN ARRIVES

My neck hurt from the long flights. It twinged as I craned it after every big guy with long hair. He's not going to be in the terminal waiting for you, dummy. Some deranged part of my brain kept imagining the crowd parting and Malakai waving at me with a teary smile and a bouquet of frangipani. I shouldn't have watched *Love Actually* on the plane...or any of the other 32 times. Shit never actually worked that way in real life.

Outside baggage claim the humid tropical air hit me with the same force of my soggy first night in Bangkok. This close to the equator the humidity was different from Michigan's swampy summer. There was nothing seasonal about this constant dampness; jungle rot and mildewed towels were a way of life. It was smothering and comforting at the same time.

The sweat gathered under my backpack straps, bit the burns on my neck and slithered down my back as I waited in the cab line. Barbara had answered my in-transit emails and recommended I start my search at the Red Cross headquarters.

The cabbie struggled to wedge Pink Demon in the backseat of his small Toyota while I hopped in the front. He spent the entire drive grumbling about tourists coming back too soon.

"You come and see the rubble and none of the resorts are open and you go back home telling people, 'Don't go to Fiji, it's not a nice place.' You gotta give us time to rebuild after this bad a disaster."

"I won't tell anyone back home I went to Fiji," I replied mildly. That would be an easy promise to keep.

The land outside the dusty windshield was stripped and bare. The lush greenery had been torn to pieces and was rotting in piles by the side of the road. Parts of the city could have been construction sites- raw materials, bare dirt and skeletal rebar. Except they were really deconstruction sites. Crews of workers crawled over hills of concrete to find evidence of their lost lives.

I wanted to tell him I was here when it happened. That I felt the shaking terror of being a fragile human in the face of Mother Nature's fury. That I had seen past the Instagramable palm trees to the harsh realities of your home being a tiny green dot in the middle of a crazy ass ocean.

Instead I offered him some of my Sour Patch Kids and kept my mouth shut.

The Red Cross headquarters was a low industrial building buzzing with people in bright yellow vests. I went to the reception desk and said I was looking for someone who had been missing since the typhoon. The middle-aged man in a polo gave me a sympathetic look and said to take a seat.

Three hours in a hard plastic chair later, I went up to the desk again.

"Please, is there someone I can talk to? I'm looking for Malakai Navakasuasua. Or an older man named Tukai. I don't know his last name. Or a middle-aged woman-"

"You see those people?" the man asked, nodding his head at a quiet knot of Fijians sharing lunch in the waiting area. "They're looking for someone too. They've come here every day for the last two months. You gotta wait your turn. When a staff member has time, they'll take your information."

Judging by the speed the yellow-vested staff members hustled in and out of the doors, they didn't have a lot of time. A terrier-sized woman in a white coat marched down the hallway and out the double doors. Everything about her, from the old coffee smell to the air of self-importance, said "doctor". Without thinking, I followed her.

She unlocked a beat-up Fiat and grabbed a pack of cigs.

"Hey" I called as I got close.

"What?" she replied, lighting a smoke. Her dark sharky eyes stopped me. One had scar tissue running out from the corner all across her cheek. The strands of hair coming out of her kerchief were bright silver and her teeth were tobacco stained. Despite her size, she would have made a very intimidating pirate.

"Help you, can I?"

"Um...maybe. Where are they treating the people who were injured in the cyclone?"

"Who are you?" she asked with the tone of someone used to holding all the cards.

"I'm a friend of someone who's missing. I thought maybe I could go to the hospital or treatment center and...ask there?"

"Busy saving lives, our staff is. The right place to start is Red Cross."

She seemed to realize she was still wearing her coat and removed it before getting in the car. I noticed the blue cursive stitching on the left breast that read *"Médecins Sans Frontières."*

"Maybe I can volunteer! You need help and I am a-"

"No," she said curtly. "Still in recovery, most of our patients are. Geriatric, very delicate, lots of complications. Medical professionals are needed not…" she took in my half-shaved head and ratty travel clothes and general Millennial-ness, "…backpackers wanting to feel good about themselves."

Well fuck you too, Hippocrates. I couldn't think of any appropriate response.

She got into the car and backed out quickly, leaving me in a chemical cloud of exhaust.

I stomped back to my orange plastic chair and plopped down. I knew this wouldn't be easy. That I would have to be patient. I knew there was more of a chance this road ended in misery than hope. Still, I couldn't help feeling a hot, rebellious anger boiling up from the acid stew of jet lag and heartbreak and Sour Patch Kids in my empty stomach.

Damn I hated asking people for help. But maybe if you never asked, you never let someone be there for you. I dug out my phone and tapped out an SOS email. Then I gave in to the smell and walked over to the group of grieving mothers, husbands and cousins and asked if they had any rice to spare. The last thing anyone on this island would ever do was be stingy with food when someone needed comfort.

The next morning I let the receptionist know I was there, delivered donuts to the group of Waiters and then sat outside the double doors. I looked worse than I had the day before. The only open hotels were way too expensive for me. No budget travelers meant no budget places were open. So I caught a few hours of sleep on a park bench, New Zealand-style. If I could pass for a backpacker yesterday, today I looked officially homeless.

After an hour the dirty Fiat rolled into the parking lot. The same woman got out, and if possible, she looked more tired than me. She lit up and inhaled as if her life depended on it.

I brushed the dried palm leaves off my butt and approached her, chin set hard.

"Good morning, Doctor," I said, shoving my phone screen in her face.

"Here you'll see my license, work record and two letters of recommendation. I am an RN with a specialization in acute geriatric care. When you've finished your business inside, I'll come with you to the care facility. You need my help and you're very lucky you found me."

Only one of her eyes moved as she tracked the digital documents on the small screen. I realized the eye surrounded by scar tissue was made of glass.

"Verify all of this, we will need to," she said crisply.

"Of course we will. And you'll find it all in order."

She nodded, still not seeming quite awake. I could almost smell the relief coming off her though.

Bless you, Shonda and Pat. Your pants may not be fancy, but you sure know how to come through for a girl with the right paperwork.

She stuck her hand out to me. "Dr. Lin."

"Charlie. But you can call me Ms. Quinn. I look forward to

working with you."

53 *MÉDECINS SANS FRONTIÈRES*

"You're looking good today Mrs. Madraiwiwi," I said brightly as I adjusted the IV.

Mrs. Madraiwiwi actually resembled an iguana that had been hit by a car and baked on the side of the road for a week. Selective truth telling is only one of the superpowers required for effective nursing.

I checked her vitals and the skin around her arm and leg casts. Poor lady had been half-crushed when a sea break failed and debris pinned her to a telephone pole. She was 87 years old, crying out in pain most of the night, and she still smiled a little when I brushed her hair. I forgot how nursing let you see the best and worst of the human condition.

"Done with the round, you are?" Dr. Lin asked, stopping to flip quickly through her chart. "Help in Exam 4, I need."

"Yup, she's my last."

She nodded and marched off. 10 days in, I think we were starting to really connect. She insisted on roughly rubbing silver nitrate into my neck burns and even offered me half her leftover lunch the other day.

Seriously though, this position was a Godsend. Once my paperwork was approved, Doctors Without Borders gave me a bunk in the converted airplane hangar that housed the overflow patients. The hospitals were crammed to capacity so the government set up this secondary center for longer-term care. I had a place to sleep, occasional meals and even access to the computers, fax machines and printers in the office to get started on the mountain of paperwork for my home insurance claim.

Best of all, this job could help me find Malakai.

As an outsider, stopping people on the street and asking if they knew a local would result in a lot of very polite rejection. But you're not seen as an outsider when you're tending someone's broken grandfather around the clock. I'd asked every patient, family member and local staffer if they knew any of my island family. One grandmother had gone to school with Nei Talei. Another one said Sam was her clansman. Nearly everyone knew of the rugby player Malakai Navakasuasua. But no one knew what happened to any of them after the typhoon.

Still, the first time I asked and a teenager broke out into a wide grin, crying "Navakasuasua was the best All Black of all time!" I felt a deep, warm gratefulness. I hadn't made him up. I wasn't crazy for chasing him halfway across the world. He was special and he was mine and I was on the right road to finding him.

After assisting Dr. Lin, I was technically off for 12 hours. I swung by the "cafeteria" a.k.a., the garage where they housed the food donations; both non-perishable disaster relief goods and fresh meals provided by local families. A crate of Mott's applesauce stood out against a wall of SPAM. I grabbed two. Mrs. Madraiwiwi hadn't moved her bowels for four days and I was on a mission to get her groove back.

"Come on, eat the second one too," I coaxed her with a spoon. "You're on a lot of painkillers and not getting enough fiber."

"This is food for babies," she grimaced. "You got any *lovo?*"

"Eat this and I'll see if anyone brought by some real food, okay?"

She grudgingly allowed me to feed her the second cup.

"I know a Malakai," she said out of nowhere.

"What?" I asked, spoon halfway to her mouth. My stomach iced over.

"You've been asking people about a young Malakai, strong guy, yeah? My cousin came the other day, said he hired a big, strong guy to help rebuild their village in Momi Bay. Lots of people named Malakai. But this one is about the right age, right build. Is your Malakai a hard worker, very handy, lots of tattoos?"

"Yes," I gasped.

"Might be the same one," she shrugged, swallowing the the last bite. "See, I'm your best patient. I eat all the baby food and I find your friend. Now go see if anyone brought *lovo* today."

I kissed her bruised cheek. It wasn't appropriate and I didn't care. Orange fireworks were exploding in my chest. This had to be him! It made sense Malakai would find work rebuilding, Momi Bay wasn't that far from here, the tattoos...it was him; I knew it!

I ran to the food garage at top speed. No *lovo* today, but someone brought a giant batch of cassava chips. I loaded a plate for Mrs. Madraiwiwi and dashed back, dropping it on her bedside milk crate, kissing her on the cheek again, and raced off.

Dr. Lin was where I expected her to be in her off hours- not in the barracks, but outside smoking while reviewing patient charts.

"I need to borrow your car," I panted.

She looked up at me quizzically. One eye did, anyway.

"What for?"

"I... left a big bag in storage at the airport. I need to get it today before the locker rental runs out."

She gave me a stare that raked the farthest reaches of my soul. I immediately regretted lying to her.

But she reached in the pocket of her scrubs and tossed me the keys.

"Back here by eighteen hundred hours you will be. New intakes to process."

I nodded and sped off to the parking lot.

"And pick up a carton of Zhonghuas, you will," she yelled at my back.

"You got it!" I shouted. I slammed the tin can into gear and whipped out of the lot.

Malakai was waiting for me 45 minutes away. I could feel it. All I needed to do was not die while driving stick on the wrong side of the road to get to him.

54 HOPE

A construction worker yelled at me to slow down as I sped into the Work Zone. Frustration and impatience clawed at my guts as the line of cars on the coastal road slowed to a stop. I drummed the wheel for the longest minute of my life before pulling the car off onto the sandy shoulder. I jogged up the line of cars and asked the Designated Sign Holder what was going on.

"This road was washed out in the typhoon. We're finishing last repairs before the detour closes and this one reopens."

"How long?" I panted.

"Maybe 20 minutes. Maybe an hour. Relax, honey. You're on our time."

He was probably a nice man so I decided not to punch him in his round stomach hard enough that he coughed up blood. Instead I ran.

Lady God help me if they towed Dr. Lin's car. But there was no way I could waste an hour (or three or four) sitting in the car when Malakai was two miles away.

I ran through the construction zone, ignoring the men who shouted out me that it was a closed site. I ran along the line of cars waiting on the other side. I ran along the sandy, trash-strewn shoulder until I saw a sign for Momi Bay, then I ran down the rutted road through the dense green forest.

I burst into the clearing of the destroyed village like a Kenyan marathoner, gasping, chest out, arms back, scrubs soaked in sweat. A young mother looked at me in concern and gathered her children to her side.

Okay, so it had been a minute since I'd had to run somewhere and I was officially out of shape.

"Ma- is Malakai here?" I wheezed at her. She pointed to the line of turquoise surf peeking out from between the piles of rubble. Of course he was in the water. I beamed at her idiotically and kept running.

There he was. Facing away from me on a yellow board 50 feet out. Broad shoulders, covered in intricate designs. Long black hair hanging down his back. I yelled but he didn't turn. I was living the dream I'd been having for months- the postcard perfection of the palms lining the bay, the hyperblue water and sky. The love of my life sitting right outside my reach, unable to hear me yelling his name.

I clumsily kicked off my sneakers, peeled off my sweaty scrubs and ran into the warm water. Razor-sharp shells growing on the rocks sliced my foot and I cursed, diving flat to swim above the rocky shallows. I swam as hard as I could. Being back in the Pacific was a reunion in and of itself. True to most reunions between long lost friends, I was overcome with the comfort of being back in her embrace and, as my lungs burned fighting the waves and salt stung my tired eyes, I immediately remembered the specifics of what a bitch she could be.

Finally, I spotted the bright yellow tail of the board and the pale bottoms of Malakai's feet right in front of me. It started to move away as his thick arms paddled.

I grabbed for it desperately and screamed, "Malakai!"

The feet popped into the water and he sat up, startled. I gasped for air and rubbed the water out of my face.

Our eyes met as a wave nosed his board upward.

It wasn't him.

A drenching defeat washed through me. It was so numbing I forgot to swim.

The clear turquoise water closed over my head and I sank, letting the soft snap-crackle-pop of the reef fill my ears. A miniature, purple-hearted jellyfish pulsed in front of my face. Strands of hair drifted in my eyes and I blinked stupidly, suddenly too tired to push them away, let alone fight to stay afloat.

A meaty hand grabbed my arm and yanked me upward.

I sprawled across the pebbly wax of this stranger's board, coughing.

He helped me sit up, facing him.

"Hi!" Imposter Malakai grinned at me. He was missing a canine tooth. "Do I know you?"

I looked down and realized I was in my soaking wet bra and panties. This was the second time in two weeks I'd snapped back to reality wearing nothing but my underwear in public. Damn I needed to get my shit together.

"Sorry. I thought you were someone else," I said sheepishly, crossing my arms over my jaunty nipples.

"I'm Malakai Cama. And you're very pretty. You sure you weren't looking for me?" he laughed.

Someday I might think this was funny. If I did find Malakai and we lived happily ever after and we told this story to our 15 grandkids at a beach bonfire while my subservient sons-in-law brought me beer. Right now? Numbness was melting into fury and I had the humiliating realization I was straddling a surfboard in my underwear with two weeks' worth of aggressive bikini line overgrowth.

"Sorry," I repeated coldly and moved to slide back into the water.

"Hang on," he protested, "You'll slice your feet to pieces walking out of the shallows. Let me give you a lift in."

Whatever. Fine. Just don't try any funny business, Imposter Malakai. I will knock out the rest of your teeth, put them in a peanut butter sandwich and make you gum that shit down. Don't try me right now.

Turns out he was an alright guy. The name Malakai must have a good vibe. He got me a plate of food from the communal lunch table and didn't mention that my scrubs reeked of old blood and new sweat and now, fishy ocean funk. When he noticed my foot bleeding from the shell cut he insisted on getting me iodine and a bandage. He even helped me ask around the village if anyone knew Real Malakai. No luck though.

I thanked him and explained I'd left my boss's car abandoned on the side of the road, so should probs get going.

"I hope you find him," he said at the road, a little wistfully. "He's a lucky guy."

Oh sweet Imposter Malakai, you should see me when my nether-regions don't look like I've got a hippie in a leg lock.

"Thanks for...thanks," I half smiled at him. "Bye."

I tried to head back down the road at a jog but the afternoon sun was balls hot, my foot hurt, the starchy taro was expanding in my stomach and the bone-deep exhaustion had crept back on me. I walked, imagining the dark comfort of hiding under the covers of my bunk until my next shift.

Traffic was moving along the brand-new pavement and I was super relieved to see the Fiat was still there.

I didn't remember Dr. Lin's cigarettes until I saw her hustling toward the car as I pulled in.

Fuck me. She was the kind who would push you out of a helicopter for a lot less.

"Glad you're back. Came early, the new transfers did. Wash up and meet me in triage."

So long, sweet bunk dreams. I nodded and followed her darting minnow frame.

I took a 30 second shower, chugged some old coffee, grabbed fresh scrubs and walked into the "triage evaluation room," which was really a corner they put curtains around at the front of the hangar.

Four spotty brown bodies laid on snowy cots with plastic tubing running out of them. They reminded me of potatoes in a class science project.

Dr. Lin was already chatting easily with one of them, making her chuckle while she took notes that I would spend hours trying to decode later.

I walked up to the first bed and plastered a smile on my face.

"Hi there Mr...." I looked at the chart and my heart skipped a step. I looked into the man's face and saw the Sea God himself, battered and bruised, but unmistakably Tukai.

55 CLUES FROM THE SEA GOD

I was frozen, locked into Tukai's face.

"Ms. Quinn!" Dr. Lin barked. "Doing your job today, are you?"

"Yes," I replied automatically, not taking my eyes off my miracle. "I'll need the translator. Tukai doesn't speak English."

His head turned to me at the mention of his name.

"We refer to our patients as Mr. and Ms. in my ward," Dr. Lin said. "Very important, respect is."

"I know this man, he's my friend," I snapped. She gave me a look over her shoulder, but kept writing briskly.

"I'll be right back," I whispered, squeezing his hand. His cataract-clouded eyes blinked slowly. I wondered if he recognized my voice.

I hurried back with one of our young volunteers. She helped me with the slow process of cross-checking all the information on Tukai's hospital chart. I could tell he was confused and barely lucid. I bitterly gave Dr. Lin the Cliff Notes version when she came to the bedside.

"Internal damage from blunt force trauma. Broken ribs healing badly. Near complete renal failure. Liver's in bad shape too. He's got two days left, maybe four. I have no clue why they shipped him here instead of letting him stay put to die."

"Need the dialysis machine for someone with better odds, they must," she shrugged, reviewing the chart with a sharp, clinical eye. But when she took his hand and spoke to him her voice was cheery and soft.

"Ms. Quinn is the best nurse here. Take good care of you, she will."

The translator spoke to Tukai and he smiled and nodded vaguely.

"Take your time with him," she said, passing me his warm hand. "Assess the others, I will."

"Tukai, it's Charlie," I said haltingly. It was strange to speak to him through a 16-year old girl.

"Do you remember me? I'm Malakai's friend. I lived with you for a while before the storm. You shared *cava* with me."

Tukai turned his head toward our voices but didn't respond.

"I'm the one who'd bring you little presents...shells you didn't need and wood you couldn't carve?"

Nothing. I sighed deeply.

"The foreigner who got too drunk and kind of lost her mind when we were in the storm shelter...?"

The teenage translator raised her eyebrows at me before speaking to him quickly. Yeah, yeah yeah, you'll make some bad choices too, honey.

Tukai chuckled softly and squeezed my hand. He remembered! My exhaustion evaporated under a wash of warm gratitude at finding a connection to my life here.

"I know you hurt, but you're with me now and I'm going to make you comfortable and happy, ok?" I said quickly. "You tell me what you need and I'll do it for you."

He nodded again and I set to work getting his bed and IVs arranged. Then I hustled to my bunk and rifled around in my pack for a minute before finding what I was looking for.

With the help of a couple burly Red Cross workers, we gently transferred Tukai into his bed next to Mrs. Madraiwiwi. Her neighbor, Mr. Lahiri, had died the day before. Heart failure.

Mrs. Madraiwiwi and Mr. Lahiri had become fast buddies, whispering dirty jokes to each other long after Lights Out, until I had to yell that they were worse than naughty kids at a sleepover. Mrs. Madraiwiwi sniffed dismissively when I introduced Tukai. A man in his condition wasn't going to swap good ones about the nun from Nantucket.

After I got lines in Tukai and administered a grab bag of drugs, I placed the small carved turtle from my bag into one of his hands. His weathered fingers closed instinctively around it and he felt the lines of the satiny wood with the sensitive touch of an artisan.

"Thank you for giving me this," I said. "It meant a lot to me."

The translator wasn't around, but he nodded in understanding.

"Can you ask him if he's comfortable?" I asked Mrs. Madraiwiwi.

"How about you ask after my comfort?" she huffed. "I'm going to chew this cast off if it keeps itching this bad!"

I rolled my eyes and went to fetch some bamboo chopsticks from the supply room.

She sighed in relief as I gently inserted one between the plaster and her skin, moving it slowly back and forth.

"A little to the left," she grunted.

"Now can you ask him?" I said as patiently as I could.

She spoke to Tukai in rapid Fijian and he answered in a weak voice.

"He's ok for now," she said, "Down and to the right."

"Ask if he knows anything about Malakai!"

"Go get one of those translators girl! I'm not a Find my Boyfriend app."

I pulled the bamboo out, walked to the trash and held it over the bin, smiling blandly at her.

She got the message.

They had a quick exchange and she reported, "He says Malakai stays at the big house. And that he's tired. Now do my leg."

Sure enough, Tukai was already asleep. I was glad to see him resting but burned to ask a thousand more questions. As I worked the stick into Mrs. Madraiwiwi's stinking leg cast one thought bubbled up over and over: he's alive.

He's alive. Tukai said he was staying somewhere. Now. As in, right this minute. But what if the present tense was a translation error? What if he meant "he was staying at the big house...before he died?" And the big house was the hospital? Or shit...what if...

"Mrs. Madraiwiwi, he doesn't mean...you guys don't call heaven, or...the afterlife 'the big house,' do you?"

"What? No, don't be silly girl. Go around to the back, behind the knee."

"Do you know what he means then, about 'the big house'?"

"No, I don't and stop bugging me now. I'm sore and tired too. I need my peace to heal, you know."

I clamped my lips together to keep from mentioning all the nights I'd scolded her for staying up too late giggling about rabbis and priests walking into bars.

For now, I would hang on to that thread of hope, that Malakai was alive, that Tukai knew where he was, that I could get more information out of him tomorrow.

I could barely keep my eyes open. I wasn't technically scheduled again until 6:00 a.m. Another nurse was already making rounds at the other end of the hangar. I should crash in my bunk, let her do her job and get some rest so I could do mine in the morning.

Instead I grabbed some extra sheets and made a nest in the corner by Mrs. Madraiwiwi and Tukai. I had barely bedded down when my eyes closed without permission and I fell into a thick, black sleep.

It was still dark when I woke up to Dr. Lin's staccato voice. I sat up and saw her holding Tukai's wrist. The carved turtle was still clutched tight in his other hand.

I knew right away.

I didn't need to feel his still chest or hear her declare the time of death.

Tukai was gone and my link to Malakai was gone with him.

56 AN UNLIKELY SOURCE

I don't know how I made it through the 12 hour shift that day. Muscle memory and acidic coffee, I guess. And working kept me from screaming.

I had been so close. Another conversation with Tukai and I could be planning what to wear to Malakai's house. Instead I'm no closer to finding him than I was when I landed on this fucking busted island. Fucking poor man's Tahiti. God*dammit.*

I kept a lid on it until my shift ended. I stripped off my stinking scrubs in the utility room where the Red Cross had installed an industrial-grade washer and dryer. I gave the washer an aggravated kick as I tossed in the soft blue cloth. It made a satisfying noise. I did it again, harder. Boooooong.

Again. Bong. Bong. Bong. All the anger and sadness and loss ran through my legs as I kicked that stupid fucking appliance over and over. My toes stung through the thin mesh of my sneakers and the pain fueled a primal scream that ran out of my throat with raw power.

I pulled back an arm to get my fists in on the action when a tight vice clamped on my bicep.

"Wrong this Kenmore has not done you," Dr. Lin said calmly.

"Drinking we are going to."

The bar was an open-air stand on the edge of a busy road. A giant wooden electrical wire spool, turned on its side, made for a makeshift table. Citronella candles lit the tables and kept the evening mosquitoes from eating people alive.

Dr. Lin brought two tall beers and popped the caps off expertly on the edge of the splintery wood.

I closed my eyes and took a long chug, feeling the tight band of exhaustion around my brain loosen a little. An image of Tukai's thick, worn hands floated behind my closed lids.

"He didn't have to die that quick. We should have had him on dialysis and-"

"Forget 'should,' you must, in times and places such as these," Dr. Lin said quickly. "There is what can be done and what cannot be done, that is all."

I shook my head and drank. No matter what she said, I couldn't help thinking I should have been able to help him more.

Dr. Lin studied me closely. Her glass eye seemed to have more perception that most people's real eyes.

"Doctor you could be, why only nurse are you?"

Well screw you too, Dr. Big Britches.

"I find nursing very rewarding," I answered coldly. "And where I practiced, a doctor could get jumped in the parking lot for saying that."

"Get more education, you should."

I paused, taking another long pull on my beer. I didn't want to lie to her.

"I want to be a physician assistant. I tried to go back to school but my aunt got cancer and I had to drop out. Then my boyfriend was going to pay for it...but he locked me in a basement and I burned the house down and left town and am never going back."

Dr. Lin gave a low whistle.

"Well, bad things happen to everyone. Very good touch you have, smart you are, go back to school you should."

"Your unsolicited opinion is noted," I said acidly. Still, a warm little glow of pride grew in my chest. If there was one thing I knew about Dr. Lin, it was that she didn't blow smoke up people's asses.

"How'd you lose the eye?" I asked, since we were doing True Confessions.

"Competitive, medical school in Shanghai is. Very competitive."

"Really?" I whispered, gaping at her.

She laughed, throwing back her head and baring her yellow teeth.

"J.K., J.K. A land mine in Sri Lanka it was. Very messy. In recovery, I start smoking. Lost an eye, gained a lifelong friend."

"Yeah...I don't know any other doctors who smoke. They all know better," I said a little righteously.

"Ah, so you never do things because they feel good even though they are not smart, huh? Very good girl, you are Ms. Quinn. Very well-mannered young lady, yes?"

"You bet your pancake ass I am," I laughed. "So well mannered, I'm buying us whiskey shots."

She didn't say no, and when I came back with the tumblers, she downed hers neatly.

"Why did you lie to me about needing my car?" she asked point blank.

Shame flashing hot on my cheeks. I chose not to ask how she knew.

"I shouldn't have lied to you. I thought...you'd think it was silly...that I was silly. I'm looking for someone- a man I knew here before the typhoon. Malakai Navakasuasua. I thought he was in Momi Bay and needed to drive there. But it wasn't him. Tukai, the man who died, he knew him. I hoped he knew where he was...but he didn't. Now...who fucking knows if I'll ever find him."

All of a sudden I felt more tired than buzzed. I chugged the bottom third of my beer to wash the thickness out of my throat. I refused to get drunk and cry in front of Dr. Lin.

"You think I don't know this?" she asked sarcastically. "Every day, you're asking my patients about this man. Malakai this, Malakai that. Never ask me though."

I put the bottle down and stared at her hard. She stared back blankly, her good eye bobbing a little.

"Do you know something about him?" I said slowly.

"Malakai Navakasuasua. Former big-deal rugby player. On Mamanuca Islands when a landslide struck, he was. Looks like a mountain you want to fuck, he does."

Now there was an accurate description. There was no way that wasn't my Malakai.

"Why didn't you say anything?" I hissed, cheeks now burning hot.

"Ask me, you never did," she said simply.

I fought the urge to throttle her bird-boned throat. My hand gripped the beer bottle so hard I could have turned the glass into sand.

"Okay Dr. Lin, please tell me everything you know about Malakai Navakasuasua," I said through gritted teeth.

"Survived the landslide, came into hospital. Only treated him briefly, I did. Then, at a fundraiser relief party at a mansion, we meet again. He says he lived there now. Very nice man. Very handsome. Why you want to track him down, I can see."

"The big house," I whispered. "Do you have the address of this mansion?"

She nodded. "Somewhere in my email, the invitation is."

"Can you please find it right now?" I asked, impatience and joy and disbelief swirling around in my tight head. I was proud of myself for deleting the "fuck" out of "right fucking now" before I spoke.

She thumbed through her phone and I stared at her, worried if I looked away this would all disappear and I'd wake up in my bunk having dreamt the entire conversation.

"Here," she said, sliding the e-vite over to me. I copied the address into my phone and saved it three different places for safekeeping. It was only 10 miles from here.

"Thank you," I said tightly. Why I had to get drunk and confess the deepest wishes of my heart to get it out of her, I did not know.

"Too late it is tonight. Get some sleep you should, take my car in the morning you will."

"I won't sleep. But I'll take you up on the loaner," I said, taking the keys she offered.

I got up to leave, but couldn't resist one last question.

"You do realize your speech pattern sounds exactly the same as Yoda, right?"

"Yes, the green elf in Star Trek! All the time people tell me this. Know, I do. Care, I do not."

As frustrating as she was, you had to admire her philosophy.

57 RESURRECTION

The tires of the Fiat crunched on the seashell driveway. The mansion was an absurd yellow wedding cake plopped down in the old-growth forest. The devastation of the typhoon wasn't as visible this far inland. Aqua butterflies the size of dessert plates fluttered through the wide porch as I approached the oversized double doors.

Was I supposed to actually knock the circle in the brass monkey's mouth? There definitely wasn't a plastic doorbell anywhere in sight. I hesitated, listening to the early morning racket of the creatures in the canopy. Ants scurried between the mossy chinks in the grey flagstone porch and into small cracks in the stucco. Must be a bitch to keep them out of the old house, I thought randomly.

Now that I was finally here, and Malakai could be right behind the 10-foot doors...I didn't know what to do. I wiped my sweaty hands on the black Prada dress. It was a weird thing to wear for a Tuesday morning house call. But getting ready at 4:00 a.m. I had to choose between this or scrubs or grubby jeggings. And it had done it's magic and transformed me from a sloppy mess into a lady-shaped Lady.

My lips were pink and raw from applying and wiping off the red lipstick multiple times. I wanted to look amazing but Aunt Mary always said only whores and stewardesses should wear red lipstick before 9:00 a.m. My fingertips lightly traced the healing burns on my neck. I wished they were hidden by my still-damp curls instead of bared on the shaved side of my head.

The one of the doors swung open with a loud creak and I jumped back, panicked.

A petite Fijian man stood in the hall, wearing a tuxedo on top and a *sulu* on bottom.

"May I help you, madame?"

From a few steps back I saw the security camera over the door and wondered how long he had been watching me fidget on the porch. I was sure I'd never seen him before but there was something familiar about the creases around his eyes.

"Yes. Sorry. Um...does Malakai Navakasuasua live here?"

"May I ask who is inquiring after Master Malakai?" he replied archly.

Right. Introducing myself. Damn I wished I could rewind five minutes and re-approach this situation with some shred of confidence.

"Charlie Quinn," I announced, thrusting my hand at him. "I knew Malakai at the Garden of Eden resort and have been trying to find him since the storm. Well...since I knew he might have survived the storm."

He eyed my crusty nurse hand with glove powder in the cracked cuticles. After a beat he took it, turned it gracefully and planted a light kiss on the top.

"Welcome to *Levu Bure*, Miss Quinn," he said, eyes twinkling. "Allow me to show to you Master Malakai's quarters."

He gestured inside and I entered the dark hall ahead of him. The walls were covered with wallpaper so rich I couldn't help trailing a fingertip across it. The jasmine branch pattern was actually embroidered silk. I folded my hands behind my back to keep from touching anything else.

Each room we passed was an elegant diorama with carefully arranged Colonial furniture and drapes that could double as ship sails. The smells of floor wax and fresh flowers tickled my nose. As my sandals clicked down the marble hallway a creeping anxiety started gnawing at my gut.

Was this "Master" Malakai's mansion? Was the failed rugby player/maintenance man who stored his homemade personal hygiene products in beach garbage...secretly rich? He hadn't said anything about having family money. Or done anything so out-of-touch and douchey I would assume he had family money. His tattoos and wild hair seemed authentic, not the flimsy bohemian badges of trust fund babies trying to cover their reek of economic security and fine leather goods.

Once or twice he mentioned the stash of money he had saved from his years on the All Blacks payroll. I got the sense it was a modest nest egg though, not a bottomless money pit. Real talk: I didn't want Malakai to be rich. I don't understand rich people. And rich people sure don't understand me. If you don't know how much a gallon of milk costs and you pay someone to pick up your dog's poop, we can't relate.

The elegant little man stopped at a shiny white door toward the back of the house.

"Here you are. Please don't hesitate to ring if you need anything."

He gave a small bow and marched back down the hall. I wanted to shout after him, "Ring what?? Is there a Servant Bell or something? Whose house is this? Come back and explain everything to delay me having to take the next step myself!"

Instead I watched him go and, still looking at his back, knocked softly on the door before I could chicken out and not knock.

Seconds ticked by with no response. I reached out and turned the cut glass doorknob.

The room was simple but expensive. Gold-framed botanical drawings lined the white walls and the king-sized four-poster bed sat on a plush Persian rug.

A big lump of white linen rose and fell slightly in the middle of the bed.

I took all that in as background noise against the high-end paraplegic wheelchair in the corner. A shaft of morning sunlight laid across it, brighter than a streak of yellow highlighter. Through the open bathroom door, I could see a handicap-accessible shower.

I hadn't asked Dr. Lin why Malakai was in the hospital. Or what condition he was in when she saw him. Finding out he was alive and nearby was all that mattered.

Staring at the mouth tube on the wheelchair...his condition mattered. I didn't have any rainbow-colored, wistful, *Me Before You* delusions about what it meant to be the primary caregiver for a severely disabled person. I had seen the reality day in and day out for years.

The bodily fluids weren't pretty, but it was the lack of freedom that really drove caregivers to deep depression. The reality that your needs were never, ever, the priority. That you could never say yes to a last-minute happy hour or weekend getaway, no matter how much you needed a little break. You were chained to someone else's needs, and the person you sacrificed your freedom, career and relationships for, could catch a common cold and die on you at any time. Leaving you broke, friendless and unmoored.

I had seen it a hundred times at the hospice center. When I was green, I expected the caregivers to seem at least a little relieved when their charge died. They were no longer a slave to catheter bags and round-the-clock medications. Instead each and every one would drift out of the building and loiter in the parking lot for a while. Like a dog set loose from a fenced yard, now that they were on the other side, they had no fucking clue what to do with themselves.

All this flashed through my mind in seconds.

I hesitated on the threshold. I could back out quietly. I could turn around, grab my stuff from the hangar and go to the airport. I didn't have much right now but I had my freedom. And I had fought motherfucking hard for that freedom. Fought the deep undertow of my family and neighborhood, always pulling me back right at the edge of wanting to be a better version of myself. Fought the swaddling comfort of financial security and a man who would consider it his job to take care of me. Fought the quicksand traps in my own mind that sucked me down and suffocated my ambition with self-doubt.

I had come a long way to stand in this doorway. When I was disintegrating on the deck of the Coast Guard ship, all I wanted was one more moment with Malakai. Now that time was right in front of me and I didn't know if I was willing to cross the threshold and embrace whatever version of him had survived.

The old mansion let out a series of sighs as some ventilation system shut off. In the sudden stillness I heard the parrotfinches calling to each other outside. The sound took me back to our beach in the pre-dawn grey, my shoulders burning as the thick ropes of kelp stubbornly clung to the sand. The resort speedboat bobbed in the low tide and I secretly and desperately wished that it needed some sort of maintenance. A burnt-out spark plug or leaking gas line, anything to bring Malakai out of his hut and across my path. I didn't even hope for a "good morning" from him, only the ability to side-eye watch his tree trunk legs enter the surf. To witness a sea creature's grace in his natural habitat and appreciate the beauty of something being perfectly adapted to its home.

Oh, fuck it. Whatever shape he was in, I wanted him.

I stepped into the room and approached the lump of white blankets. Placed a hand on the crisp cotton and shook gently. "Malakai," I whispered, "It's me."

The lump jerked and tossed. Malakai's bare torso popped out of the nest and he glared at me blearily. His broad hand went absently to the right side of his head, where an angry red scar ran under the spikes of shaved hair.

"Ha. We have matching haircuts," he laughed drowsily, then laid back down and immediately fell asleep again.

58 THE BANYAN GROVE

I stood next to the bed, dumbstruck. In the hundreds of times I'd imagined our reunion, Malakai laughing at me and going back to sleep hadn't made the highlight reel.

A note of relief panged that he had use of his upper body at least. But it was quickly drowned by hot indignation.

"Wake up!" I yelled, shaking him roughly. "It's Charlie and I came a really fucking long way to see you!"

Malakai groaned and turned over. He opened one eye and studied me grouchily.

"You're not really Charlie. You're only my brain giving me something happy after trying to kill me all night."

"It's really me," I half-laughed, confused.

"No. My Charlie doesn't wear fancy dresses. She wears torn board shorts and crowns of bug bites and kelp necklaces."

He harumphed and turned over in bed.

Did he have brain damage? Amnesia? The urge to run away swelled up again, a light throbbing in my hamstrings begging to make a mad dash.

Instead I hopped into the oversized bed and crawled over the lump until I was firmly straddling him.

I pulled hard on the long hair he had left.

"Ow!" he yelled and turned with a feral look in his bloodshot eyes. I grabbed his chin and met his lips roughly. They were hot and cracked and soft.

He didn't respond for a moment. Then his hand met mine and he tugged on the jade circle around my wrist. His mouth came to life and he sat up, pulling me to him and tasting me with wonder.

After a long minute we broke apart for air.

"You're real," he said, still looking crazy and a little lost.

"Yeah," I smiled softly. "You been seeing things that aren't real?"

"Only you. When my head hurts the worst, I sometimes see you or feel your hand on my forehead. It helps...then I'm so sad when I wake up alone."

Tears hung on the edges of his dark eyes. I let mine spill over and kissed him again, letting the wetness on our cheeks come together along with our tongues.

I could feel him rise even under the wads of blankets.

"Glad you're not paralyzed from the waist down," I smirked. "What happened to your head?"

He impatiently pulled the sheets out from between us and settled me firmly on his lap, smelling my hair and stroking my arms.

"First you tell me how the hell you got here! I've spent the last two months cursing myself for never getting your phone number or email or any way to get ahold of you. Do you have any idea how unhelpful the

Google results are for 'Charlie from Michigan with a magical ass?'"

"It's a long story. The short version is I tried to find you for a month in New Zealand...and then I went home to handle some stuff...and then I got news you might be alive...so I came back to Fiji to find you and I've been working at the spillover care facility for the Red Cross. A doctor there, Dr. Lin, do you remember her? She told me you were here."

"Wow," he said quietly, looking down at his lap.

A flush of self-consciousness crept over my bubbling joy.

"Do you think I'm crazy?"

"No!" he said fiercely, wrapping me tight in his arms. "No. I've thought about going to Michigan and hiking around, knocking on every barn door I could find until someone knew you. I wouldn't have assumed...you'd do all that for me."

"I may have painted an inaccurate picture of life in Michigan for you," I laughed. "It's not all farmers and woods...So who's Freedom Rider, Jazz Edition wheelchair is that? I was scared to death it meant you were paralyzed."

I skipped the admission that it almost scared me away. Feeling the solid warmth of his skin on mine was heaven and the last thing I wanted to do was admit I'd almost lost faith at the Pearly Gates.

"The Cravin's. Their grandfather lived here in his last years. This is their winter retreat."

"So, this...this isn't your house then?"

"Ha!" he barked. "I wish. Our families go way back. They're letting me stay here till...well, till they come back to Fiji or I'm fully back on my feet, whichever comes first."

"Right, so what exactly happened to you? The last thing I saw was the whole damn side of the mountain collapsing."

Malakai's wide mouth twisted. Instead of answering he tightened · his grip and kissed me.

I hadn't imagined or romanticized the heat. It was real and it was back instantly. Our connection went down to the cellular level, as if my ribosomes were trying to holler at his chloroplasts. I dug my fingertips into the textured skin of his back and sunk my teeth into the meat of his shoulder while he explored the hint of cleavage coming out of my dress with his tongue. I could feel him through his thin boxers, impatient and rock hard.

"Why do you feel so good?" he groaned, "Every inch of you is so soft."

His hands crept up my thighs and pushed at the tight skirt, trying to work their way higher.

A knock at the door made me jump so hard I cracked my nose on his chin.

I scrambled out of the bed and stood there panting, nose throbbing and bright red from ears to nipples.

"What?" Malakai shouted hoarsely.

The door creaked open and the butler stood there with a shining tea set and a merry twinkle. I could have sworn he knew exactly what he was interrupting and was enjoying himself a lot.

"I thought Master Malakai and Miz Quinn might enjoy some morning tea," he said innocently. "And then perhaps the Master could show his guest around the grounds?"

He turned to me, "The banyan grove is quite lovely this time of year."

I nodded seriously. Oh yes, yes, the banyan grove. I definitely wanted to stand around in some trees instead of fucking Malakai so hard his fillings fell out.

"Thanks Dad," Malakai said tightly. "We'll be out in a minute."

The door closed and I could definitely hear a chuckle echoing down the long hallway.

"Dad?" I asked, eyebrows up to my hairline.

"Ughhhh I know," Malakai said, burying his face in his hands. "It's mortifying. Yes, I am a 33-year old man living with his parents. Not even in their house, in the house where they're the help. My mother is the gardener, that's why he wants me to take you on the grounds, so she can meet you. Also, there's nothing more my dad loves in life than busting my balls. I swear this is temporary, once I-"

I crawled back into bed and shut him up with a kiss.

"I'm glad you're not a spoiled rich kid. And that you're not paralyzed. And," I slid a hand under the sheets and gave him a rough stroke, "That you're happy to see me."

He rolled me on top of him and pawed at the zipper on my dress.

"I'd be happier if I was seeing more of you."

"Later," I said, untangling myself from him. "I don't want to meet your parents with we-just-fucked hair."

He grumbled as I crawled out of bed on all fours, wagging my ass at him.

I straightened my dress and ran my fingers through my curls. Took a deep breath. I promised myself I would do this right away if I found him. No more secrets, from him or from myself.

"Besides, you should know...Before I left Michigan the first time, I killed my aunt and stole a lot of money from a shady guy. I still owe him $20,000. And I'm sort of engaged to his nephew."

Malakai blinked at me, mouth a little ajar.

"Do you still want me to meet your mom?"

59 COMING CLEAN

Mrs. Navakasuasua was built sturdier than a Green Bay Packer. Her hug was an aggressive smothering in sun-warmed, dirt-scented cotton. She was the absolute ying to the yang of Mr. Navakasuasua's quiet elegance.

Malakai hadn't told me to get out when I confessed my sins. He'd been quiet since though, trailing along behind his chatty mother as she toured me around her impressive beds and greenhouses. Finally, after the famed banyan grove, Mr. Navakasuasua called us to a tray of lemonade on the sweeping back porch.

"Alright Kalara, we've had our fun torturing the young ones. Let's leave them be for a while."

"We're so glad you're here Charlie," she nearly yelled, squeezing my forearm with a racquet-sized hand. "Kai Kai needs a strong woman to help him heal."

"That's lovely mom," Malakai sighed, "Thank you. Goodbye. I'll come round to help in a bit."

The Navakasuasua's retreated to the house, giggling and whispering to each other.

"Kai Kai?" I asked him.

"Does being around your family ever make you feel about 12 years old again? I want to yell, 'Do none of you people remember that I'm a grown man who sent you money for the last decade?'"

"You have no idea how much I understand," I said. "When I was home...yeah. I get it."

He leaned back in his chair, watched me and waited. I took a sip of the icy, bruisingly tart lemonade. It was the perfect drink to cut through the swampy atmosphere, it would only be better with some vodka to loosen my tongue.

"I- I don't know where to start," I admitted.

"The beginning," Malakai replied. "I've got time."

I had forgotten the power of his patience. Maybe it was the fisherman in him. With his easy lean and distant stare, I had the space to think about what I wanted to say. To take long pauses in the story without feeling pressured to keep talking. I didn't miss the American insistence that head nodding and eye contact and finishing your sentences for you were required to demonstrate active listening.

I watched delicate, jewel-colored birds' flit around a golden cage perched on the railing. They helped me concentrate as everything came out over the course of an hour. From Aunt Mary getting sick all the way to burning down my childhood home. I didn't pull many punches when it came to Diego. It made me wildly uncomfortable to tell Malakai about our plans to move in together, about the comfort I felt in our shared experiences. But it was part of the truth and I wanted to tell him the whole truth.

Okay, so I didn't mention the sex had been pretty lights out. That just seemed mean.

"...and then I decided I didn't need to track down my mom right now. That I needed a new path. And if I could find you...maybe we could start a new thing together. Anyway, I got on a plane. The end."

He was quiet. Despite the whooshing of the wicker-bladed ceiling fans, I was sweating through the black linen dress in the morning heat. I waited for him to call me a murderer, or a con artist, or worse. And tell me to get off his lawn.

"That's a lot to take in. I only have one question..." he paused and a bolt of anxiety hit my gut. I gulped the last of my lemonade.

"What kind of motor's in Sally, the '69 Chevy Impala?"

I pulled my eyes away from the birds and met his. They were filled with teasing laughter. I carefully pulled a piece of ice out of my mouth and threw it at him.

He dodged it and said simply, "Come here."

I walked over and he pulled me down into his lap.

"I knew you were running from something. Even fiercely independent 23-year olds text their mom or best friends once in a while. Every time I asked you something personal, you blew me off. I figured you'd tell me your story when you were ready."

"You don't care? About any of...that?"

"That you helped your dying aunt pass away the way she wanted? That you stole stolen money to escape a bad situation? No. I don't think less of you for that. Besides, you don't know me that well, Charlie. I wasn't exactly a model Catholic school boy, and when people let you get away with being an arse because you're a star athlete...it's hard not to go ahead and enjoy being an arse. If you stick around long enough, I'll tell you some of my stories. Then we'll decide which one of us is more crazy than we should be."

He took my hand and pressed it to his face. I closed my eyes to better feel the texture of his stubble over the chiseled features. When my fingers stroked toward the right side of his head, he flinched hard and moved my hand away.

"All that said, I am furious that you got back with your high school boyfriend and he tried to hold you hostage in a burning building."

"I was the one who set the fire," I said quickly.

"Is that how you got these?" he asked, taking a turn tracing the outline of the the burns on my neck.

I nodded. He kissed my collarbone below the healing flesh.

"I wish I had been there."

I hesitated. Fuck it. He'd already seen into the dark fissures of my mind in the storm shelter. I wanted to fling the doors wide open and let the light in. To stop trying to hide the damaged terrain in there, to bleach out the shame and the fear.

"You were there," I said, meeting his dark eyes directly. "I heard your voice. When I was coming apart, pissing myself with fear, I heard you say, clear as anything, 'You're a tiny, fierce speck of life on the edge of infinity. You are free.' And it gave me the courage to stomp down the panic and try to find a way out."

"Really?" he whispered, the crinkles around his eyes deepening in wonder. "That's amazing."

"Really," I shrugged. "So. That's me. Now I need you to tell me what happened to you! And Nei Talei and Litia and Sam."

"Ask Sam yourself," Malakai grinned, pointing to a figure coming out of the brush with a shovel.

"You're kidding!" I gasped.

"Go see," Malakai smiled. I ran off the porch and collided with Sam's sweaty frame.

"You're alive!" I yelled, hugging him tight. He had somehow grown two inches in the past two months.

"Yeah I'm alive. Where have you been?"

"The government wouldn't let me come back for a while. And I thought you all died. Then I had to track down Malakai. I'm volunteering at the Red Cross overflow center, taking care of the people who can't fit in the hospitals."

"Well, it took you long enough to find us," he grumped.

"He barely got a scratch in the landslide," Malakai said, joining us. "The joys of youth. He's helping my mom with some of the heavy work for now."

"You're at that Red Cross center, yeah?" Sam asked, eyes lighting up. "You seen Tukai? The people at the hospital said they had to move him there this week."

The fizzy bubbles of joy popped and I looked down at the perfectly manicured grass. I reached for Malakai's hand before I spoke. I was still hyper-aware of where his body was in relation to mine at every second. Like if he fell off my psychic radar, I'd lose him forever. I squeezed his hand tight.

"I'm so sorry guys. Tukai is dead."

60 DEDICATION

"Come on."

Malakai led me into the house through the kitchen door. The metallic smells of light sweat and need drifted from the damp fabric on the back of his blue Billabong t-shirt. As soon as we were in the cool tile room his mouth was on mine.

His hands circled my waist and he lifted me onto the countertop. My sticky thighs squeaked on the marble surface as he wedged himself as close as possible to my center. I ran my hands up and down his arms, thrilled that the reality of the thick muscles lived up to my memory. His breath came in ragged gasps as he tried to puzzle out the miniature hook at the top of my dress zipper.

I told you death and loss made people extra horny.

"Is this thing locked?" he grumbled. "I don't care that it looks fucking amazing on you, if you don't help me get it off, I'll tear it off."

"Don't you dare, it's the nicest thing I've ever owned!"

I reached back to help, arching myself into him. Goddammit he felt right. All I wanted was to get our stupid clothes out of the way and rub on him like a lion scratching an itch against a tree.

He abandoned the zipper to me and bent down. The two sides of his head felt completely different on my inner thighs, one silky long hair and one prickly new growth. He pulled at my thin underwear with his teeth and I closed my eyes. I had forgotten how a hot, stubbly man mouth felt against me and it was all melty tightness with a little prickle of pain.

"You taste so good. I could eat you all day," he murmured. His breath tickled so bad my eyes popped open.

That's when I saw the digital display on the oven.

"Shit! My shift starts in 20 minutes!"

"What?" his voice was muffled.

I fought the undertow sucking me toward him with all my willpower and scooted back on the counter.

"I have to go. My shift starts soon."

He looked up at me with legit horror in his eyes.

"No. Please no. Aren't you a volunteer? Stay here."

"You need to understand, it's a war zone over there. If I don't show up people will miss their pain meds and be left to sit in their own shit. Besides, if I don't bring Dr. Lin's car back, she'll stick her foot so far up my junk I'll be out of commission anyway."

Malakai stood up and kicked the cabinet baseboard hard enough to rattle the pans in the hanging rack. I jumped. He suddenly looked older, worn out and defeated.

When I'd told him about Tukai his shoulders had slumped and they hadn't straightened back to their usual swagger since. I tried not to mentally replay the way Sam's face had crumpled like a used napkin at the news. The poor kid had stalked back into the bushes instead of letting us see him cry.

"It kills me to leave you. Can you come to the center when I'm off? Shift change is at 11, I know that's late."

He nodded, resting his head on my shoulder.

"I don't sleep much these days. I'll be there."

I pulled his face up and kissed him almost violently. He squeezed me so hard I couldn't breathe.

He rubbed against me desperately. "Stay five minutes? I promise it won't take long."

I laughed and gave him a rough tug through his shorts.

"Tonight. Believe me, I don't want to wait either. But I can't no-show on my patients."

"You're awfully responsible for a girl who stole $40,000 and skipped town."

"I know, right?" I said, sliding off the counter, "I'm pretty much Florence Nightingale over here. One time I read she was a very randy minx, too."

He walked me to Dr. Lin's car. I kissed him quickly and got in before I could change my mind. Then I saw the pair of scrubs in the front seat and got an idea. I had to change anyway…

Smiling at Malakai through the dirty car window, I unhooked the little clasp that had driven him crazy, unzipped the dress and took my time peeling it off. Kneeling on the seat, I took a little longer than totally necessary to pull the scrubs over my underwear, and leaned forward, pressing my breasts against the glass to get it done.

His eyes were glued to me and I saw him mouthing, "That's not fair."

Then I blew him a kiss and high-tailed it out of the driveway, spewing broken shells behind me. I made myself not look back at his figure in the driveway. If I looked back, I might jinx everything. I'd see him in 12 hours. Stop fucking crying. There was no way he could disappear and I'd never see him again. No way.

That's what I told myself over and over on the drive and through the endless hours of bedpans, linen changes and charting, "He won't disappear again. You found him. He won't disappear."

It didn't keep me from glancing at the door every five minutes. Dr. Lin yelled at me for being slow so many times she finally cuffed me upside the head in frustration.

"Hey!" I protested. "That's workplace harassment!"

"File a complaint with human resources, you should," she snapped, "Out back next to the pig living off garbage, the office is."

Finally (finally, finally, finally), it was 11 p.m. I took a three-minute shower, twisted my curls into a messy braid and did the best I could with the grainy remains of my makeup in the dim bunk lighting. I dug through my pack, half-hoping a new dress would magically appear for the occasion. No luck. Instead I pulled on a white eyelet sundress that had seen (many) better days. I ignored the coffee stains on the skirt and focused on the fact that it was what I had been wearing the first day I visited the island. I grabbed the canvas Walmart bag I'd been using for a purse and headed out, happy there wasn't a mirror around to give me feedback on my Date Night Look.

Even at night, heat rose in waves off the center's asphalt parking lot. I wandered restlessly around the dusty cars.

"What if he doesn't come?" a little voice piped up over the racket of the insects. "What if you never see him again?"

A thin light rounded the corner through the palms. The whine of a moped intensified along with my heart rate.

Friends, when your prince (or princess, or qween, or non-binary royalty of any sort) comes, I hope they look half as good as Malakai did in gas station flip flops and faded board shorts, riding a rusty moped for a stallion.

I ran to him and almost knocked the bike over. We got lost in each other until the volunteers on a smoke break whistled and broke us apart.

"Want to go out on the boat?" he asked.

"Yes! You have a boat here?! I'll get my bathing suit. Should I bring the Pink Demon?"

"We won't surf this time. And the bathing suit is highly optional," he smiled.

My laugh had an edge of crazy on it. I swung a leg over the seat and we sped off into the thick night air.

61 THE WAYFINDER

The slick catamaran gleamed in the sulphur dock lights.

"Um, are we stealing this?" I asked quietly. "This isn't your standard fishing boat."

"Courtesy of the Cravens, once again," Malakai answered, "I maintain it for them. Got to knock the dust off the engine once in a while to be sure she's running well, right? Shoes off please."

I kicked off my flips, took his hand and stepped over the chrome railing onto the smooth white leather seats. He handed me a Fiji Bitter and worn hoodie with a polite, "M'lady."

"It's 90 degrees out?"

"When we get moving on the open ocean, you'll thank me."

"Where are we going?"

"For a ride."

Malakai hopped around expertly unmooring the boat and soon we were putting out of the port while I guzzled the deliciously cold beer.

When we hit open water, Malakai cranked the speed and the powerful engine kicked until I was tilted back at a 45-degree angle. He was having a blast at the helm, deeply banking turns. I giggled and lifted my face to the cool salt spray that pattered across my face, appreciating the thousand little kisses from my ocean. The stars multiplied and stood out in deeper relief as we left the city lights behind us. The ocean was flat black carpet in every direction.

"How can you tell where we're going?" I yelled into the wind.

He shaped his left hand into an "L" and gazed up at the night sky.

"My people are ancient wayfinders. We can find our way across thousands of miles by the seas and stars alone."

I was impressed for a minute. Then I noticed the weak blue light on his face from the console.

"You've got the GPS on, don't you?"

He grinned and nodded.

After a half hour of racing through the night Malakai slowed and tied up to a large buoy.

"We're here!"
"Where's here?"

We were in the middle of featureless, open water. I could only make out a dark bulge of land blocking the stars ahead of us.

"Somewhere special. We call it Ray Alley. Let's go for a swim."

He lifted a seat and pulled snorkel gear from the storage bin underneath.

"The last time you took me 'somewhere special' it was claustrophobic as hell and you exploited my blind panic to make out with me."

"True. It was a brilliant plan," he handed me a mask, snorkel and fins. "Don't worry, this is wide open ocean. There's only one problem...that dress doesn't go with your fins. You should probably take it off."

"Fine."

I pulled the stretchy fabric over my head and put the mask and flippers on. Then I struck a pose in my thong and snorkel gear.

"Better?"

"So much better," he said, eyes travelling up and down and back again.

Suddenly I couldn't wait a second longer to get in the water. I climbed on the rail and dove headfirst into the pitch black. The soft salt water slid over my bare skin like a blessing. I'd never been in the sensory deprivation chamber of open ocean at night. There was nothing to see and everything was out there. It was probably the closest I'd come to experiencing the weightless infinity of outer space. Then something silky and massive brushed my leg. A scream bubbled in my throat- was that a Space Shark?!?

A bikini wasn't going to protect me from Jaws but suddenly being nearly naked in the vast expanse made me feel as vulnerable as a turtle without a shell.

Malakai knifed into the water nearby and illuminated a streak of the world around us with a high-intensity flashlight.

A manta ray the size of a SmartCar flapped silently through the beam of light slicing the greenish water. I spun around and stared down the ribbed gullet of a gaping mouth. The monster flew over my head, it's pale, dalmatian-spotted underside shining in the flashlight glow. Three more followed, almost brushing my bare sides. The leisurely pace of their rolling wings seemed in direct opposition to the speed they carried through the water. Within seconds their whip tails trailed out of the light beam.

My heart thumped at top speed and goosebumps rose across my arms and legs. I had missed being Good Scared. The edgy burst of adventure adrenaline was so different from the sucking dread that smothered my senses back home. Both feelings made me want to do wild shit. The difference was Good Scared pushed me toward risks that build me up instead of ones that tore me down.

Malakai ran his hand over my back and the goosebumps tightened. He pointed the flashlight down and revealed a colorful reef beneath us. Here and there the delicate structures had been smashed by debris washed out by the typhoon. The reef was already healing itself though, with small polyps of coral growing over the chunks of concrete and lumber.

We floated 10 feet above the reef, watching the night creatures forage and dart around the purple fan coral. The anemones waved their pale arms in the current to welcome their clownfish home. A fluorescent parrotfish cruised by inches from my nose and gave me the stink eye like I stole his parking spot.

Malakai pointed to a dark section of the reef and handed me the flashlight. He took a deep breath at the surface and dove, kicking his way down to a bed of inky black mussels. I tried to swim in place and hold the light steady as he pried clusters off the rocks with a steel knife. The light played over his back tattoos as the muscles worked against the shells. Finally, a large chunk popped off and he tucked them carefully into a net bag at his waist.

After a gulp of air at the surface, he took my hand and gave me a slow-motion tour of the reef. We cruised over the intricate patterns and deep black troughs. More manta rays cruised through the dark water, each one first spooking me with their size then amazing me with their efficient grace. Once in a while the light would disappear from the corals below and I'd realize Malakai was tracing my curves with the beam, watching me swim in a halo of glowing light.

Yeah, I'd allow that.

We circled back to the boat and climbed up the rear ladder. He wrapped me in an oversized towel that smelled fancy. The rear of the catamaran housed a spotless galley and he dumped the haul from his net bag into a pot.

"We have five to seven minutes to rinse off," he said, setting a timer. "Let's not get into too much trouble yet."

The spray of the outdoor shower stripped the salt off my skin and chased away the chill. Malakai joined me and I took my time massaging lavender shampoo into the remaining hair on the left side of his head. He closed his eyes as I scratched his scalp and brushed against him. When he lathered his hands and ran them over me, I remembered our first shower at his hut.

"Do you think Pinchy is still alive?" I gasped.

"Let's say he is," Malakai smiled, teeth flashing in the dark. "That butt-ugly crustacean was a survivor."

He picked me up and pressed my back into the tile wall. My legs wrapped around him and I felt the wash of internal heat that seemed to be my body's automatic biological response to the slightest hint of an erection on this man. We kissed until he wasn't hinting any more. My pruned fingers were struggling with the knot at the waist of his board shorts when the stove timer went off.

"Let's leave it," I complained as he set me down.

"You aren't hungry for fresh mussels after a 12-hour shift and a swim?"

My stomach answered for me, loudly declaring that my lady parts weren't the only bodily system with needs around here.

I re-wrapped in the towel and joined him on the wide leather seats. He set a wooden bowl between us and squeezed half a lemon over the gaping shells. We dug in, gulping the salty, chewy meat and chucking the shells overboard. In minutes we cleared out the bunch.

I laid back and licked the last of the briny flavor off my lips.

"So good. Any way you want to hop back down there and get another round?"

"Maybe later."

He stretched out beside me. "You don't have to be back until 11 a.m. tomorrow, right? No more running off on me?"

"Right."

"Excellent," he said, nuzzling my neck. "Then I promise that every single hour between now and then I'm going to make you come."

62 REALITY

Malakai took my hand and led me to a sleek spiral staircase.

"Let's see how the other half sleeps."

I climbed the stairs and intentionally hiked the towel up so he got glimpses of my ass as he walked behind me.

His fingers brushed the crease and then somehow, I was on my hands and knees.

"That's enough teasing now," he growled from above in my ear. "Enough."

I arched against his hold on my hips. The wood hurt my knees and the no-slip surface on the stairs was gripping my skin.

"Let's make it upstairs," I said.

"No," he replied simply. "You stay put now."

He tossed the towel aside, yanked my damp underwear down and licked me in a single, long stroke. Then he was inside me. Fully and possessively.

Out of a defiant reflex I crawled up a stair, pulling away from the heavy pressure splitting me open.

He followed. Grabbed my shoulder and thick braid and reeled me back to him. We tussled, thighs pushing against and away. My body betrayed me- I was so wet we slid against each other like we were still underwater. But I kept struggling to climb the stairs because the more I pulled away the harder he chased my flesh and I could feel the fight stoking something primal in both of us.

Malakai trapped me at the top. He hooked a powerful leg over my left hip, twisted me on my side and pinned my hands against the smooth bannister poles.

"I said to stay put," he gasped. His face was dark red and his hands were sweaty on mine.

"Fine. You got me. Now what are you going to do with me?"

In answer he reared back and drove into me as hard as he could. Over and over. The last stair cleat bit into my ribs but I pushed against it to meet him each time. We were greedy; mindless and inconsiderate of anything as mundane as pain.

His eyes locked into mine as he lost control. I loved seeing the abandon on his face but the aching fullness between my legs wasn't satisfied, only intensified by the shudders that ran across his abs like a wind ruffling the water's surface. Still, I cradled his heavy head tenderly against my chest until he caught his breath.

He eased off me carefully, gathered me from my sprawl across the stairs and carried me to the wide expanse of the king bed.

"Damn, you always have the best beds," I moaned, rubbing my toes against the silky fabric.

As soon as we settled, he replaced his ear right above my heart. I was happy he didn't flinch when my hand carefully travelled from the healed scars on his temple to the fresh head wound. His fingers played with the jade bracelet on my wrist.

"This is what convinced me you were real. When you came to the house. I thought I was still asleep until I felt this. You were never wearing...well, anything, when I would dream about you."

The stone circle shone pale in the moonlight coming through the wraparound windows. I hoped everything had gone smoothly with the Chinese woman's labor and delivery.
"How dumb was that rescue? Going into the water with a drowning guy alone, no floatation. I need to wise up."

Malakai picked up his head and glared at me, wrapping his hand around my chin.

"No. Before that day I thought you were beautiful and funny. After I knew you were brave, the kind of person who does what needs to be done when other people would walk away. I think that's when I fell in love with you."

Seabirds swooped around carelessly in my chest, calling out in abandon and joy.

Wanting every inch of my skin to be touching him at the same time, I wound myself around him until even the bottoms of my feet were tucked in. I half wondered if his tattoos could rub off on me- wondered if we got close enough the geometric designs could newsprint transfer to my skin.

"This sounds ridiculous...I think I fell in love with you the first time I saw you," I said, burying my face in his shoulder. "At first I thought it was only a hard crush. Then I thought it was the sex. I knew when I came back from Nadi it was more than that. But it wasn't until you were gone in a split second that I realized...it had been there from the start."

Malakai kissed me then. And didn't stop for a long while.

Eventually he left my mouth and worked his way down, making each nipple stand and deliver. His fingers brushed my stomach, tracking the dips between my ribs and hips. One strong thumb worked its way deep into the tight muscle that wrapped around to my glutes. The other played pinball on me. I little groan escaped me.

"If I promise you something, Charlie, I will do anything I can to make it happen. I want you to know that."

A spike of anger pierced my happy bubble. I grabbed his hand and made him stop.

"You promised you weren't leaving me. When you put me on the Coast Guard ship? Then you died in front of me. Don't promise things you can't control."

"Well I didn't die, did I?"

"You could have! And what if I hadn't come and found you?"

"I would have found you," he said simply, "I want you to know that. Your stubborn arse just beat me to it."

He kissed my hip.

"I get it. A lot of people you trusted have broken promises to you. I won't promise you anything that's out of my control, okay?"

I nodded and released his hand.

"Now will you let me do what I said I would? It's almost been an hour, after all."

"I guess. But you're lucky I'm not more mad about you dying on me."

"So very lucky," he said, licking the skin along my tan line.

That was the last thing he said for a good long while.

The fluttering throbs came harder and faster and I started to see streaks of iridescent fuchsia and teal behind my closed lids.

I yanked his head away, dragged him upright on the cool sheets and climbed on him, sliding his ready cock inside me with zero resistance. Just like our first time in a bed after the cave, I was sore and tender and I didn't give a shit. I could tell from his sharp inhale that he was a little raw too. The sheets stuck to the abraded skin on my knees. Neither of us were getting out of this unmarked.

I dug my nails into his mounded pecs and leaned back. The strong lines of his face were barely sketched in the shadowy moonlight. As many times as I tried to recall exactly what he looked like, I had never quite been able to remember how all his features came together to form something so fierce and soft at the same time.

I took my time, rocking to a slow, thudding rhythm that beat in every cell of my body. As close as I had been while he was eating me, the release stayed just out of my reach. I chased it with the mild, then building panic of searching through a pile of clothes in the dark for a wallet. Please. Please let me find it. I'm tired of searching.

Malakai put his hand to my face and traced the bow of my lips with his thumb. I slipped it into my mouth, rubbing the calloused flesh with my tongue. He sat up and took the Lesser Breast into his mouth. We sucked each other's flesh in at a building pace and suddenly I didn't have to chase anything anymore.

The sensation hit so hard I couldn't breathe. Everything was water, boiling water, freezing water, rushing in deep rivers away from the mountain source at my core. Tributaries spreading all the way to the roots of my hair. I dragged in a deep breath around his thumb and called his name. His body answered to the sound of it.

We fell asleep almost immediately after, still tangled in each other. I think I woke once more in the dead of night to feel him inside me again and that time was slow and sleepy and maybe not real. Reality didn't matter though, as long as he didn't let go.

63 THE *VAKATARAISULU* CEREMONY

The pink glow of dawn woke me up. The ocean was quiet, lapping the double hull of the catamaran peacefully. I sat up and gasped. Straight outside the windows was our island. The dark landmass I'd seen against the stars in the night was the ridge behind the hotel. It was bare rock now. My eyes scanned the lagoon and shore. There were no landmarks, only piles of muddy rock and torn palms.

Malakai stirred beside me and sat up. He wrapped the sheet around us and warmed my back with his chest. The hairs running down the center of his torso tickled a little.

"It looks...everything's gone," I said softly.

"Well, the structures are all gone," he answered just as quietly. "The land remains. See there on the cliffs? The choke vines are already growing back. Mr. Craven said the resort investment group is going to rebuild. It will take years though."

"Can we go closer?"

"No. The lagoon waters are off bounds. Out of respect for the dead. After 100 days the taboo is lifted with a *vakataraisulu* ceremony."

"When's that?"

"Today," he sighed. "For Nei Talei and Litia. Now, we will honor Tukai in the same way, so the taboo starts again from the day of his death."

"So..."

"Yes, they died right away. Buried in the kitchens. Litia's husband and two sons will come later today for the ceremony. I wanted to be here early so I could pay respects and leave the tie up free for them."

"I didn't know she had a family."

"Everyone has a family, Charlie."

Not everyone, I thought. And not the way you have family here. I didn't say anything though, choosing to simply kiss the solid, patterned forearm wrapped around my shoulder. I thought about Litia's warm practicality, how she had always made me feel better without letting me feel sorry for myself. Of course she was a mom. Those poor boys.

"I'm sorry. I know they were special aunties to you."

He nodded, kissing my cheek, and untangled himself.

"Come on," he called, heading down the stairs.

When I came down, he had a backpack and a sort of little wooden float. He pulled handmade *masi* mats, fruit and strands of frangipani and orchids from the bag and carefully arranged them on the float.

"Hand it down to me?" he asked, then hopped the railing. I brought the float to the ladder and passed it to him, then slid into the smooth morning water as well. My ribs hurt and the salt stung the patches on my skin where his stubble had rubbed me raw.

Malakai ran his fingers over the intricate designs on the mats, then gave the float a shove.

His eyes followed it closely as the small waves pulled it gradually toward the shore.

"I should have been able to help them."

"In times and places like that, there is no should. There's only what you can do, and what you can't do." I replied, thanking Dr. Lin in my head for that pearl.

We hung on to the ladder, bobbing up and down a little.

"When the slide happened...all I remember is a wall of dirt and then a cracking deep in my head. It sounded like a coconut splitting. When I came to, Sam had me tied to a piece of dock, floating in the lagoon a kilometer from shore. We hung off the sides, and there was barely room on top for Tukai. I still can't believe Sam found us both. That kid is tough."

I wanted to ask a ton of questions. Instead I let the fish come to me.

"I don't know how long we were out there in the waves. I was in and out. I mostly remember the rain and the noises Tukai made. He was in so much pain and there was nothing I could do."

"I wish I could have helped him more too," I said. It killed me that simple treatment sooner could have saved his life.

The float with Nei Talei's *masi* mats was almost to shore when he spoke again.

"A Coast Guard patrol fished us out after four days of hell. There was nothing I could do for Tukai then, and there's nothing I can do for myself now. The headaches and dizziness come and go as they please. They can knock me out for days at a time. Sometimes I can work all day and be fine. Other times I find myself in the shop with something in pieces in front of me with no idea how to put it back together. I can't hold down a job in this condition and I don't know how to get better. When I broke my hip, I was painful and angry. At least I knew if I put in the work I'd walk again. With my head...I don't know."

Loss and emptiness smeared his face when he finally looked at me

"I need to be honest with you. I don't know if I'll get better. And I don't want you stuck with damaged goods because you're too stubborn to leave."

I fought the urge to swim over to his side of the ladder and wrap my arms around him. The last thing his bruised ego wanted was easy comfort. Instead I used my Nurse Voice.

"I won't lie to you and say I know you will make a full recovery. No one knows that for sure at this point. I can say with confidence that you have very typical post-concussion symptoms. We will get an MRI done to reassess where you are and set a benchmark for recovery. Then we'll find a physical therapist who specializes in vestibular therapy. It will take time and you will probably experience some setbacks along the way. But if you stick with it, I'll be next to you every step of the way. Deal?"

I stuck out my hand. Malakai stared at it a while.

"You promise you'll leave if you feel trapped or I stop trying?"

"I promise, and I don't plan on breaking any promises to you either."

He took my wet hand and shook it with determination.

"Deal. Damn. I can see how you make a good nurse."

"Actually, I want to be a doctor," I said.

The words shocked the hell out of me. I'd never thought them before, let alone said them out loud. PA school was the biggest I'd let myself dream.

"No way!" Malakai cried.

I was a little stung.

"Well I mean yeah, it's a crazy idea. A decade of school, hundreds of thousands of dollars in student loans...if I can even get in to a med school..."

"You'd be Dr. Quinn! Like *Dr. Quinn, Medicine Woman*! That show was huge here. I had the world's biggest hard on for Jane Seymour growing up. Any way you could wear a prairie skirt with your scrubs?"

"Oh my God, you are old," I laughed, climbing the ladder. "Dr. Quinn...damn. That does sound good."

Malakai gave my ass a swat on the way up.

"You want some cranberry scones? My dad made them fresh yesterday and insisted I bring you some. I think he's keen on you."

That idea made me stupidly happy. And I was glad about Malakai's dad's good opinion too.

I nestled into a towel and savored every bite of the crumbly scones while Malakai boiled water for tea.

"So where do we go from here?" he asked, bringing over two steaming mugs.

"My next shift, first of all," replied. "We have to go soon."

"You know what I mean."

"Well, I'm serious about my job here. I think I want to stay on with

Doctors Without Borders until…"

I tried to think of when it would be okay to walk away. When can you say a tragedy of these proportions is over?

"I guess until they don't need the spillover center anymore. When everyone who needs care can be seen in the real hospital."

I dug my phone out of my Walmart bag and checked to see if I had email service. No luck.

"And I need to keep the home insurance claim moving. It'll be easier to stay in one place while I get that sorted out. I need to pay that money back ASAP to be able to…for everything in Flint to be done."

Malakai stopped chewing and his eyes darkened.

"I don't want to ask you this, but I need to know. Are things over with you and that guy? For good?"

I stared out at the eastern horizon. Somewhere really, really far that way Diego was going on with business as usual. He'd probably already started a great new job. If I had to bet, I'd say he chose one in Detroit. Maybe he got a generically chic apartment in the downtown high rises. Or maybe he was still living in his bedroom at Uncle Lou's. Either way, it wasn't my concern whether he grew up or not. Just like I let go of knowing where my mom ended up and how she had survived herself. They were both my past and I had chosen to stop letting my past define me.

I dug in the Walmart bag again. The dark pearls Diego gave me rattled around the bottom. I had put them on when I got dressed to go to the mansion, then took them off on the drive. I wanted to avoid bad juju by wearing them while searching for Malakai.

I slid them through my fingers, enjoying the sensation of the perfectly symmetrical orbs. Then I dropped them into the 40-foot water beneath us. Go free, little pearls, and find your way back to the South Seas oyster bed where you were born.

"It's over," I said to Malakai.

"Good," he replied.

I scooted closer to him and brushed scone debris off his bare stomach. The happy little roll of fat above his trunks was gone. I missed it. I'd make sure he started sleeping and eating well again until it came back.

He took my right hand, tugged the silver Claddagh off my finger, turned it, and replaced it with the heart facing my hand.

"There. That's been bugging me since you showed back up."

"How do you even know what that means?"

"Once upon a time, I was married to an Irish lass. For all of six months."

"Oh really?" I said, straddling one wide thigh and pinching a nipple. "Tell me everything about this slutty bog-trotter immediately or else."

"Nope. We have lots of time for old stories. I still want to know where we're going next. Once you're done with the Red Cross and when I'm better. I have rugby mates in South Africa, France, Australia. We could roll around the world surfing until Fiji recovers more."

I played with a strand of his hair, wrapping the salty silk around my finger.

"I don't know. You have brain damage and I have some major trauma and anxiety issues I probably need to work on. Maybe we shouldn't make long term plans yet."

He lifted my chin up so I met his gaze. He was battered and scarred and brimming with crazy, joyful optimism.

"Maybe the plan is simply for you to help me remember, and for me to help you forget."

I leaned in and brushed his lips with mine. They felt like some kind of home.

"You know, it's been more than an hour since we woke up. I thought you were a man who lived up to his promises."

Malakai grinned and rolled me over on the damp towels.

"Don't you worry, Dr. Quinn. I'll keep my end of the bargain. I'm going to make you scream until we scare the fish and then I'm going to make you figure out how to drive a $250,000 catamaran back to port."

***

I had never driven a boat before. I loved how I could feel the waves echo through the steering wheel as we sliced over them.

I tried to imagine the girl who left Great Lakes State last fall standing here in my place. With her crunchy gelled curls and ignorance and tacky Victoria's Secret nightie. In case you were wondering, it is absolutely possible to have secondhand embarrassment for your own self. She'd probably be scared as hell to pilot an expensive boat and would do something wild and dumb to prove she wasn't scared.

Smirking, I cranked up the speed until we bounced over a wave and Malakai shot me a look. Ok, ok, Debbie Downer, I'll back off. I didn't have to prove anything to him. But I still had a lot to prove to myself.

ABOUT THE AUTHOR

Maria Martinico is the author of many epic meal plans that never came to fruition. A graduate of a middling state college with a completely obsolete degree, she enjoys using her job in marketing to observe the darkness of the human condition. She lives in the Rocky Mountains with her crested gecko and a number of carefully-tended grudges.

Made in the
USA
Lexington, KY